A Widow's Wife

By Rachelle Woods

This is a work of fiction. Names, characters, places, and incidents either are the product of the author's imagination or are used fictitiously. Any resemblance to actual persons, living or dead, events, or locales is entirely coincidental.

First Edition: March 2026

Cover Art by Rachelle Woods

ISBN 979-8-9946677-0-5
E-book ISBN 979-8-9946677-1-2

A WIDOW'S *Wife*

By Rachelle Woods

To anyone who has lost a loved one: You
aren't grieving too much or for too long.
You aren't "doing it wrong".
Feel your grief, honor your loss.
They will always be with you.

You are not alone.

Content Warning

This book discusses themes such as cancer, infertility, death and the grieving process which some readers may find upsetting. While approached with care, please be aware of these and other possible triggers.

Chapter 1

Melody

Maybe it was her best friend getting married, or another Valentine's Day passing by without her. It could be the fifteenth anniversary of losing her parents last month, but she was forced to admit that she was lonely. Melody had been on her own for a long time, her small circle of loved ones held close, but sometimes she felt like there was something missing. Not often. Just every once in a while, a sense of isolation crept in. Usually, it wasn't too hard to distract herself, but on days like today she couldn't shake the feeling.

She wasn't sure what she was looking for as she scrolled through the ads. Just...something. One caught her attention. *Wife Wanted*. It sounded kinda sketchy, but also, who does that? Her inner nosiness won out and she had to read it.

(Nathaniel) Male (35) looking for a single female (32-40) willing to marry. Not interested in dating, just trying to keep this as simple as possible. My family and friends are starting to worry and won't drop it. Serious

inquiries only. Interviews will be held and more details discussed in person.

Definitely weird. But there had to be something wrong with her because she found it intriguing. Besides, this guy could be a complete troll. She hated it when she was reading something and there was no description of the person. She was left to fill in the blanks, and her imagination ran away with her...sometimes she couldn't ever picture them correctly going forward – oh wait, he included a selfie at the bottom.

She found herself looking at what could only be described as a very hot lumberjack. That was probably not intentional on his part – he actually gave off the whole, "no nonsense, carrying the weight of the world on his shoulders" kind of vibe – but it probably was the plaid flannel that really did it. He looked tall and muscled underneath the flannel. The photo wasn't close enough to really determine the color of his eyes. He had light brown hair, which was a little long and a full, but nicely kept, beard. The kind that looked like it would prickle in the most delicious ways.

Hot damn. Well, that settled it. She might end up murdered by a serial killer, but at least she'd have a hell of a view going out.

She clicked to reply and introduce herself.

My name is Melody Parker (34) and I came across your ad. I would love to meet you and learn more. I thought I'd return the favor and include a photo so you can put a face with the name. I look forward to hearing from you!

Twenty minutes later, she decided on a selfie. She wasn't particularly vain or self-critical either, but she could not photograph to save her life. For every ten photos, seven were just not usable. Her eyes would be half closed, making her look high, or her mouth was open, or she was mid-turning or gesturing, so she would be partially blurred out. She didn't know what it was – she was just a little chaotic apparently.

Otherwise, she had always felt fairly average physically. She wasn't thin, but also not noticeably big. Just full figured. She had long dark brown hair and hazel eyes. More brown than green. Nothing too memorable, but she liked her body. It had gotten her this far, and she happened to think her face was adorable, thank you very much. She attached the photo and hit send before she could overthink it.

Oh god, she was pretty sure she sounded like she's interviewing to be his secretary, not trying to get him to marry her. Oh well. What's done is done. She'd just have to make an impression in person.

Chapter 2

Nate

Understandably, he had only gotten a few serious inquiries. You'd think that specifically listing "serious inquiries only" would help with that, but not when it comes to the internet. Between the overtly sexual propositions, offers to join some kind of pyramid scheme and one offer to help by taking some "very tasteful" photos, he realized that he really should have known better. But it was too late now. Six women had responded and also seemed reasonable, and he decided that it made the most sense to meet them all at once, so he could see how they behaved with people besides him and narrow down his options at the same time. This was, in all honesty, probably a horrendously bad idea. But he just didn't have it in him to start dating.

He had no interest in actually falling in love. He'd had that with his wife before she died, and that was enough. He just needed everyone in his life to stop worrying about him so much. He really was fine. They just cared too damn much. So, he could do this and ease their minds.

The women started to trickle into his home and Nate realized two things: he probably shouldn't have given out his home address to all these strangers before he even met them, and he probably should've made a game plan for what they would do once they got here. He didn't have snacks or anything to drink besides water. He didn't even really have all that many questions prepared to help him figure out which woman would be best...he just kind of expected that he'd *know*.

Nate glanced around his living room in a panic, looking for anything to do with these women. The only thing he spotted was a deck of cards that his sister had left here the last time she'd talked everyone into a game night. But that could work.

"Uh, anyone up for a game of Bullshit?" he asked, picking it up. "We could go around and introduce ourselves first."

A round of agreements sealed the decision. They all settled around his living room as best they could, a few of them squeezing onto the couch while one took the recliner, leaving him and a brunette woman on the floor on the other side of his coffee table.

As he started to shuffle the deck, a blonde on the couch chimed in, "Well, I'm Veronica."

They took turns going around and he learned that the redhead next to the blonde was Evie, the blonde on her other side was Meredith, the woman with long black hair was Monica, the woman with the short black hair was Brandy.

Lastly, the brunette on the floor next to him introduced herself, saying "I'm Melody. My friends call me Mel." He remembered her face – she had included a photo back to him in her reply to the ad.

Once he was satisfied that the cards were decently shuffled, he set them on the coffee table and stood. "Someone want to deal? I'm going to grab water bottles for everyone."

"I got it," Veronica said, quickly grabbing up the cards with a smile.

Melody stood as well and offered, "I can help you carry the water, if you want."

"Sure, thanks," Nate said.

She followed him to the kitchen and waited as he pulled seven bottles from the fridge, handing her three while he took the rest.

They passed them out, taking a seat and examining their hand of cards in relative silence. "Everyone know how to play?" Nate asked.

"Oh, yes," Veronica answered with a smirk.

"I actually don't," Evie said.

"No worries. Basically, the goal is to get rid of all the cards in your hand. We go around the circle and whoever's turn it is gets to lay down cards for the number we are on. So for example, if Veronica – right?" He gestured to the blonde to make sure he was not mixing people up. She nodded with a slightly sour look on her face, as if she was offended that he had to ask her name. "– so, if Veronica here was playing threes, you would lay down fours. You can lay down however many you actually have, or you can lie and put down extra cards while saying that they are all fours. The catch is, someone else could call your bluff, and if they are right, you have to take all of the cards in the pile and add them to your hand. If you call Bullshit and you're wrong though, you have to take all the cards instead," he said.

"How are we supposed to know if they are lying?" Evie asked.

"Well, reading people comes in handy. Most people have a tell. But you also will need to pay attention to the cards. Like if you have three fives in your hand, and on the next turn she says she is playing three fives, you know she's full of shit because there are only four total in the deck," Melody said.

Nate nodded in agreement. "Exactly. So put on your best poker face and we'll see who comes out on top. Everyone good?"

"I think so," Evie said. The others nodded.

"Since Veronica dealt, Evie will go first. We will start with aces," he said.

The first round was quiet as everyone eyed each other suspiciously and tried to dissect their game play. He felt multiple sets of eyes on him regardless of whose turn it was though, and the attention was slightly unnerving. But he couldn't really object since he had been the one to invite them all here under these circumstances. Glancing up, his eyes were snared by, he wanted to say Monica?

The look on her face was intense, and she tried to subtly lick her lip in what he was sure she thought was an appealing gesture, but really just made his skin crawl a bit.

"Bullshit." Melody's voice broke through the awkward tension, and he thankfully glanced over to see Veronica snatching up the entire pile of cards with a sulky look on her face. When she noticed his attention, she tried to quickly replace it with a playful smile as if she hadn't been a sore loser just seconds before.

Melody had her eyes back on her cards and was doing her best to keep a neutral face as a small smile tugged on the corner of her mouth. He felt his lips twitch in response.

Around and around they went, accusations of "Bullshit!" becoming more frequent. At one point, Meredith and Brandy decided they would rather start a conversation with him instead, and so they kept trying to speak over the gameplay to tell him about themselves.

"I'm a yoga instructor. My flexibility is off the charts," Meredith said.

Brandy scoffed. "Well, I'm a paralegal and I'm putting myself through law school."

Evie on the other hand couldn't seem to get a word in edgewise. The poor thing would start to talk, only to be interrupted and spoken over repeatedly, but instead of trying again, she just seemed to shut down.

"Well, I –" Evie started.

"I'm the regional manager at my cosmetics company. Two Aces." Veronica leaned forward with her cards.

"Well, *that's* bullshit. I'm sorry, Evie, what were you trying to say?" Melody asked.

Veronica shot Melody a narrow-eyed glare as she picked up the stack of cards once again.

Evie gave Melody a grateful smile. "Oh, I'm a first-grade teacher is all. What about you?"

"That's really cool. I'm a painter." She returned her smile and stretched her legs out in front of her. Nate couldn't help but notice the swaths of creamy skin and toned muscles that her shorts showed off.

"What do you paint?" he asked her.

"Oh, it just depends on the day. Not to sound pretentious, but I let the universe tell me what it's going to be if that makes any sense. I tend to work in the abstract mostly." Melody said.

"That makes perfect sense to me actually," Nate said. She turned her smile on him, and he felt it in his chest. Out of everyone, Melody seemed to be the one he was connecting with the most so far.

This could work. Now he just had to figure out how to get rid of the rest of these women so he could get her alone and learn more about her.

She had been leaning back on her arms with her lovely legs still stretched out before her as they continued playing, when she suddenly uncrossed her ankles and got up to head into the kitchen with her finger raised in the "one minute" gesture.

"Excuse me, ladies. I want to make sure she's okay..." he said as he got up to follow her and see what she might need.

He found her leaning against the kitchen counter, waiting for him and he paused.

"So, when are you going to kick the rest of them out so we can get down to it?" She smiled with a wink.

He was taken aback for just a second.

"Bold of you. But you're not wrong. Question is, are you sure you don't want to leave as well?" He raised an eyebrow.

A look passed over her face that he couldn't decipher, and she stepped towards him. He thought she might stop, but she came right up to him and the next thing he knew, she had wound her arms around his neck and placed a kiss on his lips.

He tensed. He hadn't been kissed in.... a long time. But this awakened something in him, so before he even realized it, his body had responded. His arms wound around her waist, one hand snaking down to cup her ass and draw her more firmly against him. God, this felt good after so long.

Her lips were soft, her ass was full and firm in his palm, and he could feel every point of contact where their bodies touched.

It took some willpower, but he managed to break the kiss and pull away enough to look at her.

"I know what I'm here for," she said.

He searched her eyes for any sign of hesitation but found none. He wasn't sure what to make of her.

He released her and stepped away. "My landlord is actually supposed to be dropping by soon to give me a replacement key for my mailbox. I can just tell everyone that she is coming and so they need to leave now."

She was already nodding her agreement as he finished, "I can ask to use your bathroom as we are all leaving and just hide out in there until everyone is gone."

"That will work. It's straight back through my bedroom, off of the living room. You can actually see the bathroom door from the front door – I don't know whose brilliant design idea that was," he said, shaking his head and rolling his eyes.

"That's not the worst design I've ever seen though. That would have to go to the bathroom located at the bottom of a flight of stairs. No door, just a toilet and tub open to a full flight of stairs! Can you imagine tripping and falling down the stairs, only to end up with your head in a toilet or on top of someone taking a bath?" She laughed.

His brow crinkled. "I will never understand people."

"You and me both."

"I better go tell them that it's time to go now."

"I'll join you."

They walked back into the living room where everyone else was still chatting.

"Well ladies, I hate to cut this short, but my landlord is coming by to do some work, so I'm going to have to call it an afternoon. I'll be thinking things over and will reach out if I decide that I'd like to speak with you more. Thank you for your time."

They tittered and batted their eyelashes as they stood and gathered their purses. He heard Melody quietly mention she was going to use the restroom and saw her head away. The rest of the group made their way to the front door, where he let them out and said his goodbyes. As they started driving off, he could see his landlord pulling into the driveway. Good timing. And Melody had parked a little ways down the street because of the other cars, so it didn't look like he had company any longer, which was also good. No sense in getting Shirley's hopes up about him seeing someone until he was sure.

She walked up to the front door as the last of them left. "Looks like someone was having a party. Hope you didn't send them away on my account."

"Oh no, just had some people over for games. I've got some things to take care of after this, so it seemed as good of a time as any to send them on their way."

Shirley had gotten that look on her face. The one that had a tinge of pity, but she meant well, and it was all just so damn awkward. Yes, he missed his wife every fucking day. But the intensity of the pain changed over time and he had learned to carry it. After a certain point, no one wanted to really hear about it anymore; they just wanted to hear he was doing better, to see him going back to some semblance of normal in their eyes. He knew whatever it was she was about to say, he didn't want to have another one of these conversations.

"It's good to see you socializing. Getting back out there. You're such a good guy, I just hate to think about you rattling around here all by yourself..."

He cringed internally. Everyone cared. Everyone just wanted him to be happy. But they just couldn't accept that his version of happiness wouldn't look like theirs. Not anymore.

"I'm fine," he replied in what he hoped was a polite but firm tone, hoping to end the conversation there. But Shirley clearly missed the hint.

"It's just that ever since –"

He was trying to listen. He really was. But he'd happened to glance over at the mirror that hung next to the door. The way he was standing, with the front door only opened partially, Shirley could not see past him. But next to him...that damn mirror reflected the bathroom back to him. The bathroom, which until thirty seconds ago, had the door shut. Now however, it had been opened. And much to his disbelief, Melody stood there, with her eyes locked on his in the mirror, as she slowly started to remove her clothing.

This could not be happening. This woman he had just met, could surely not be stripping in front of him – getting naked in his home. He wasn't exactly angry about this development, but he was definitely surprised.

He was trying so hard to appear like he was listening to Shirley. He'd throw in a "mmhmm" and an "I know" or a "sure" every once in a while, but his biggest struggle was tearing his eyes away from that damned mirror. Finally, once all her clothing was gone, she gave him a sultry smile before turning and heading further into the bathroom.

God, she had a good ass.

He heard the shower turn on and decided that it was time for Shirley to go.

"Shirley, thanks so much for coming by. I know how much you care, and I can never thank you enough for it. I'll take care of myself, I promise," he told her genuinely. While he did need her to leave now, this woman was like family to him, and he wanted to make sure she knew that. "I think I left the sink running though, so I better let you go."

"Oh, you know, I do think I hear some water now that you mention it." She squeezed his arm and her face softened. "You call if you need anything."

"I will. Drive safe."

He quickly closed the door behind her and locked it. What the fuck was he going to do now?

It wasn't like he was celibate. He wasn't against what she seemed to be offering, but this was something he hadn't done in a long time. He'd had some casual dates that led to sex in the last couple of years; he'd worked through the initial guilt and feelings of wrongness that came with being with anyone besides Angela. It just became clear quickly that he couldn't offer them more and so he let things fizzle out. Eventually he just stopped altogether.

He ran his hand down his face before walking back across the living room, into his bedroom, and finally into the bathroom.

He stood there in the doorway for a moment, just taking her in. She was standing under the waterfall shower head with her eyes closed and was clearly enjoying the heat. He cleared his throat, and she opened her eyes. A small smile played around her lips.

"What are you waiting for?" she asked. "Would you like to join me?"

He paused, his heartbeat pounding in his ears. And then decided, well, fuck it. She clearly wanted this, and it would be one more area he could see if they worked well together. Just because his heart wouldn't be involved didn't mean that the rest of him couldn't be.

He strode forward while ripping his shirt over his head. That was one good thing about not having an active social life, it left plenty of time to go to the gym and hone your body. He was more thankful for that than he had been in a long time as her eyes devoured his sculpted chest and abs.

He kicked off his boots and socks before starting to undo his belt. Here, he hesitated.

"Oh, come on, I showed you mine," she teased.

It had the desired effect, taking some of the tension off of him. He shoved his pants off and stalked towards the shower. It was one of those fancy ones with no door – the shower head was set far enough back to where it wasn't needed. He hadn't designed this house, but this seemed like a perk at the moment. One less barrier between them, one less thing to waste his time.

He entered the spray with her, and she immediately reached for him, drawing him into another kiss. He let himself fall into the sensation, cupping her face with one hand and the back of her neck with the other; his mind blissfully blank. She moaned and opened for him, so he swept his tongue in, deepening the kiss. God, it had been too long.

He jerked suddenly as he felt her grip his cock. He was so hard already, he didn't know how long he would last. So, he pressed into her and backed her up to the wall as he continued kissing her, sealing their bodies together so that she had no room to touch him. She drew her hand back up his abdomen to rest on his chest. He lowered his hands and gripped her hips, then slowly caressed his hands all the way up the sides of her body, taking her arms with him as he went, so that he could restrain them above her head. She made a small noise in the back of her throat that he took as encouragement.

Shifting so that he held both of her arms in one hand, he broke their kiss and drew back slightly to look at her. Her eyes were hooded, pupils dilated, and her lips were parted slightly in anticipation.

"We'll get to that later. But first, I get to taste you." With that, he dropped his mouth to her collarbone, making a path of searing kisses towards her breasts. She arched her back, which thrust her breasts out further, much to his delight. He captured one in his mouth, swirling his tongue around her tightened nipple before lightly dragging his teeth over the sensitive peak. She let out another noise then, this one no longer subtle.

He chuckled darkly before asking "Mmm, like that, do you?"

She nodded enthusiastically, as if speaking were too much at the moment.

He moved onto her other breast, repeating the torment, and her breathing turned ragged.

As she released another loud moan, he let his free hand drift down. He could feel her stomach tighten under his fingertips and he increased the pressure of his tongue on her breast. Her head lolled back as his hand met her entrance, and he gently explored her.

Fuck, she was so wet already.

He circled and teased until he could feel her trembling, and then he pushed a finger inside her.

"Oh my god." She moaned.

He pulled back to watch her face as he added a second finger and curled them inside. She made the most perfect "O" with her mouth, and he couldn't resist capturing her mouth in another kiss. She kissed him back hungrily, and he could feel her start to rock against his hand, in time with his fingers thrusting. She was beginning to flutter, to tighten, but he didn't want to send her over the edge yet. He withdrew his fingers, much to her dismay as she let out a small whimper.

He gave her a smirk as he released her arms and dropped to his knees.

"Shift your weight to your other leg," he instructed as he ran his hand up her left calf. When she did, he raised her leg and draped it over his shoulder, bearing her to him and opening her wide. He heard her inhale sharply and glanced up to make sure she was okay. The look she gave him was smoldering.

"Hold onto my shoulders," he warned her, before tightening his grip on her hips.

He felt her hands settling on him as he leaned in and tasted her. If he thought her moans were loud before, they were nothing to the sounds she made now. He chuckled again and she let out a strangled sounding "Yes."

He set to work, teasing her opening, and sucking her clit before fucking her with his tongue. He'd forgotten that women could taste so sweet. He could stay down here for hours. Every noise, every squirm, every taste and scent of her were only serving to turn him on further.

He went back to focusing on her clit, finding a rhythm that she responded to most. Once he was sure she was teetering on the edge, he drove two fingers into her as well. She came with a cry of pleasure, and he could feel how tightly she squeezed his fingers. This was going to be heaven.

He continued through the aftershock of her orgasm and when he felt her start to go slack, he started to lower her leg. Not all the way though. In one swift motion, he stood and brought her with him, wrapping her legs around his waist and positioning himself at her opening.

"Do you need a second?" he asked.

"God, no. I need you inside of me now."

"You don't have to tell me twice."

He started to ease into her. God, he wanted to just slam into her. But he didn't want to hurt her, he'd heard plenty of stor—

She suddenly tilted her hips and thrust down onto him, burying him to the hilt.

"Je-*sus*," he grunted. She was so fucking tight and perfect. He wasn't going to last. He was never –

"Oh, you feel so good." She moaned as she took over and started driving herself up and down, her slick skin sliding against his everywhere they met.

It took a second to regain his head and a tiny bit of control. He leaned in, pinning her to the wall once more as he thrusted into her. She was tightening again; it wouldn't be long now. He just had to hold on, there was more he wanted to do with her.

He dropped his hand to her clit, and she came again, fluttering around his cock and almost sending him over the edge with her.

He decided to change it up before it was too late. Gripping her ass, he backed away from the wall and walked over to the built-in bench on the other side of the shower. He sat down with her on his lap, still buried deep inside her.

This new position had him seated even further in, and he could feel himself hitting a spot deep inside of her. The way her eyes were rolling back said she liked it too. Now it took her a moment to collect herself, during which time he used his grip on her hips and made her ride him. She took over soon though, and kept him deep inside, in that position to hit that sweet spot over and over while grinding on his pelvis at the same time.

Her breasts bounced in front of him like his own personal show, and he couldn't think of anything better at the moment.

This time when she came, he went with her.

Chapter 3

Melody

They sat there for a few moments, catching their breath. She looked up at him and smiled, a little sheepishly to be honest, after everything they had just done. Especially considering the bold strip show she had decided to put on and start all of this.

He rose to his feet and took her with him, back over to the stream of water.

"Let's get you cleaned up."

He reached out of the shower and grabbed a clean washcloth from a basket on a nearby shelf. Lathering it up, the scent of his body wash floated to her, smelling crisp and spicy as he began to gently wash her. It was incredibly sweet, and very quickly also became incredibly hot.

When he reached her breasts, the touches became teasing again – brushing the material over her sensitive flesh before lightly tugging. His calloused fingers caused the most perfect friction against her smooth skin, and goosebumps broke out over her body. This man was going to be the death of her. She was already starting to ache for him again.

He continued washing her, moving down her body. But when he got to where she wanted him most, he skipped down to her legs.

After more teasing touches to her thighs, he stood and turned her around to face the wall. She pulled her hair over her shoulder to keep it out of the way and pouted where he couldn't see her face as he started washing her back.

They were both quiet, but it didn't feel uncomfortable. This surprised her honestly. She had expected things to get awkward after all the fun had stopped. The fleeting touches were getting frustrating, but overall, this was nice.

She suddenly felt him closing in behind her. His arms snaked around her waist from behind and she could feel him, hot and ready again against her ass.

Finally.

"It's difficult to clean you, when I keep having all these dirty thoughts," he whispered.

"Maybe you should act on them then."

He stepped back a couple of steps, pulling her with him before leaning them forward and gesturing for her to raise her arms and rest her hands on the wall.

He then nudged her legs further apart and licked a trail up her spine as he leaned back over her to speak in her ear.

"Brace yourself."

She felt him simultaneously bite down where her shoulder and neck met, while he thrust into her savagely. She would likely have a bite mark to show for it, but the thought of it only made her wetter. It was the perfect balance of pleasure-pain, and she could tell she wasn't going to last.

He didn't try to go slowly this time, he pounded into her, taking what he needed. There was something so primitive, so animalistic about this time and, fuck if it wasn't sexy. Every thrust made his beard scratch deliciously.

He reached down once again to tease her clit and soon she was squeezing him and coming with a string of unintelligible words flying from her mouth.

She was starting to think answering this ad may have been the best decision she had ever made.

He pounded into her a few more times before stilling deep inside, where she felt him pulse and spill himself.

Ugh, why was that so hot?

He released his bite and placed a gentle kiss on the mark. After a moment of catching their breath, he eased them back up and finished washing her. He was still gentle, but it was all business this time. Once she was taken care of, he quickly and efficiently washed himself down before turning the water off. She watched the water run over him, noticing a tattoo on his left bicep that she had missed in all the excitement. There was another on his shoulder blade as he turned away from her.

He grabbed a fluffy towel from another shelf and then turned to her, patting her dry and fluffing her hair. He made quick work of drying himself well before turning back to her and surprising her by picking her up.

She let out a startled “Oh!” As he walked them into his bedroom towards the bed.

“I don't know about you, but I could use a nap right about now. That was fucking amazing, and my body feels like jello.”

She laughed. “I will not object to that. Everything feels pleasantly leaden. If you hadn’t picked me up, I don't know how I would’ve made it this far.”

“Then I did my job right.” He smirked.

He pulled back the covers and laid her down, climbing in next to her. As he closed the distance, she asked with narrowed eyes, “Wait, you actually want to snuggle? Guys never want to snuggle.”

“Men who don’t like naked cuddles are either idiots or liars.” He crossed his arms. “Now roll over and be a good little spoon.”

She snorted a laugh and shrugged before doing as he asked. None of this made sense. It was bad enough she went to a strange man’s house that she met through an internet ad. Then she slept with him. Pretty much immediately. Now she felt perfectly at ease to fall asleep in his arms. This was the part of the movie where she’d wake up, tied to a pipe in a basement. But she couldn’t bring herself to move.

They fell asleep quickly.

She awoke sometime later, though how much later, she had no idea.

Why were there no clocks in here? Also, where did her phone end up? She didn't even remember what she did with it during her impromptu strip tease.

She was so warm and cozy. As she gained her bearings some more, she realized they had shifted a little. His arm was now under her head and wrapped around her chest, with his hand resting on her opposite shoulder, while his leg had snaked its way over hers. She was firmly pressed up against him, and she wasn't sure she could escape.

Not that she particularly wanted to, but she really did need to know the time. Though, she could feel his erection pressed up against her from behind – my god, this man was insatiable!

She squirmed a little, and her hair must have tickled his nose, because she felt him twitch slightly before rolling onto his back, releasing her. She rolled over to look at him, finding him still asleep.

"Nate!" she whispered, trying to gauge how deeply he slept. He groaned softly.

So, almost awake.

Then she came up with a devious way to perk him up and help take care of...well, you know.

"Nate..." her voice came out low and husky. His eyelids fluttered, and she started to run her fingers down his chest and over his abs. He had a sexy trail of hair leading down from his navel that she was itching to follow. "If you wake up, I'll make it worth your while."

He quirked an eye open at that. She leaned forward and replaced her fingers with her mouth, running her tongue through each indentation and rivet on his abdomen, paying special attention to the enticing V of muscles at his hips. He made a noise in the back of his throat and when she glanced up again, he was fully awake now, staring at her intensely. His eyes were such a piercing shade of green, it was like he could see into her soul, even as hazed with lust as they were right now.

She maintained eye contact as she made her way down to his cock. Once she reached it, she licked him, all the way up his shaft to the head, where she swirled her tongue around his tip.

His hips jerked and he released another noise. She smiled as she took him into her mouth, until he was drawn almost to the back of her throat. Then she began to lick, and suck and tease as he had done to her earlier.

His hand came down and tangled in her hair, while his hips thrust up, making him hit the back of her throat. He let out a satisfied groan before doing it again. His back arched off the bed and his eyes grew hooded. She kept up her rhythm with her tongue as well, and soon she could feel him pulsing again. He tried to draw her off of him, but she gripped his hips and refused to move, swallowing down every last drop and licking him clean before releasing him.

The look he gave her was filthy and heated, but utterly sated too.

"I could get used to wake-up calls like this," he murmured. "Though it's hardly fair to expect me to get up now that you've gotten me all relaxed again."

She grinned. "I know, but I really need to know what time it is."

He lazily reached over and pulled open the drawer in his nightstand, grabbing his cellphone.

"It is 5:47."

"Shit! Fredrick is going to kill me."

He sat up suddenly. "Who is Fredrick? I thought you were single."

She choked back a laugh. "Oh god, sorry. No, it's – Fredrick is my dog. A husky. A very needy and demanding husky who is very particular about his dinner time and is most likely carrying on like he is on the verge of death right now."

"Oh," he said, his shoulders relaxing. "Well, let's go take care of him then."

"You want to come with me?"

"I mean, yeah if that's okay. We haven't actually talked yet since you skipped straight to jumping my bones, so I thought we could talk in the car and maybe grab dinner after?"

She nodded and blushed. Dammit. She was doing so well up until now. But she hadn't shown up today planning to seduce him. He just looked so... edible... and he seemed nice, and respectful, and her imagination took off and took her panties with it. But he was right; they hadn't talked at all yet.

Oh god.

"You're not a cat person, are you? My dog is my world, and I've had him for years. He's been with me through the deaths of both of my parents, and he's pretty much the only family I've got. If you hate him, that's kind of my only deal breaker on this, so I really need you to not be a cat person." She realized she was rambling and talking too quickly, so she forcibly shut her mouth to keep from going on.

The look he gave her was amused and for a moment, she thought she caught a glimpse of sad understanding, but she couldn't be sure because it was gone almost as soon as it had appeared.

"Don't worry, I love dogs," he said.

She let out a relieved sigh and got up to find her clothes and phone. Once she was dressed, she pulled up the nanny cam on her phone to check on Fredrick.

It was about as expected. He was howling like a siren while repeatedly pressing the "food" button on his canine keyboard. Why she thought jumping on this trend of training your dog to speak via buttons was a good idea, she'd never know. She'd only given him another avenue to yell at her.

What a diva.

As they were walking through the house, she cleared her throat. "Speaking of us not talking beforehand, I, uh, also didn't stop to think about using a condom..." Her voice came out a little higher than normal.

His eyes widened. "Oh shit. It's been a while for me, so I forgot about it. Are you – do we–?"

"I have an IUD, so we don't have to worry about me getting pregnant at least...but what I meant was, is there anything I need to worry about? I know you said it's been a while, but.... I mean, I've been tested recently, so I'm clean... do you...?" She could feel her palms starting to sweat.

"Oh!" he said, letting out a breath. "No, you don't have to worry on my account. I'm clean."

She ran a hand through her hair. "Awesome. Phew. I swear, I don't normally just go around jumping guys like this. There's just something about you that feels... right. And comfortable. Not to mention you're fucking hot. Anyway." She blushed again.

Dammit, she really had to stop rambling.

He gave her a small smile. "I feel the same way. Now, let's go feed that mini ambulance you call a dog."

She laughed. "You heard that?"

"From across the room." He snorted.

Chapter 4

Nate

He locked up the front door as Mel headed down the porch and ran her hands through her hair as though she was trying to smooth out the sex, shower and nap. While they walked over to her old beat-up red Jeep Cherokee, she asked over her shoulder "So where do you want to go eat after this?"

"Ladies choice," he said.

"I would kill for some tacos honestly."

"I'm pretty much always down for Mexican food, myself. There's a great hole-in-the-wall place called Rudy's near here if you want to try it."

"I love Rudy's. Sounds like a plan."

They hopped in and she started the car, using an aux cord to turn on some music from her phone. He had no idea what was playing, except that it was not in English. He could see the start of a blush on her cheeks and ears as she tried to nonchalantly adjust the volume down and get buckled in, but she didn't comment on her music selection.

As she drove off, he cleared his throat and asked, "So are you bilingual?"

She laughed abruptly before clapping her hand over her mouth and looking at him apologetically. "Sorry, no. I'm just a big anime fan."

"At the risk of sounding completely ignorant, may I ask what anime is?"

"Oh, we are going to have so much fun rectifying this obvious lack of exposure. Anime is the beautiful practice of taking manga, which is sort of like Japanese comics and animating them. Some of the most beautiful and profound stories I have ever experienced have been through a manga or an anime. Now, some people shrug it off as just for children or perverts, but there are some real gems. This song, for example, is from one of my favorites: Demon Slayer. We are totally going to watch it together sometime soon so I can see your face as you understand just how amazing it is." She let out in one breath.

He chuckled. "All right then. So, I see you enjoy reading and watching shows. What else do you enjoy?"

She paused in thought.

The song shifted to a slower song, in English this time, the singer talking about how if they had a choice, they would choose their life again. It was sweet and had a comforting feeling about it.

"Sorry – what is this one called?" he asked.

Her face broke into a soft smile. "This story is called Frieren: Beyond Journey's End. Another of my favorites. I feel like it is one that has to be experienced more than it can be explained though. We'll add it to the list. To answer your other question, I enjoy leisurely bicycling and yoga. I volunteer at the local animal shelter when I have time, which is where I found my fluffy freeloader. And I paint. Nothing too crazy. What about you?"

"Well, I'm a woodworker. So, I do that both professionally and also as a hobby. I've got a storefront over on Main. I do more practical things professionally, so a lot of furniture, cabinets, and stuff like that. On my own time, it's more of an outlet for me and I make sculptures. I'm kinda boring other than that. I work out and spend time with my family."

"That's amazing. I would love to see your work sometime if that's okay. What all family do you have around here?"

"Well, my dad took off when I was young. So, it's just my mom, Naomi, my two siblings and me. I'm the oldest, then there is my sister Natalie, but everyone calls her Nat, and then my little brother Nash. And before you ask, yes, my mom had a weird thing for alliteration which is why all of our names start with N." He laughed while rolling his eyes.

"I think that's sweet." She cleared her throat. "I don't really have family around. My parents passed away in a car accident when I was nineteen, and I went to live with my aunt for a while after that. Once I got out of college, I decided to move away from our hometown and start fresh. My aunt and I are still fairly close and talk on the phone every week, but she doesn't live around here."

“I’m sorry to hear that.” He hesitated before starting again. “I…my wife passed away almost five years ago. It’ll be five years in May actually. She uh, she was sick. Cancer. By the time we knew anything was wrong, it was too far gone and she went quick.” He looked out the window for a second. “That’s why I’m doing this. Why I placed the ad, I mean. Angela was…everything. I loved her with every piece of me. I’ve had no interest in being with anyone else like that. But my family, they worry. They mean well and I love them for it, but they just don’t understand. They can’t. So I figured, if I can find someone I like okay and is willing to be my friend, we can make an arrangement. It will ease their minds if they think I’ve moved on. I can’t promise to be your great love or that this will be some kind of fairy tale. But I can offer you friendship and respect. And apparently seriously hot sex if this afternoon was anything to go by.” He laughed nervously. “I realize that this is not fair of me to even ask you. You deserve to find someone who isn’t broken and who can give you their heart. So, I totally understand if you want to walk away from this.”

She didn’t reply right away, and he glanced over to see what she was thinking. Her face was contemplative. Finally, she said, “I’m sorry for your loss. I know more than anyone how little those words help or change anything, but I need you to know all the same. And I appreciate your honesty. I would like that. To be your friend, I mean.” After another pause, she added, “And if I get amazing orgasms out of it too, all the better.” She grinned mischievously.

He leaned his head back against the headrest as he laughed, relaxing at her response. "Well then, let's get to know each other a little better and decide if we're getting married this weekend."

Chapter 5

Melody

Melody pulled up into the driveway of her town home and switched off her jeep.

"You're welcome to come in, but if you value your eardrums and would rather wait out here, I totally understand," she said.

"I think it's about time I meet the man in your life." He snorted.

"Don't say I didn't warn you."

They walked up to her front door and could already hear Fredrick faintly from inside. With a grimace she said, "At least I have the end unit and dear old Mrs. Fern next door is hard of hearing..."

She led him inside, locking the door behind them and dropping her keys into a pottery bowl that was sitting on a small table in the entryway. An automated voice chanting "Food" was getting louder the further into the house they got.

She saw him glance around as if he didn't know where to look first. Her home was comfortable, but also slightly chaotic like her. She mused it's what people probably call "organized chaos". Her painting occupied a good amount of her time and inspiration struck everywhere. Aside from the many finished pieces hanging on her walls, there were several partially finished pieces on small easels throughout the space. A warm piece was over by one window that was inspired by the afternoon light that glowed through there; a multicolor piece was by the backdoor and reminded her of the trees against the sky at different times of year.

They made it to the living room, and they could finally see the cause of the ruckus. Fredrick, on the other hand, ignored Nate completely, focusing solely on Mel.

In one of those voices that every dog owner seems to use, Melody said, "Hey buddy. I know, I'm late and I'm sorry. I promise you're fine, though. No, really, you're fine. I'm going to feed you right now."

Nate leaned against the kitchen counter to stay out of her way as she went about putting food in the dish before letting him out of the gated area of the living room. Fredrick descended on the bowl like he hadn't eaten in a week while she shook her head and told Nate, "I swear, you'd think he never gets fed. Anyway, this is home." She threw her arms out to both sides in a ta-da motion.

"It's beautiful. Is this all your work?" He motioned to one of the abstract paintings on the wall.

"Yes. I tend to make it faster than I can sell it, and sometimes I also get attached to pieces, so they often end up hanging around a while. Pun intended." She winked.

"I'm going to ignore that last part." He laughed and looked around some more. "Your art is so diverse. Some of these feel intense while others are soothing. You're very talented."

"Thank you. It pays the bills. And I love it, so win-win, I'd say," Melody said with a wide smile.

"I know the feeling."

Fredrick finished eating and decided to finally investigate the stranger. Running up to Nate, he started to sniff around to assess him fully. Nate ran his hand over his ears, eliciting a contented sigh. Once he looked up at Nate, the light caught his face, showing off his one brown and one blue eye. Nate squatted so he could pet him more easily, and Fredrick used the opportunity to lick him straight across the face. Nate fell back, laughing and wiping his face on his sleeve.

With a mixture of a groan and a laugh, Melody said, "I'm so sorry – Fredrick, we've talked about this. Not everyone likes kisses. And you have death-breath. Come on, you need to go potty."

He perked up at that and without a backward glance, ran to the back door. She let him out into her fenced-in backyard.

"I've heard huskies can sometimes tend to be runners. He doesn't give you any problems with the yard?"

"Maybe in his "teenage" years I would have been concerned. But he's an old fella now and the running you just saw is the extent of it most days. He mostly sticks to talking to me via the ambulance noise as you dubbed it, or his buttons."

Nate laughed. "I can't believe you actually trained him with buttons. I can't tell if that is genius or insanity."

"A bit of both most days to be honest." She joined in laughing. "Anyway, you want a quick tour while we wait for him to do his business?"

"Sure. Lead the way."

She gestured around. "Clearly this is the living room and the kitchen attached here. Open concept floor plan and all." She led him back towards the front door and the room they had passed on their way inside. "This I think is supposed to be a dining room, but since I never host, I turned it into a painting area. It's got good light."

"I can tell." He paused as he took in the room, looking over some of her pieces in progress. She wished she could see them through his eyes, feel his reaction. Hearing other people's thoughts on her work was one of her favorite parts of making art. She wouldn't push though, opinions should be freely given.

After a minute, they moved on. Upstairs was her bedroom, and she showed him the way. "And this concludes our tour," she told him with a flourish. Her room was fairly small, with just a little bit of room surrounding her queen size bed. A dresser was pushed up against the wall across from the foot of the bed, but not much else was there.

"It's cozy." He smiled. "Though if we decide to really do this, I think we are going to have to find a bigger place to live. We both kinda live in shoe boxes." He rubbed the back of his neck. "What you saw of my place is basically it space-wise."

"You're probably right. I guess we'll see how the rest of this week goes and cross that bridge when we come to it?"

Nate nodded. "Sounds like a plan."

They headed back downstairs where she let Fredrick back in. After a few minutes of sitting on the couch and showering him with attention, they decided to head to dinner.

She drove them a couple of blocks to Rudy's, and they went inside where they were met with the familiar scent of onions and meat fried up with spices.

From behind the counter, a wiry older gentleman greeted them, "Miss Melody, Mr. Nathaniel! Two of my best customers, and here together – what a day."

They glanced at each other in surprise, having not realized that they both frequented this place.

"Hey Mr. Miller, how have you been?" Melody asked as Nate shook his hand.

"Oh, you know. My arthritis is acting up since we had rain earlier this week, but I'm still kicking. The missus has been on me to keep up with my PT, so it's not as bad as it could've been."

"She knows what she's talking about, that one. Best to listen to her," Nate said.

"Yes, yes. Not worth the headache of arguing at the very least." Mr. Miller chuckled. "But how have you two been? And what are you doing here together? I didn't realize you were acquainted."

They glanced at each other before Nate answered, "Well, we recently met and are getting to know each other. I asked her to have dinner with me."

"That's wonderful. She's a good girl. And he's a gentleman, Miss Mel. I trust him to treat you nicely. So, one ticket then, right? The usual for you both?" He looked back and forth between them expectantly.

Melody started to object, "Oh, no –"

Nate waved her off with a scoff. "It's a date, Mel. Of course I'm paying."

Mr. Miller nodded in approval before ringing up their order and handing them a couple of empty cups for their fountain drinks. "Be right out."

Melody accepted her cup and chose a booth in the corner after filling it. Nate joined her shortly, sliding into the seat across from her.

"So clearly you come here often." Nate chuckled.

"I could say the same thing about you."

"It's true. Especially these last few years. I can cook, but it's been hard to work up the motivation to cook for one all the time."

"Agreed. But in my case, I'm also not so good at cooking in the first place. I don't have that natural instinct for it, and for some reason, reading the directions on packages is a real struggle."

Nate laughed. "Where does the struggle lay exactly?"

"Ummm well, the retention, I guess? I obviously can read, and I generally understand what I read. But then I turn to go measure something out and it's like the numbers flee my brain. So instead of two cups of milk and five cups of water, I'll try to use five cups of milk and two cups of water. Obviously, some mix ups are more disastrous than others." She said, shredding her straw wrapper between her fingers.

"Got it. So cooking is not your thing. Well, I'm decent at it, so no worries there. Other than that, what would you say your least favorite household chore would be? Division of household labor is one of those things Angela and I never thought to talk about before we got married since we were basically kids, but in hindsight, setting healthy expectations up front is huge." He took a sip of his drink and rested his forearms on the table.

She tucked her hair behind her ear. "I've never been married, so I'm pretty much used to doing it all. I'd have to say laundry is my least favorite though. I tend to enjoy most of the work involved in taking care of Fredrick, and I don't mind things like dishes. I invested in a Roomba years ago because the fur was going to drive me insane, so vacuuming isn't too much of a chore thanks to that. I'll be honest, I pretty much never bother with dusting though because it feels pointless. What about you?"

"Well, if we do this, I don't expect you to do it all. I tend to be fairly neat, but half of the mess will be mine, and it's not fair to either one of us to be expected to be a maid on top of our day jobs. I personally don't mind laundry, but I don't particularly like cleaning bathrooms. I'm pretty good about just rinsing my dishes and putting them in the dishwasher immediately, so dishes aren't too bad. I have to agree with you on dusting. The only places I really worry about are in my workspaces since it's less dust than wood particles everywhere."

A waitress dropped off trays with their food then. "Need anything else?" she asked as she backed away from their table. Shaking their heads no, she headed to the back of the store, and they settled into their meal.

"What did you get?" he asked.

"I love their fried avocado tacos. You?"

"That looks amazing. I usually get the steak fajita tacos."

"Want to trade bites?" she asked and held out one of her tacos to him.

After a moment of hesitation, he leaned forward and took a bite. She saw his eyes flare as he chewed, then he said, "Damn, that's good. Here."

He held out one of his own tacos for her to try. She let out a satisfied sigh as the flavors hit her tongue and once she was finished with the bite, she said, "That's pretty good too."

They ate quietly for a little bit before he started the conversation back up. "So, on a more serious note. How do you feel about kids?"

She coughed on the sip of drink she had just taken and cleared her throat. "I mean, I like them fine. I've never really wanted any of my own though. I don't mind being around them and if I'd had siblings, I know I would be a great aunt. But I've just never had that *maternal instinct* or had the urge to procreate. It's just not my thing. Honestly, I'd have probably taken a more permanent approach to things if doctors weren't so hesitant to do it. So, the IUD is the closest I've been able to get. Is that a deal breaker for you?"

"God no. That's a relief actually." He sat back in his seat. "It was always part of the plan with Angela because it's just kind of an unspoken expectation placed on young couples. I know she wanted kids and would've been an amazing mom. But it just never happened for us. Looking back, I know now that was clearly due to her health issues that we were unaware of, but back then we weren't worried about it. We were just enjoying each other, and figured it would happen when it happened. At the time, I didn't realize that I felt that way more than she did though. I found out later that she had a really hard time with it all. But after losing her, part of me was relieved that I didn't have a little one depending on me to get them through that dark time. I barely got myself through. And now that a few years have passed, I realize that I was always kind of indifferent about the whole thing. I wanted it because

Ang wanted it, not because I have this burning desire to be a dad. I would have loved any child we would've had, but I know that it's not something I would actively choose now. It probably didn't help that with my own dad skipping out, and being raised by a single mom, there were a lot of times I felt like a stand-in father for my siblings. My family kinda has this unspoken rule that we don't talk about him ever since he left, and my mom is wonderful, and she did her best, but managing three kids while working to support us all was a lot. I had to step up for the family and grow up a little faster than my mom wanted. It kinda feels like I've gotten a small taste of being a dad, and I grew up just wanting to be able to be a kid for once. Just worry about being my own person without having someone's whole future being on my shoulders. So, I'm glad to hear that you feel similarly." He glanced down at the table for a moment before meeting her eye again. "Like I said, I can't offer you some epic love story and I can't promise you a family in the traditional sense. I would never forgive myself if I stole something like that from you if it's what you want in life."

She reached out and placed her hand over his. "It sounds like we are on the same page here."

He traced a thumb over her knuckles. "I know this is all sudden. I'm throwing a lot at you and we just met, but I meant what I said in the ad. I'm not looking to do the whole drawn out dating thing. The more time that passes, the more everyone seems to want to set me up on blind dates and encourage me to meet someone.

Everyone always means well, but I'm just not interested. As crazy as it sounds, I know my family, and they are more likely to accept someone in my life if they are my wife instead of just a girlfriend. Cutting out all the scrutiny that comes with dating should help things along – all the opinions people are more likely to share if they think there's a chance it's not permanent. I've never been one for rash decisions, so I feel pretty certain that they will accept you if we do this. That being said, I'd like to be able to tell everyone at our next family gathering coming up here soon. So, if we do this, I want to do it fairly quickly. Am I scaring you off yet?"

"I understand. And I'm still in if you are."

"I am. I still think we should take this week to get to know each other a little more and then if we still feel this way, we can go to the courthouse on Saturday."

"Sounds like a plan to me. Since it's Sunday, that gives us almost a full week. We can grab meals between work and can exchange numbers if you're comfortable with it, so we can text and stuff."

Nate snorted a laugh. "You've seen me naked and know where I live, so I don't think giving you my phone number is out of the question."

Feeling her face flush once again, she pulled out her phone and set about adding him as a new contact before handing the phone to him so he could enter the number.

He took the phone and not only entered his number, but also took a selfie and set it as his contact photo for her with a wink. Taking his offered phone, she typed her number in quickly before handing it back.

"What? No picture for me?" Nate asked with a teasing pout.

"I'm the queen of taking bad photos." She fidgeted with her straw.

"I find that hard to believe with how gorgeous you are," he said in a low voice.

She couldn't help but smile, and he took the opportunity to snap a quick picture.

"See? Look how perfect you are." He turned the phone to her and much to her surprise, it was a good photo. Her smile was soft, the light was hitting her face in a flattering way, and for once, no part of her was blurred out.

"A rare photo indeed. Half the time, I can't sit still long enough for it to take. But you're kind of a sweet talker, aren't you?"

"What? I may be a little out of practice, but I know how to talk to a woman. Plus, it's easy when it's true."

Melody shook her head as she scooted out of their booth, "Okay, Casanova. You ready to get out of here?"

"Propositioning me again, Mel? Just can't get enough, can you?"

With a snort, she said, "I was planning to just drop you off at home seeing as I've already had my wicked ways with you this afternoon. Be a good boy and maybe we'll play again soon."

"Yes, Ma'am."

They waved goodbye to Mr. Miller, who had been behind the front counter, trying to look like he hadn't been watching and attempting to eavesdrop. "Come back soon!" he called after them.

As they drove back to Nate's house, Mel said, "Just thinking about it all, maybe we should agree here and now that we won't have sex anymore this week. It was incredible, but as you pointed out earlier, it doesn't leave much room for talking. I feel like we should focus more on that the rest of the week so that we are sure about all this."

"As much as I hate to admit it, you're probably right. I'll do my best to keep my hands to myself."

They pulled up in his driveway, and she got out to walk him to his front door. "So, I'll text you tomorrow?"

"Sure. We can figure out schedules for the rest of the week." He fished out his keys and started unlocking the door.

"You know, you don't have to one hundred percent keep your hands to yourself...I do think we should slow things down a little, but if you wanted to kiss me goodnight, I won't say no."

With a half smile, he turned back to her and said, "Can't leave my lady hanging, now can I?" He stepped into her personal space and ran a thumb over her cheek before angling his face down to meet hers.

She had intended to give him a quick and chaste kiss goodnight, but as soon as their lips met, her body reacted on its own, pulling her closer towards him like a magnet. His scent of citrus and timber enveloped her, as if his work was so deeply ingrained inside of him that they were one and the same. Her hands ran up his biceps and his tangled in her hair as the kiss lingered.

Finally, he broke away. "If I don't stop now, I'm not going to be able to keep my word." He placed one more soft kiss on her lips and then released her. "Goodnight Mel."

"Goodnight, Nate."

She drove home in a daze, not sure the day had really happened. It sure felt like some kind of fever dream.

Going about her evening routine with Fredrick and getting ready for bed, she tried to think about it all rationally. Curling up in bed and placing her fingers to her lips, she realized that rationality was going to be hard to come by this week with this man. All she knew for sure was that she wanted to see where this went.

Chapter 6

Nate

Nate drove to work the next morning like it was any other Monday. He did his best to focus on his tasks and appointments for the day, but the compulsion to check his phone every five minutes was strong. He didn't want to pressure Melody though, so he had resolved to let her be the one to reach out.

He could hear Sean talking with customers up front while he finished up some paperwork at his desk. He had met Sean through Shirley, and he was a good kid. He had decided to take some time off before going to college, so Nate was giving him some work experience in the meantime.

Signing order forms, checking budgets and project proposals kept him busy for a couple of hours, and once he was done with that, he went to the next room to work with his hands and get some energy out.

Settling into the familiar routine, he set music playing and started working. Something about it always settled him and helped him get out of his head, which was exactly what he needed right now.

This current piece was a simple rocking chair, a gift for a new mother from her doting husband. Smoothing out each spoke, each curve, Nate did his best to imbue the wood with the comfort and peace he felt while crafting it. Once he was satisfied with the construction, he tested it out, seeking any areas that needed extra attention. He found none, and moved on to staining it. The man had requested a rich honey brown to compliment the nursery. After finishing the first coat, he left it to dry as he went to get some water and take a break in his office.

Pulling his phone out, he saw it was about two in the afternoon, and he finally had a text from Melody. Breathing out a sigh of relief, he texted her back.

With a game plan for the evening in mind, he focused in and finished up what he needed to for the day. He flipped off the lights to his workroom and office before heading up front and telling Sean that he was calling it a day.

"Have a good evening, boss," Sean called after him.

"You too, man."

Nate hopped into his truck and drove home, lost in thought about what to fix for dinner. He decided on his version of Spanish Paella since he had everything on hand already and he knew that Mel liked Mexican food.

He headed into his bathroom to grab a quick shower, needing to wash the sawdust and chemicals off his skin. The bathroom held memories now though, and flashbacks of the day before went through his mind as he set the water running in the shower.

If he was going to keep his word and keep his hands to himself, he was going to have to get a handle on this. With a snort, he realized that he would probably have to take that literally since he was already hard and aching just thinking about his time with her yesterday.

He threw his clothes in the hamper and walked into the steaming water, letting the heat relax him. When he closed his eyes, all he could see was Melody standing there, beads of water running down her bare skin. The sound of her moans filled his mind and remembering the look on her face as she came was too much for him, so he gave in and gave his cock a firm stroke. Memories of her riding him, of her mouth around him as he woke up spurred him on to his release.

Feeling a little more clear headed, he finished getting cleaned up and dressed again before heading to the kitchen to get started on dinner.

The timing was just about perfect, with five minutes left on the timer, he heard her knock on his front door. He set the lid back on the pot and answered the door, where he was greeted by a very excited husky.

"Fredrick, good to see you too."

"I know you said you didn't need me to bring anything, but I thought hard lemonade sounded good. I hope you don't mind."

"Not at all. That should go pretty well with the food actually."

"Well, it smells delicious." Melody sat her purse down on the side table by the couch and released the dog from his harness. As soon as he was free, he took off to explore his new surroundings. "He won't hurt anything, but I can keep him here if you don't want him running around all over."

Nate waved her off as he headed back to the kitchen. "He'll be fine. If all goes according to plan, we'll be roommates soon anyway, so we might as well get used to having each other around. Do you need a water bowl for him though?"

"I brought one actually, if you can just point me to the best spot to set it out of the way."

"Maybe the corner by the fridge?" He took the lid back off the pot and stirred the rice dish.

"Sounds good." She filled the bowl and set it on the floor. "Anything I can do to help?"

"Nah, it's ready. Go ahead and grab one of those plates." He gestured towards the table where he had set them out along with some toppings. She took two of the drinks she had brought and set them down, exchanging them for plates.

He dished them both up a decent sized helping and led her back to the table where he pulled out her chair for her.

"So fancy. Thank you, sir."

"I try." He winked. "So, I enjoy adding sour cream and fresh avocado to mine. You'll have to see what you prefer – I have salsa in the fridge too if you'd like."

"I'll try it your way first." She smiled as she dabbed some of the toppings onto her food. He watched her take the first bite, waiting for her reaction. She closed her eyes and tilted her head back saying, "Oh my god, this is perfect. What is this?"

"It's Paella. Maybe not the strictly traditional version, but the version I tinkered around with and enjoy the most. It's rice, chorizo, chicken, peppers and spices. I'm glad you like it."

"You weren't kidding when you said you cook."

They settled into eating, chatting about their day between bites. He told her about his shop, and she told him about her latest painting, sparked by the chipped paint on the fire hydrant down the block from her home.

The evening passed quickly and before they knew it, the clock read 10:30pm. With a sigh, Nate said, "I hate to cut this short, but I have an early morning, so I better call it a night. I had a nice evening with you though."

"Me too. How does tomorrow night look for you?"

"I usually hit the gym after work on Tuesdays and Thursdays, but I'm free after that."

"Well, I think it is high time to start your anime education. Want to come over to my place tomorrow night for dinner and a mini marathon? I need to make sure you don't have trash taste in anime before I commit." She sniffed.

He laughed. "Sounds good. I can pick up pizza on my way over?"

"No judgement here, but you want to eat junk food immediately after working out?"

"Hell yes. It's called self-care. I work my ass off so that I *can* eat all the pizza I fucking want."

"I like that." She got up and took their plates to the sink, rinsing them off before loading them into the dishwasher for him. Nate started putting the toppings away and dishing up the leftovers into a Tupperware container.

"Do you want to take this for later?" he asked her.

"Umm most definitely." She took the container over to her bag. "Fredrick, come here boy!"

Nate gave him an affectionate scratch behind his ear once he was buckled into his harness, and then he walked them to her Jeep.

"Thank you for dinner," Mel said, leaning against the SUV once Fredrick was loaded up.

"You're welcome." Bracketing his arms on either side of her body, Nate leaned in to kiss her goodnight. They weren't able to get too carried away tonight however, because after a few seconds a keening whine was heard from inside the Jeep, effectively killing the mood. With a dry chuckle, Nate backed up with hands raised in surrender and said, "Okay, okay. She's all yours for tonight buddy." Placing one more soft kiss on her cheek, he left her with an "I'll see you tomorrow."

After seeing her drive safely down the street, he headed in and finished cleaning up the kitchen before bed.

The next day was much like the day before, but work did go a little faster at least. Before he knew it, he was heading into the gym, eager to get his workout over with. He stored his bag in a locker and made his way over to the various weight machines, headphones in hand.

He had gotten in a few sets when he saw his brother come up behind him in the mirror. Nate carefully set the weights back down and pulled up one side of his headphones so he could hear what Nash was saying.

"Only forty pounds today? Slacking."

"Pssh, is that inferiority I smell? What are you up to these days? Fifteen?" Nate shot back. They tussled like brothers often do, dodging halfhearted punches.

"How much more are you doing? I got here late today," Nash said.

"Probably another thirty minutes or so. I have a few more sets."

"I can do a short routine today. Want to grab dinner after?"

"I actually am meeting up with a friend for dinner after this, so rain check?"

"You're going out on a school night? By all means! We'll hook up later this week or something."

Nate laughed. "Shut up. I'll hit you up after this weekend. I've got some deadlines coming up, so I'm going to be a little distracted the rest of this week."

"Don't push yourself too hard, man."

Nate started to reply, but Nash cut him off, "I know, I know, 'You're fine.' So, you always say."

"I say it because it's true."

"Uh-huh."

"Are you going to work out or just watch me?"

"Just seeing what not to do." Nash moved to the next machine over and adjusted the weights to his preferred amount before settling in.

They finished their workout in relative silence, commenting on technique here and there, but mostly focusing on their own work. Walking to the locker rooms together, Nate said, "I'm going to grab a quick shower here. You heading home?"

"Yeah, I'll shower in private, thanks."

With a snort, Nate shrugged. "Can't say I blame you. Well, see you later brother."

"Have fun tonight, man." Nash waved goodbye as he headed back out with his bag slung over his shoulder.

Once Nate was finished, he gave Melody a quick call from his truck. "Hey. I'm about to head that way. What are your favorite pizza toppings?"

"Great. Honestly, I'm a fan of good ol' pepperoni."

"Noted. I'll probably be there in about twenty minutes or so. See you soon."

"See you in a bit. Bye."

A little bit later, he walked up to her front door and rang the doorbell. Inside he heard the telltale sound of Fredrick getting closer right before Melody opened the door to let him inside. He followed her in and set the pizzas on the kitchen counter as she convinced Fredrick to calm back down.

He reached down to pet Fredrick in greeting before turning his attention back to Mel. She looked adorable in an oversized sweatshirt which featured an angry looking orange cat and a surly looking man with equally orange hair. It said "Year of the Cat" underneath. She had paired it with some little running shorts which showed off her toned legs and soft skin. He knew that would distract him all evening if he wasn't careful, so with some effort, he pulled his attention back up to her face only to find her taking him in as well. Considering he was just in some casual clothes after the gym, he felt a little confused by the look on her face.

"What?" He asked.

She gave an indelicate snort. "You know what. You men and your grey sweatpants, I swear."

His brow furrowed. "What are you talking about?"

She raised her eyebrows. "You've seriously never heard about the grey sweatpants thing? The trend on social media?"

"I have no idea what you're talking about. I don't really do the whole social media thing." He crossed his arms over his chest.

She laughed. "Basically, you're wearing women's equivalent to lingerie. I mean, you've got the fitted white t-shirt to show off your muscles, you've got the backwards baseball cap thing going on, and then...the sweatpants. Ah, the sweatpants. I'm guessing you've never noticed, but they tend to show off how well...*endowed*...a guy is. They leave little to the imagination."

He felt mildly horrified. "You're joking, right?" He looked down, expecting to see that they were somehow see through and that he had never noticed.

Laughing again, she said, "Here, come with me. Let me show you what I mean." She took his hand and led him upstairs to her room where she closed the door behind them, exposing the full-length mirror fixed to the back of the door.

She sat down on her bed and told him, "Okay, walk towards the mirror and watch your pants."

He hesitantly followed her instruction and saw what she was referring to. "Holy shit. I knew these were comfortable and gave me plenty of breathing room, but I had no idea that would be so visible." He twisted his hips once more before running a hand down his face.

Melody devolved into laughter, pulling her knees up to bury her face. Nate couldn't help but join in. "I can't believe no one has ever said anything."

Collecting herself slightly, she said, "Why spoil it for everyone? I mean, you're basically doing a public service every time you go out in those. It's really quite unfair."

Nate dropped to his knees in front of her and cupped the back of her calves with his hands before saying, "Then I guess we are even. It's also unfair to display these gorgeous legs like this."

Her eyes dilated, and his gaze snagged on her lips as Melody slowly lowered her legs to the floor around him. He let his hands slide up to her thighs as she moved, not wanting to stop touching her yet. He realized he had also started to lean in without thinking, the distance between their lips shrinking.

She crossed the remaining distance, breaking the tension with a tentative kiss. Nate let himself sink into the sensation and pulled her a little closer by his grip on her legs. Melody responded by winding her arms around his neck and running her fingers through the hair at the nape of his neck, underneath his hat.

He could tell they were getting carried away as he shifted her back further on the bed, settling over her and his hat got knocked off completely, but he didn't want to stop. She clearly didn't either, opening for him and teasing his tongue with her own and nipping at his bottom lip. When she rolled her hips though, he knew he would be in trouble if he didn't pump the brakes now.

Finding the willpower to break their kiss and pull back so he could look at her, he said, "I hate myself for even saying this, but we should probably stop. I want to honor your wishes and not take this further until you've made up your mind about everything. So maybe we should go eat and cool things down."

"You're probably right," she said, still a little out of breath.

He kissed her nose before standing up and putting his hat back on. He took her hand to help her back up as well and kept hold of it as they went back downstairs.

After filling their plates, they settled on the couch and Melody said, "Okay, so which anime do you want to start with? My top ones are: Fullmetal Alchemist, Demon Slayer, Frieren, and Fruits Basket. I can tell you about any of them if you want to know more."

"Frieren was that softer song I heard in the car the other day?"

"Yes, the one you had asked me about and seemed to like."

"Let's give that one a try."

"Sounds good. Fair warning though, you are going to immediately want more when we reach the end of this first season. It's that good."

She was right. He had been a little skeptical about watching a cartoon in any form, but it drew him in from the first episode. He found himself caring more about fictional characters than he could ever remember doing in his life. They made him laugh, they made him think, they made him feel. The next thing he knew, it was almost two a.m., and they had finished the final episode available.

"Shit. I did not expect to get that invested." He stretched.

"I know. The writer is a genius. If the books were finished, I wouldn't be able to help myself – I would have to read them all and find out what happens. Unfortunately, the world must wait though."

"I'm going to feel like garbage tomorrow for staying up this late, but, no regrets. Thank you for showing me this."

"Yeah, I didn't realize we would binge all of it. But I'm so glad that you love it. That's one point in your favor."

"How many points am I up to then?"

"Well, you know, like a million for orgasm skills. At least seven points for being a good cook. Ten for the sweatpants." She tapped a finger against her lips.

"This seems like a fairly arbitrary grading system."

"Maybe. Either way though, you're coming out ahead."

"Hmm. So, a million whole points for orgasm skills, huh?" He put his arm around her and drew her closer to his side.

“I mean, it was pretty mind blowing if memory serves.”

Brushing his mouth over hers, he said against her lips, “Well, if you decide to marry me, I’ll be sure to refresh your memory.”

Melody let out a soft whimpering sound and Nate gave her what she wanted, kissing her soundly. He was careful not to get carried away this time and pulled back after a moment. “I should let you get some sleep. Thank you for tonight.”

“Thank you for giving it a shot. Talk tomorrow?”

“Absolutely.” He gave her one more soft kiss before disentangling himself and standing. They said goodnight and he headed home, feeling pretty good about this arrangement so far.

Nate was correct, he did indeed feel like garbage as he headed into the shop a few hours later. “I’m too old for this,” he muttered as he nursed his coffee and went inside.

In a much too cheery voice for this hour, Sean greeted him, “Morning boss. No offense, but you kinda look like shit today.”

“Thanks, Sean. You know just how to make a guy feel special.”

“My bad. You good though?”

“Yeah, I was just up too long last night. I’ll be fine once I get more caffeine in my system.”

He left Sean to run the front of the store like usual and sat at his desk with an exhausted sigh. The paperwork piled up for the day would probably take a while, and he felt his eyes glazing over already. Instead, he chugged the rest of his coffee and headed into the breakroom for a refill.

Maybe he'd start with the hands-on stuff today. Movement surely would help keep him awake. Today he was working on a dining room set. A sturdy oak table for six and solid chairs to go along with it.

The music and the work flowed, and soon it was lunch time. He had planned to drop off the newly finished rocking chair today, so he decided to take care of that while he was out getting food.

After loading the chair up and securing it in the back of his truck, he decided to give Melody a call while he drove. She picked up after a couple of rings.

"Hey stranger," she answered.

"Hey there. Just wanted to check in."

"That's sweet. I'm definitely dragging after the late night last night, but other than that I'm good. How are you today?"

"Same. It's days like this that remind me that I'm definitely not twenty years old anymore."

"Sorry. I promise not to keep you up so late the rest of this week." She laughed. "Actually, I really need to get some cleaning done tonight because I had made plans for a friend to come visit tomorrow night. Are you okay if we just talk on the phone and text today and tomorrow? I'm sorry. I made these plans before all of this happened."

"Don't apologize. Of course that's fine. I'm happy to just talk with you. This helps us with the hands-off rule anyway." He chuckled.

"True. Oh – I've got a short day on Friday; do you want to grab lunch? I think it would be good to get together and make a final decision too."

"Sure. I can take a half day. That's the beauty of being your own boss."

"A definite perk. Want to meet at that little cafe off the town square?"

"It's a date. I just got to my customer's house for a delivery, so I better let you go for now. I'll text you later?"

"Sounds good. Have a good afternoon. Bye."

"Bye, Mel." Hanging up, he got out of his truck and finished up his delivery.

They spent the next thirty-six hours exchanging many phone calls and texts to get to know each other better. He felt like a teenager, being so glued to his phone.

One evening they'd talked about their home lives and people in their lives.

"So, tell me about your mom and your siblings," she'd said.

"Well, my mom is at that age where she keeps trying new and odd hobbies. She never bothered dating again after my dad, so she's nurtured a pretty strong relationship with a group of women, and they do all kinds of shit together. She's independent and strong but loves having us all around as much as possible. She loves to garden." He cleared his throat. "Natalie is the middle child. She gets her fierce independence from my mom. She's brilliant and fearless. She has the mouth of a sailor. She kicks ass at her marketing job and kind of makes me crazy with her dating practices – she's always got some new guy for the night or the weekend, but she never lets anyone get close enough to get attached or hurt her, so it's all surface level, physical, a means to an end. But if you do manage to get past her defenses, she's the most loyal person out there. She will tell you what you need to hear whether you want it or not." He chuckled. "Nash on the other hand is the laid back one. He just loves to travel and have a good time. He's brilliant too, the things he can do with computers... I won't pretend to understand, but he's not one to show off. You'll probably get along with him immediately. He's easy to talk to." A smile pulled at his lips. "What about you? You mentioned an aunt?"

"Yeah, I lived with my Aunt Bea for a while after my parents died. She is also fiercely independent. She's a handful." Her laugh filled his ear. "One time when I was little, she came for a visit and I'll never forget how my mom spent the whole weekend in a frenzied mixture of being happy to spend time with her sister, and trying to make sure I didn't go around repeating all those fun new words I was learning. Or how just because someone was being stupid, didn't necessarily mean you could just up and say it to their face. But at the same time, Aunt Bea taught me to be bold, to be honest. I'll never be quite as bold as her, but whenever I'm trying to navigate a situation, I think – what would Aunt Bea do? It's gotten me through a lot in life. She definitely saved me after I lost my parents."

The next, they texted about random things.

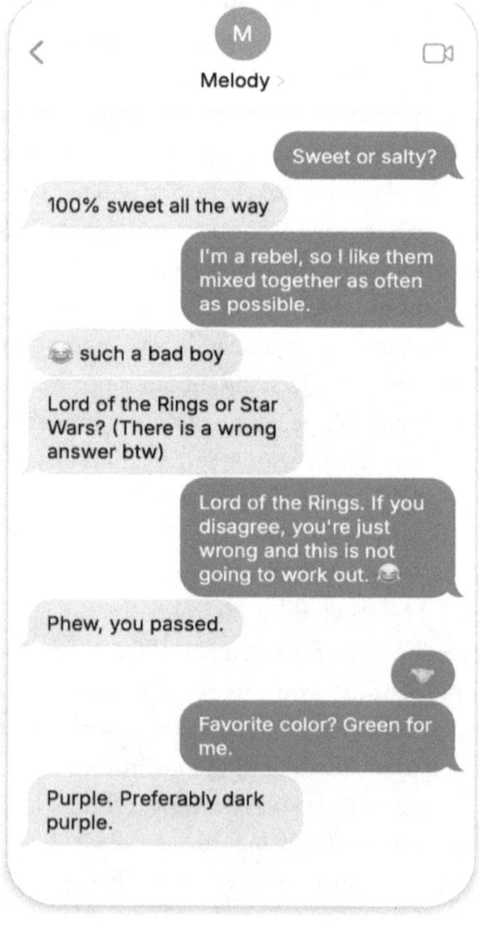

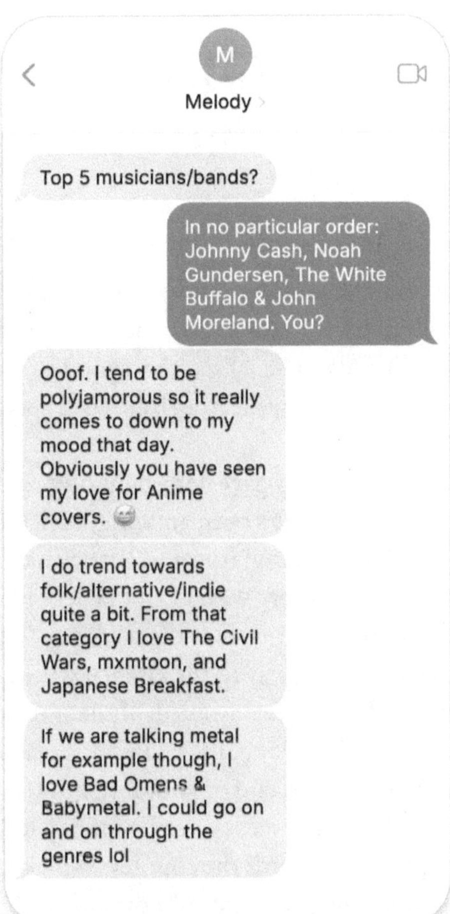

He found himself smiling like an idiot when her name popped up, laughing at things she'd say on the phone. She was nothing like Angela, but that was probably for the best. He awaited Friday, eager to find out what she would decide.

Chapter 7

Melody

Her doorbell rang, announcing Emily's arrival, and Fredrick sped to the door to greet her. Melody let her inside with a wide smile. "Em, it's so good to see you. How is life as a newlywed? Marriage looks good on you."

It really did. Emily gave her a tight hug, and she was practically glowing. "It's been amazing, Mel. Our honeymoon was so much fun, and Patrick has been utterly attentive in every way. I can't believe it's already been almost two months since the wedding."

They made their way to the kitchen where appetizers and margaritas awaited. "It definitely doesn't feel like it's been that long. I feel like I just watched you hop into the car at the end of your reception, but somehow it has been weeks since I've seen you." Melody gestured towards the counter. "I picked up some random stuff, and most importantly – the good stuff." She poured them both a glass, raising hers to clink against Emily's.

With full plates, they got comfortable on the couch and Emily asked, "So anything new in your world since we last talked?"

She finished her bite of food and said, "Well, actually I met someone. We've been on a few dates, and it's going pretty well. I really like him."

"Really? Girl, spill. What's his name? How'd you meet? What does he look like?"

"Um, so his name is Nate. He's a carpenter." Melody pulled out her phone and showed Emily his photo. "We, uh, met at a coffee shop."

They had not established a cover story yet, so she said the first thing that came to mind. Hopefully Emily would not pry further right now. She would have to remember to talk to Nate so they could get their story straight going forward.

Emily grabbed the phone to take a closer look. "Oh, my god, Mel. He's hot. Damn girl. And a carpenter? So, he works with his hands, huh? Nice."

"Yeah, he's great." She took her phone back.

"So have you guys...you know...?"

Melody laughed nervously. "Em."

"Holy shit, you did! This is huge. You haven't seriously dated anyone in ages. I was a little bit afraid your pussy was going to seal itself off like a tomb or something." She laughed. "But seriously...how was it?"

Melody's face burned and she dropped her gaze to her knees and sighed. "It's been the hottest sex of my life." She flopped back against the back of the couch and stared up at the ceiling with a laugh. "Em, I didn't know a man could get me off that many times in one day. Like, have I seriously just been missing out on good sex my entire life? Is it like this for everyone else?

Because Nate makes it feel like none of the other men I've been with had a clue what they were doing."

"That is entirely possible. Some of those idiots didn't know their ass from a hole in the ground. I'm so happy for you though. It's about time you met someone who treats you right. And he's kind to you outside of the bedroom?"

"Yeah. He's thoughtful and sweet. He makes me laugh. And he's not just looking for a good time. He was married before...and she died. It was a few years ago. As morbid as it sounds, it feels like we share this understanding because we've both lost people. I don't know, Em. I just feel like this might be what I've been waiting for."

Emily reached over and took her hand. "This is wonderful, Mel. I totally want to meet him when you're ready. You're one of the best people I know, and you deserve all the happiness in the world."

When Emily left a few hours later, Melody leaned against her front door and let a breath out. Even though she didn't have all the details, having Em's support felt good. And thankfully, they had the kind of friendship where they might not talk for a few days or sometimes even weeks, but when they did, they were always able to pick up right where they left off. She was there anytime Emily needed her, and she knew Emily would be there too, with no hesitation.

Hopefully by the time they ended up getting together again, she could gloss over the speed of her wedding. The less questions the better.

Friday rolled around quickly. Melody's heart raced, thinking about their lunch and the discussion that would follow. But as crazy as it was, she knew what her answer would be.

A little before it was time, she headed out on her bicycle to meet Nate. It was a beautiful day, and she wanted to enjoy the fresh air on her way.

She saw him parking his truck as she locked her bike onto the nearby rack, so she walked his way once it was secure. "Hey. How are you today?"

Holding the door open for her, he said, "I'm doing alright. Did you have fun with your friend last night?"

"Yes. It was good to see her. We haven't caught up since before her wedding. We had lots to talk about."

"Oh yeah? Like me for example?" he teased.

She scoffed. "Obviously. There's those million orgasm points and all."

Nate laughed. "Naturally."

"But seriously, I just left it at that we are dating but obviously didn't tell her all the messy details."

"And how are you feeling about those messy details exactly?" He kept his face blank.

She made sure to maintain eye contact as she said, "I want to do this."

"You're sure? I don't want to pressure you into this, and I don't want you to have regrets."

"I'm sure. Are you?"

He studied her face for a moment. "Yes."

"Okay, then. Let's get some food and make a game plan."

They ordered their lunch and Nate once again insisted on paying. As they ate, they decided on what time to meet at the courthouse the next day and looked up what else would be needed as far as paperwork went.

"Oh shit. I forgot about rings," Nate said.

"Mmm, right. Well, there's actually an antique mall across the square, and I know they have a jewelry section. Want to walk over there once we're done?"

"I'm happy to buy you a real ring from a jeweler – you don't need to feel like you should settle for some old piece of junk."

"They actually have some beautiful old rings in there. They're real, just a little untraditional. Which honestly is right up my alley. If we don't see anything good, I promise I'll let you drag me to the over-priced jeweler and we can pick out something obnoxiously expensive."

"Deal." Nate gathered up their trash and threw it away as they went back outside and walked down the sidewalk towards the antique mall. "So, what are we looking for? What do you think you'd prefer?"

"I don't really know. I was just planning on seeing what speaks to me." She shrugged.

They arrived at the front door and followed directions from an employee towards the jewelry cases located further back in the store. Melody looked through rows and rows of rings with Nate quietly trailing behind her, letting her browse without interrupting.

One ring caught her attention, and she asked the worker behind the counter, "Can I see that one, please?" She pointed at a ring in the second row with a square sapphire nestled on either side with small diamonds.

He pulled it from the case and handed it to her explaining, "This is a wonderful piece. Genuine 1.5 carat sapphire and melee diamonds on either side, set in sterling silver. There's actually a matching band that goes with it if you're interested."

She nodded silently and slipped the ring onto her finger. It was a perfect fit.

"You like that one?" Nate asked her softly.

Melody gathered herself and said, "It reminds me of my mom's ring."

The man came back with the matching band, a delicate silver ring with a light filigree etched onto it. "We also have this men's band that compliments the set beautifully, if I may be so bold."

Nate tried on the men's ring and found it fit as well. "We'll take them."

"Are you sure? We haven't even seen the price yet!" Melody said.

"We'll take them," Nate told the man again.

"Very good, sir."

Melody started to remove the ring and hand it back, but the worker told her, "No need, miss. I have the box here; you are welcome to wear it out of the store once it is paid for."

Nate followed him to the cash register as Mel continued to study the ring, a lump in her throat. It was moments like this that she missed her parents the most. There were countless moments in her life that they had missed, and she had always known that if she ever got married, they would not be there to see it. She would never experience the joy of announcing her engagement, of gushing over the ring with her mom, or dress shopping with her, of having her dad walk her down the aisle. Most days it was just a fact in the back of her mind and an old ache she had learned to live with, but it was harder to push down when the big life events popped up.

Part of her knew they would probably also be concerned about this decision she was making. They would ask her how well she really knew this man, and why she wasn't trying to find a more normal relationship. She had no idea what she would tell them if she had been faced with that conversation, other than she had a gut feeling that this was where she was meant to be. Nate needed a friend, he needed her. And other than the constant butterflies in her tummy, she felt at ease with him in a way that she did not with most other people. Something about him made her feel safe. It may not be picture perfect, but it felt right.

Nate had finished up and came back to her, rubbing a reassuring hand over her back. "Are you alright?"

Clearing her throat, she said, "Yes, I'm fine. Ready to go?"

He nodded as he took her hand and walked her back outside. As they approached her bike, he said, "I'll drive you home if you want to throw that in the back of my truck."

"Sure." She unlocked it and let him lift it into the truck bed for her.

They were quiet on the drive back to her house, and once they arrived, he turned off the truck before turning to look at her. "Are you sure you're okay?"

With a sigh, she told him, "I am. It's just one of those things – another moment in my life that my parents aren't here for. I hadn't really let myself think about the fact that they're going to miss this. I've gotten used to the everyday things I miss: not being able to call my mom for advice or telling my dad the corny joke I heard that I know he would bust a gut over. But it's been a while since I've had anything big happen in my life. But getting *married*. That's a milestone. And yes, our situation has its complications, but still. It's another part of my life that they should be here for."

"I'm sorry. I wish they could be here for you. And I wish I could do something to make it better. I know first-hand that there isn't anything that takes the pain away, but I'll sit here with you as long as you need." He took her hand and gently squeezed it.

"Thank you."

They stayed like that for a long time, silently taking comfort in each other as best they could.

Chapter 8

Nate

Nate rarely had a reason to wear his good suit. It felt strange buttoning it up as he got ready to meet Melody. Or maybe it was just him that was feeling strange. The sensation of buzzing bees under his skin and a tightness in his chest had been growing all day. He was doing his best to ignore it.

He drove to the courthouse, but once he parked and turned off the truck, he found he couldn't get out. His hands gripped the steering wheel and his breaths were coming in quick pants that he could not slow.

Could he really do this? Was he really ready to let someone into his life again, in any capacity? Was he crazy for trusting Melody so quickly? What would Angela think of this mess? What would his family do if they found out the whole truth?

Forehead pressed to the steering wheel, he shut his eyes against the barrage of thoughts. He needed to pull it together. Everything would be fine. He just needed to breathe and get out of this truck. One foot in front of the other.

A brief stint in therapy after losing Angela had taught him a trick to try to gain control when anxiety was spiraling: he just needed to look around and list out every blue object he could see. Count them off. It didn't always work, but it was worth a shot in times like this.

"Blue canopy. One. Blue car. Two. Blue sky. Three. Blue jeans on that man. Four. Blue stroller. Five."

Slowly, his breathing regulated. He took another moment to collect himself, running his hands through his hair and smoothing it back before exiting the truck.

Once he was inside, he saw Melody sitting on a bench outside of the courtroom, waiting for him and their turn. She was in a simple white dress that hit a few inches above her knees and matching white high heels.

"You look beautiful," he said.

She looked up from her phone with a start and stood, a slight flush rising on her cheeks. "Thank you. You look very handsome." With a soft touch, she smoothed his lapels.

He smiled. "Are you ready for this?"

"I am. How are you feeling?"

"I'm a little nervous if I'm being honest."

"Oh, thank God. Me too. I want to do this, but it is a little intimidating."

Nate tucked a stray hair behind her ear. The sound of the door opening behind them drew their attention and a man called over to them, "Nathaniel Blackwell and Melody Parker? We're ready for you."

They followed him inside and the man asked, "Do you have your marriage license?" Nate handed it over to him. "Very good. Will anyone else be joining you or would you like to use the courthouse witnesses?"

"It'll just be us, so we will use your witnesses. Thanks," Nate said.

"No problem. I'll summon them. We also have a photographer if you'd like a few photos taken during the ceremony."

Nate glanced at Melody, who said, "That would be great, thank you." To Nate she said, "We should probably have a few shots for when people ask, don't you think?"

"Good call," Nate said.

The witnesses were gathered, soft instrumental music played in the background, and the judge instructed them to join him in front of the stand as he began. Thanks to his nerves, the words blurred together at first, and the next thing he knew, it was time for the vows.

"Nathaniel Blackwell, do you take Melody Parker to be your wife, to live together in the honorable estate of matrimony, do you promise to love, honor and comfort her in sickness and health, do you promise to be faithful and keep yourself only unto her as long as you both shall live?"

For a moment, Nate couldn't find his voice. After what felt like an eternity, he said, "I do." He slid the silver band onto her finger.

"Very good. Melody Parker, do you take Nathaniel Blackwell to be your husband, to live together in the honorable estate of matrimony, do you promise to love, honor and comfort him in sickness and health, do you promise to be faithful and keep yourself only unto him as long as you both shall live?"

"I do," Melody said, her voice slightly choked as she slid his ring home.

"I now pronounce you husband and wife. You may kiss the bride," the judge said, and the witnesses clapped politely.

Nate stepped forward and gently cupped Melody's face in his hands, brushing her lips with a soft kiss. She pressed up into him, meeting him halfway, and he allowed himself to get lost in her for a short while. Once they pulled back, the photographer snapped a couple more quick shots of them together and finally they were instructed to sign off on the marriage license along with the witnesses.

Nate took care of paying the bill while Melody was handed the memory card which held their photos and then they were done. It was official, they were married. They quietly headed outside, both lost in thought.

Not knowing what to say now, Nate decided to switch gears and asked, "So, want to grab some dinner?"

"That sounds nice."

"If you want to drop your Jeep off at home, I can follow you in the truck and then drive us there."

She nodded her agreement and they headed towards her town home. When they arrived, she ran inside to let Fredrick out for a bathroom break and then met him back outside. "Where are we headed?" she asked.

"Well, we're celebrating, so I thought we'd go somewhere nice. Amore Vitto sound okay?"

"Mmm, yes."

The food was tasty, the drinks were smooth, and they picked up where they had left off the day before, choosing random topics to learn more about each other. The conversation flowed easily, which Nate was grateful for, and he walked her to the door once they arrived back at her home.

There was an awkward pause once they arrived, not having talked about how the rest of the night would go or expectations either of them may have.

They started to speak at the same time, laughing nervously at the mishap and then Melody said, "Please, go ahead. What were you going to say?"

Nate cleared his throat and said, "We didn't really talk about what happens next, and I want you to know that I don't expect anything. I can just go home now if that would make you more comfortable. We could talk more tomorrow."

After a brief pause, she said, "Well, you could go home. But I seem to recall a promise to *refresh my memory*...so how about making good on that instead?"

Nate let out a dark chuckle. "As you wish."

Melody turned to unlock the door without any further delay, and Nate closed in behind her, sliding her hair over one shoulder to expose the column of her neck. While she fumbled with her keys, he wrapped his arms around her waist and started a path of searing kisses from her shoulder to her ear. Her breathing turned ragged as he lingered on a sensitive spot, and the keys continued to rattle as if she couldn't focus long enough to locate the correct key.

He whispered in her ear, "Do you need help with that?"

"You're so distracting," she grumbled half-heartedly, finally getting the door unlocked.

They stumbled inside, hastily locking the door behind them again. Nate ran his hands up to cup her breasts through the fabric of her dress, wishing it was gone already.

"I need to let Fredrick out one more time for the night," Melody said as she gently pulled away.

He didn't let her get too far though, following her through the house. While she took care of the dog, he removed his suit jacket, laying it on the counter before kicking off his shoes and socks, not wanting to waste any time. As she turned back to him from the sliding glass door, he walked towards her, slowly undoing the buttons on his shirt as he went. He loved the way her eyes tracked the movements of his fingers lower and lower down his torso.

"First thing I'm going to do when we find our new place is install a dog door, so we don't have to wait at times like this," he said.

"Waiting isn't always bad. It can...build anticipation."

With a hum, he pressed her back against the wall and said, "Oh yeah? Let's see how much anticipation you can stand." He skimmed his nose along her collarbone as his hand traced up the inside of her thigh and hitched up her dress. “Mmm, lace,” he murmured against her skin as he reached her panties. He lightly teased her over the fabric, not quite touching her where she needed it most. “So wet for me already.”

He kept up his indulgent touches as her breathing grew faster, and they were finally interrupted by the sound of a paw scratching the door. Nate released her and threw his shirt on the counter with his jacket as she went about putting Fredrick away for the night. She turned to follow him as he backed down the short hallway towards the front door and the stairs. He watched her kick off her heels and stalk after him, catching up to press him back against the door. She wasted no time in winding her arms around his neck and claiming his lips with her own.

He gave her control for a minute, and then steered her back towards the stairs, perching her above him as he knelt between her thighs. His lips made a path up her leg, and he eased her panties off, holding them up once they were free. “You’re going to kill me, wearing little scraps of lace like this.”

“It was a special occasion.”

He tucked them into his pocket and resumed his journey. Teasing and taunting her a little more, he asked, “So, have you had enough anticipation yet?”

She breathed out a frustrated, “Yes.”

Nate didn’t waste any more time, flicking his tongue over her clit and soaking up her moans. He chased her orgasm until he felt her coming on his tongue. He scooped her up as she came back down and carried her up to the bedroom, kicking the door shut behind him.

Setting her down, he faced her away from him so he could unzip her dress. She turned back to face him as it slid from her body, and he was greeted with a matching lace bra which left little to the imagination. Her taut nipples were raised through the sheer fabric, and he couldn't resist leaning forward to suck one into his mouth.

He felt her fumbling for the clasp before the bra fell away too, and then she was reaching for his belt to rid them of the final barrier between them. She hurriedly undid the buckle and pulled down his pants as she dropped to her knees before him. Before he could even think to protest, she had slid him into her mouth with a greedy moan.

He tangled his hands in her hair and watched her for a moment before groaning. "You look so fucking perfect with your lips wrapped around my cock."

She made another noise in the back of her throat as she began to touch herself in time with his thrusts. It would be so easy to let go, but he didn't want to finish yet. He let himself enjoy the sensation for a few moments longer before he gently pulled her back and helped her to her feet as he said, "I need to be inside you."

He lifted her and she wound her legs around his waist as if it was as natural as breathing. Walking them over to the bed, he settled onto his back, letting her straddle him as he leisurely explored her lips. Finally, she reached between them and lined him up with her entrance, bearing down on him until he was fully seated. They moved together, hands and lips roaming, desperate for friction.

Nate's hand once again found her clit, and his mouth moved to her breast, fanning the flame as high as he could. With a few more deep thrusts, he felt her next orgasm roll through her. He rolled them, pinning her down to the mattress as he sought his own release now, finally stilling deep inside of her as he spent himself.

He rested his head on the crook of her neck, and she softly ran her fingers through his hair as their breathing and heart rates slowed to a normal rhythm. Before letting himself get too relaxed though, he asked, "Where do you keep your washcloths?"

"Under the bathroom sink."

He gently untangled himself and rose, heading into the ensuite to set the hot water running. While he waited, he quickly cleaned himself and once the water had heated, he ran a cloth underneath the tap and went back to Mel. He used a damp cloth, followed by a dry one to make sure she was clean as well before depositing them in the clothes hamper. Nate hesitated in the doorway, unsure again what to do next.

Melody raised a hand from the bed and sleepily asked, "Stay with me?"

He joined her once more, a soft smile playing on his lips as he drew her to him. They lay there for a few minutes before he placed a kiss sweetly on the top of her head and whispered, "Thank you."

She was already asleep.

It was always disorienting to wake up in unfamiliar surroundings, but the scent of lavender from Melody's shampoo was becoming familiar and helped align his sleep-tangled thoughts. She was draped across his chest with an arm wrapped around his middle.

However, it didn't fully stop that familiar panic from starting to bubble up again in his chest. She began to stir and made a contented noise, squinting an eye open against the morning light, and he felt the tension in his chest ease as he watched her.

"Good morning," he said.

"Morning," she mumbled.

As if he was summoned by her consciousness, Nate could hear Fredrick begin to whine downstairs.

With a groan, Melody rolled out of bed and said, "Breakfast time."

"That's the second thing I'm getting for our new place: an automatic feeder, so you can sleep in as late as you want."

"That sounds glorious." She shut herself into the bathroom to take care of her morning necessities before coming back out and grabbing an oversized t-shirt from a drawer and slipping it on. This one had another anime character, with red hair and a checkered jacket. "I had an extra, unopened toothbrush from my last dentist appointment. I left it on the counter for you." With that, she dropped a quick kiss on his forehead and headed downstairs.

He called after her, "Thank you!" and then headed into the bathroom for his turn. Once he had freshened up, he realized he did not have a change of clothes, only his suit from the day before. He also had left half of said suit downstairs in his hurry to seduce Melody last night. He wasn't sure which would be weirder – heading downstairs in only his boxers, or with his suit pants on but no shirt and shoes. He felt oddly self-conscious as he tried to adjust to this new dynamic. He knew it would take some getting used to living with someone after being on his own for so long, but he hadn't thought much about this in-between part where they would still be sorting out the living arrangements.

Should he bring some things over? Did she want to use his place or hers? Did she want to stay together in the first place before they officially moved? They had talked a lot this past week, but there was still so much they had not discussed.

Eventually, he gave up and headed down wearing his boxers, pants in hand. The closer he got, the clearer the sound of music and Melody singing along became. He rounded the corner into the kitchen to find her dancing around with Fredrick, anime music playing from her phone on the counter, as she waited for coffee to brew nearby.

She was mid-spin when she noticed his arrival, and stopped, tucking her hair behind an ear. "Umm hi."

With a chuckle, Nate said, "Hello to you too."

"I, uh, was making us some coffee if you'd like some."

"Coffee sounds great."

Melody went over to a nearby cabinet and pulled out a couple of mugs for them, the hem of her t-shirt rising to expose the curve of her ass just a little as she stretched. Nate was not going to complain about the view.

"How do you want it?" she asked.

"What?" He asked as he tore his eyes away from where they were still fixed on her ass. She held up one of the mugs, indicating coffee and he pulled his mind out of the gutter long enough to say, "Oh, just some creamer if you have any."

She let out a snort as she opened the fridge. "If I have any...well, let's see, I have: one, two, three, four, five kinds actually. I may have a problem. What flavor do you usually like?"

"Surprise me."

As she fixed their cups, he went about folding his clothes into a neat pile from where they had been tossed the night before. Once she was done, he followed her over to the couch and they sat, sipping the much-needed caffeine in silence.

Broaching the obvious first, he said, "So, I don't exactly have a change of clothes with me. I should probably run home at some point and take care of that. I don't know what your plans for the day look like..."

"I don't have any plans today. We didn't really establish what happens now though, so we should probably figure that out, right?"

"Yeah. I think we've already agreed that we will need to find a bigger place to fit us both, but that could potentially take a while, and I don't know what you'd like to do in the meantime. I know we are technically married now, but I don't want to just assume that you'll be comfortable in my space or that you'll be comfortable having me in yours." He gripped the coffee mug in his hands.

"It's definitely going to be an adjustment, but I think the only way to get comfortable is to just do it. I mean, honestly, we could take turns staying at each other's places until we sort it out – that way we could work on packing both places up in the meantime too."

"That's a good idea. And actually, I may have a solution to help us expedite finding a new place too. My landlord is awesome, and she manages a bunch of properties around town. I can give her a call to see what else she has available, if that's okay with you?"

"That sounds great. I haven't moved since I first came to town, and it would make the process so much easier if we have someone we can trust to pick out good places for us to see."

"Cool. Do you care if I give her a call real quick?"

"Go ahead." She waved a hand.

Nate picked up his phone and dialed Shirley's number. She answered after a couple of rings.

"Nathaniel, it's so good to hear from you, sweetie. How are you?"

"Morning Ms. Shirley. I'm good, how are you?"

"Oh, just movin' and groovin'."

Nate chuckled. "I know you keep busy. Well look, I don't want to take too much of your time this morning, but I wanted to talk to you about your available properties."

"Oh? Are you looking to move again? There's nothing wrong with your place is there?" she asked.

"No, no, it's been great. I'm just looking for a place with more space. My circumstances have changed a little, and I'll tell you more about that later, but I'm hoping to find something with two to three bedrooms and a couple bathrooms, that kind of thing."

"You know, I do have a home that I think would be a good fit. Honestly, when I bought it up, I thought of you. I've been fixing it up, so I hadn't listed it yet, but it's about the size you're describing, and the part that really brought you to mind is the large, detached garage out back. I think it would be just the perfect workspace for your carpentry."

"Really? I'd love to take a look, if that's okay."

"Absolutely. Actually, I was planning on popping over this afternoon to meet the contractor and make sure the bathroom upgrades are done the way I like. You know how picky I am with bathrooms. Do you want to meet me there for a tour around 2:00?"

"Let me check on something real quick. Can you hold on just a second?"

"Sure thing."

He muted the phone briefly and asked Mel, "Are you cool with us going to see a place this afternoon?"

"That was quick. Sounds good to me."

He nodded and unmuted the call. "Ms. Shirley, that would be perfect. Thanks so much."

"You're so welcome, sweetie. I'll text you the address and see you later."

They hung up the call, and he turned back to Melody, "All set. We are supposed to meet her at 2:00. If you want, we can run by my place so I can get changed and then go get some lunch before we go?"

"Sure. I'm going to go grab a shower real quick...would you like to join me?"

"Hell yes," he said and followed her back upstairs.

Chapter 9

Melody

As they pulled up to the address on the GPS, Melody could already tell that she loved this house. It had a big, covered porch, and a tidy flower bed filled with Black Eyed Susans, Coneflowers and Lavender plants that lined the sidewalk, adding a pleasant aroma to the breeze. The neighborhood seemed friendly and quiet so far too.

"This isn't very far from my mom's place," Nate said.

"Oh yeah? That's nice."

They headed up the walkway, ringing the doorbell to let Shirley know they had arrived. While they waited, they looked around the porch and Melody said, "This would be a great spot for a couple of chairs and a little table. Ooh, or a porch swing. Coffee out here in the mornings would be so peaceful." The sound of the lock turning drew their attention back to the front door as Shirley opened it.

"Nathaniel, welcome, welcome. And who might this be?" Shirley smiled, looking between them.

He wrapped an arm around Melody's shoulders and said, "Ms. Shirley, I'd like you to meet my new wife, Melody. Melody, this is Shirley. She's kind of like my bonus grandma."

"*Wife*? Nathaniel Blackwell! You never even told me you were seeing anyone, let alone seriously seeing someone!" Shirley braced her hands on her hips. To Mel she said, "It's so nice to meet you dear."

"It's nice to meet you too." Melody was doing her best to hold back laughter at the look on Nate's face and the obvious earful he was about to get. She figured this was good practice for telling the rest of the world though, and they would have to learn how to deal with reactions like this, so she waited to see what he would say next.

Nate's eyes dropped to the floor, and he cringed before meeting her gaze again. "To be fair, I didn't tell anyone. I haven't even told my mom yet. I'm sorry to be secretive, but I didn't want all the pressure of everyone watching. I needed to make this decision on my own."

Shirley studied him for a moment. "Well, you're a grown man and can do what you please. But those of us in your life love you and only want what's best for you. You should tell your mama sooner rather than later or there's bound to be some hurt feelings."

"I promise, I will. I'm sorry if I hurt your feelings, Shirley." He reached out and drew her into a hug.

She quickly returned the embrace. "Oh, I can never stay mad at you, you rascal. Well, come inside and see the place."

With that, she led them inside and took them on a tour of the home. The inside was as beautiful as the outside. Hardwood floors graced the main living areas, while soft carpet was in the three bedrooms. There was a spacious kitchen that overlooked a cozy living room with a fireplace in the corner. Shirley pointed out the pulldown stairs that led to an attic space for storage, but otherwise everything was on one level.

"And finally, here is the master bedroom," Shirley said, leading them into the last room. The room was large with windows on either side of the space. "The contractor did a marvelous job on the bathroom. Wait until you see this tub."

It was a beautiful tub, indeed. Jetted and big enough for two, it looked like something from a magazine. Melody had never lived anywhere this fancy in her life.

"Naturally, the shower is similar to the one at your place, Nate. I insist on that upgrade on all of my properties. Nothing like a good soak after a long day. So, what do you two think?"

"It's beautiful," Melody said.

"It seems just about perfect. You mentioned a garage out back too?" Nate asked.

"Oh, of course, let me show you." Shirley led them to the back door located off the kitchen, and into the backyard. Melody was glad to see that it was fully fenced in with a six-foot privacy fence, perfect for Fredrick.

The garage was decent sized, and as Nate walked around the space, it was clear he was already planning where everything would go. "This is great. Plenty of space. The garage doors will make getting larger pieces of lumber in and out easier." He nodded to himself as if checking off a mental checklist. He asked about the rent next, and between the two of them, it sounded doable.

"Now, I will say, if you decided you'd be interested in changing over to a rent-to-own situation, I would be more than happy to work with you guys on that. It's not something I offer everyone, but you're practically family and if this ends up feeling like a good fit long term, I'd love for you to have it. No pressure, you don't need to make a decision on that today, but I just wanted to throw it out there," Shirley said.

"We'll definitely keep that in mind," Nate said as he glanced around the space once more.

"Good. For now, should we look at paperwork? With the bathroom renovations complete, everything is pretty much ready to go, so you can move in as soon as you're ready. I'll have no problem filling your old place."

Nate looked at Melody for confirmation. "I'm guessing we'll need two to three weeks to get our places packed up and prepped. What do you think, Mel?"

"That sounds about right to me. I'll have to reach out to my landlord as well about ending my lease."

"Alright then. I've got my bag inside with the papers. I was hoping this would work out after we talked this morning. I'm so pleased." Shirley clapped her hands.

They followed her back inside, using the countertop to look over and sign the forms. Once that was done, they all headed back out front and Shirley locked up behind them. "Please let me know if you need anything at all with the move. I'll drop copies of your new keys off a little closer to moving day, but feel free to call if you have any questions or anything."

"We sure will, Ms. Shirley," Nate said and gave her another hug goodbye.

"Thank you again, it was so nice to meet you," Melody said.

"You too dear, you too. It was a delight. And I'm so happy for you both," Shirley said and reached over to squeeze Mel's forearm.

Climbing into the truck, Nate asked, "So what do you want to do now?"

"Well, if you want to hang out at my place, I believe it is time to introduce you to Demon Slayer."

With a laugh, Nate said, "Sure, sounds good. If I'm spending the night again, I'll drop by my place on our way and pack a bag this time."

Chapter 10

Nate

It had been two weeks since they got married and tomorrow was the next monthly brunch with his family. That night, he finally worked up the courage to fire off a text.

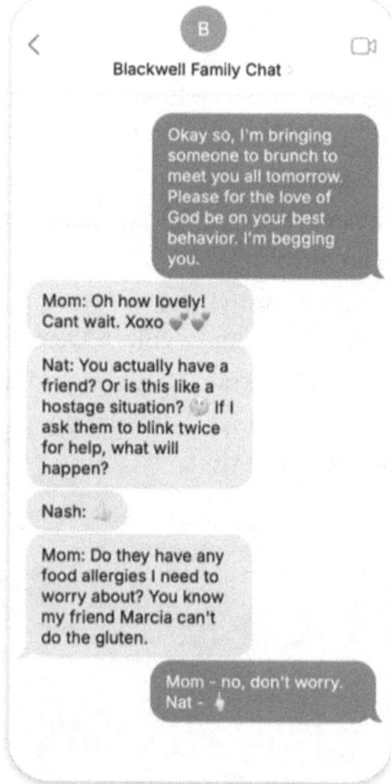

He blew out a breath and plugged his phone in on the nightstand before heading into the bathroom to brush his teeth and get ready for bed. When he got back, he saw that Melody had already dozed off, her book laid open on her chest. He gently picked it up, being careful not to lose her page and placed her bookmark inside, setting it back on the side table.

Drawing the blanket up to cover her, he turned off the lights and crawled into bed. He hoped he would be able to get some sleep.

As they pulled up into his mom's driveway and parked, he could tell Mel was nervous. Turning the truck off, he reached for her hand and gave her a reassuring squeeze. "You have nothing to worry about. They might give me some shit, but they'll be kind to you. We'll just keep things light like we talked about, keep our rings in our pockets until we are ready, and break the news at the end of the meal. That way we can make a run for it if Natalie gets too out of hand." He smiled to take the bite out of that last sentence.

Melody breathed in deeply. "You're right. It'll be fine. We'll just steer the conversation away from anything likely to give us away. We've got this." She nodded.

Nate kissed the back of her hand and got out of the truck with the loaf of banana bread in tow. They walked up to the front door where he let himself inside, a hand on Mel's back, calling out "Knock, knock. Coming in."

He led her through the entryway and to the right. Voices were spilling out of the kitchen through the doorway on the other side of the table, so he continued on towards them.

Upon entering the kitchen, he saw his mom pulling something out of the oven, Nash leaning against the breakfast bar and Natalie at the sink rinsing grapes. "Good morning," he said again to get their attention.

They all turned in his direction now, Nash straightening up while his mom and Nat both wiped their hands on a towel or apron and headed towards them.

"Everyone, this is Melody. We've been seeing each other. Melody, this is my mother, Naomi, my sister Natalie, and my brother Nash."

"It's so nice to meet you all," Mel said and reached to shake Naomi's hand first. Naomi pulled her in for a hug instead, catching her off guard.

"I'm a hugger," Naomi told Mel unapologetically. She released her from the hug but held onto her hands. "Anyone Nate thinks enough of to bring home is welcome here anytime."

"Thank you," Melody said. "You have a beautiful home."

Naomi squeezed her hands once more before she released them. "Thank you, dear. Oh, let me take that from you sweetie." She turned to Nate and relieved him of the banana bread before turning to cut it into slices.

Natalie used the opportunity to get closer, asking Nate, "So why am I just now hearing about this?"

"Because this is when I decided to tell you." He flicked her on the nose. Natalie tried to smack his hand but was not fast enough.

Ignoring his siblings, Nash whispered to Melody, "You'll get used to their bickering. They're just too much alike for their own good."

Melody chuckled. "Who normally wins these little spats?"

"Oh, I wouldn't say there's a winner per se. More like survivors. If sarcasm was an Olympic sport, they'd be duking it out for the gold."

"What nonsense are you filling her head with?" Nate asked.

"Nothing," Melody and Nash said at the same time. Unable to keep straight faces, they both burst into laughter. Nate and Natalie looked at them with narrowed eyes.

Still chuckling, Mel said, "The resemblance is uncanny when you both make that face." It wasn't the first time someone had made that observation. Natalie shared his coloring, her hair and eyes matching his exactly, inherited from their father. Nash was the only outlier with blue eyes that matched their mom.

Before things could devolve further, Naomi said, "Okay, everything is ready. Boys, please grab the rest of the food off the counter and bring it in with you." She threaded her arm through Mel's before she could attempt to try and help carry anything. "Come dear, let the big strong men do the manual labor."

Nate picked up a couple of things while Nash grabbed the rest, and they followed the women into the dining room. His mom had seated Mel next to her where Nate would usually sit and had shifted him down to the head of the table. A small lump grew in his throat at the sight. This was how they used to sit when Angela was with them. For the past few years, it had just been the four of them again, and none of them had brought an outsider in to join them. It hurt a little more than he was expecting. But he had learned a long time ago that more often than not, the first times were always the hardest. The first brunch after Angela died was a blur.

His mom gave him an understanding look, as if she could read all of the emotions roiling inside of him, so he gave her a smile back to let her know that he was fine. He didn't want her to worry.

Settling into the familiar routine, they passed the food, laughing and talking. Nash updated everyone on how work was going and where he was headed off to travel to next.

Natalie shared borderline inappropriate dating stories, punctuating her words with a stab of her fork here and there. Naomi talked about her book club and her progress with learning how to crochet.

Questions for Mel were worked in here and there, "So what do you do Melody?" (She told them about her paintings.) "How did you guys meet?" (They had rehearsed a story about meeting at the coffee shop after their drinks had been mixed up.) Finally, his mom said, "Tell me about your family."

Nate started to interject, but Melody placed a hand on his arm and said, "It's fine," giving him a grateful smile and cleared her throat. "I lost my parents fifteen years ago in an accident. I'm an only child, so it's pretty much just me and my aunt Beatrice. Aunt Bea."

"I'm so sorry. I had no idea," Naomi said.

"It really is okay," Mel said. "It's been a very long time. Most days it feels like a lifetime ago. I will always miss them, but it's not so hard to talk about it now. It's how I can keep their memory alive."

Naomi's eyes were full of unshed tears as she laid a hand on Mel's forearm. "They will always be with you." She collected herself and turned to Nate. "I'm glad you found each other."

Needing to break some of the emotional tension in the room and also wanting to rip off the band aid, Nate said, "Me too. We actually have an announcement to make." He looked at Mel, who nodded and took his hand. "We, uh, we got married."

Nat, who had just taken a sip of her orange juice, spewed her drink all over the table. Naomi stared between the two of them with an open jaw. Nash looked fairly unphased, just nodding to himself as if this made sense.

Recovering slightly, Nat pushed away from the table with a pinched look on her face. "Excuse us, just a *real quick* side bar in the kitchen Nate?" She took his arm and dragged him into the next room and Naomi said, "Pardon me, dear, I'm just going to..." She trailed off as she quickly followed her children.

Nash, on the other hand, finally burst out laughing and wiped a hand down his face. "Welcome to the family, Mel."

As the kitchen door swung shut behind them, Nate turned with his hands raised as if trying to hold off the onslaught brewing inside Natalie.

She didn't bother lowering her voice when she rounded on him. "What the *fuck*?"

"Natalie Blackwell, language," Naomi said in a voice he had heard so many times over the years. The struggle of trying to convince Natalie to stop being vulgar was a losing battle and despite how wary his mom was of the fight, she'd never stop chiding her.

"Mom, if there was ever a time for strong language, it's fucking now!"

With a sigh towards her daughter, she turned to Nate. "She's lovely, honey. How come you didn't even tell us you were seeing anyone though? This is a bit of a shock."

Before he could answer, Nat cut in with, "No shit."

Ignoring his sister, he said, "I didn't say anything before now because I didn't want to get everyone's hopes up. We were getting to know each other and once we realized we worked well together, I didn't see the point in wasting time. Melody and I aren't kids. And I know you all have meant well the past couple of years, but with all the pressure to *get back out there,* I just wasn't ready to talk about it all." He paused here, cringing internally and already hating himself for what he was about to say, but knowing it was the trump card that would put an end to this conversation. "Besides, if I learned anything from everything with Angela, it's that time is precious, and you never know when it will be stolen. I'm making the most of it."

It had the desired effect, making them both go quiet. A tear rolled down his mom's face as she reached out to hug him, and a pang of guilt went through him at playing on her emotions. Even Natalie looked like she was holding back tears.

"Get over here," he told Natalie as he pulled her into the group hug. She let them hug her for a minute before pulling away.

"Okay, okay, enough with the mushy shit. I get it. I guess I'm just glad you're not going to spend the rest of your life as some kind of hermit," Nat said and tried to regain her composure.

Nate scritched her head as she batted his hand away. "I love you too."

Walking back into the dining room, they found it empty. He found Mel and Nash on the couch in the living room, as Nash was showing her some old photo albums full of their childhood photos. With a groan, he plopped down beside Melody and rested his arm across the back of the couch behind her.

"Not the photo albums," Nate said.

"She deserves to know what all she signed up for." Nash flashed him a grin.

Melody looked over with a wide smile on her own face. "You were the cutest baby. Also, I can't believe I didn't see it before, but when you were younger and without the beard, you looked a lot like the older brother from that show – Supernatural. You know the one I'm talking about?"

Nate barked out a laugh and nodded. "I guess I missed my calling as a stunt double or celebrity impersonator."

"Do not feed his ego," Nat said.

The rest of the afternoon passed with laughter and shared stories. At one point, Natalie made sure to harass Nate into adding Melody to the family group chat.

As things wound down, Nate remembered the rest of the news he needed to share. "Oh yeah, obviously we won't really fit in the tiny place I've been renting, so Shirley helped us find a new place. We move in next weekend. I'll text you the new address, but it's pretty close to here."

"So much news for one brunch," Naomi smiled.

"There's no other surprises, right? No surprise kid or lotto win?" Nat narrowed her eyes.

Raising one hand and placing the other over his heart, Nate said, "This is it, I swear."

"It better be," Natalie tossed a throw pillow at Nate's head.

After saying their goodbyes and getting buckled into the truck, Mel smiled and said "I think that went well, don't you?"

Chapter 11

Melody

It was moving day. They had started at Nate's place, leaving the logistics of moving Fredrick for last. Natalie and Nash had texted a few days ago and volunteered to help, so things were moving along fairly quickly. Though, Natalie seemed to be more interested in supervising than doing any actual heavy lifting. Melody didn't mind; it was an amusing distraction for her at least.

She walked into the garage to retrieve some boxes. Since space was limited, Nate had used it as his woodworking space, and it had also doubled as storage, boxes lining the back wall even before he had started packing to move. It was cramped with all of his tables and supplies shoved into the space with the boxes, so he was excited to have a proper space to work out of at home going forward.

As she moved a box, one of his sculptures caught her eye where the cloth covering it had slipped off. It was an abstract rendering of a man hunched over himself, hollow in the middle as if he was trying to hold his broken pieces together. She studied it for a few more seconds before forcing herself to turn away. This was clearly a personal piece, not meant for her eyes. She had a gut feeling that this was a self-reflection of Nate.

On second thought, she turned and fixed the sheet, covering it once more before picking the box back up and loading it onto the truck.

Several trips later, they had gathered up the things from her town home and were unloading them into the new house. Fredrick was firmly underfoot, and Natalie had taken a quick hiatus with a promise to meet them back here when she left them at Nate's old place earlier that day.

Now that the shop was closed for the day as well, Sean stopped by to help for an hour or two before he headed home for dinner. Introductions were made, but he mostly followed Nate and Nash around helping where he could. It was obvious to Melody by the way he watched Nate and was quick to emulate him that the boy clearly looked up to Nate a great deal. The sight brought a smile to her lips.

Melody was doing her best to organize the boxes into the rooms they were intended for while the guys handled the big furniture. They had whittled down quite a bit between the two of them since they didn't need duplicates of everything.

It had been decided that they would keep Melody's living room furniture as it was more comfortable, but Nate's TV since it was bigger; they would use Nate's bed since it was a king size and Melody's old queen size bed would serve as the guest bed since they had a spare room for that now; Melody hadn't actually owned a dining table, and Nate's was one of his own creation, as were most of the side tables. All of those pieces made the cut, especially since Melody's were generally cheap items, she had no attachments to.

In the distance, Melody heard when Natalie arrived. "Oh my god, no one told me that I gained a nephew." The sound of a satisfied husky followed, along with some unintelligible baby talk. She made her way back out to the living room to see Nat collapsed on the floor, squeezing Fredrick's face between her hands as she told him what a good boy he was. The look on his face said that he knew it well and that it was about time that someone else acknowledged it.

Nash and Nate came through the front door, hauling one of the mattresses between them and Nash grunted, "Fuck Nat, can you get out of the damn walkway? This shit is heavy."

She scrambled out of the way, but remained on the floor, unbothered. Sean was nowhere to be seen, so Melody assumed he had headed home to his parents for the evening.

Melody made sure to clear out of their way too and went to stand by Nat. "This is Fredrick. Fredrick, this is Auntie Natalie. You be on your best behavior."

"Oh, he could never be anything but the best boy," Natalie said and continued to pet him.

The guys passed back through and Nate called over, "So Nat, are you actually going to help or?"

"I'm bonding with my nephew. You got this," she called back without moving.

Melody laughed and went back out to see what else she might be able to carry. Looking in the truck though, all that was left were big items, so she headed back inside to see where she could get started there instead.

She tackled the kitchen while they continued trips to and from the moving truck. By the time they dropped off the living room furniture, she had gotten the kitchen mostly put away and had started a stack of broken-down boxes to help save space. Natalie was still with Fredrick, but at least the attention was keeping him out of the way.

Melody set about scooting the couch and loveseat into place, followed by the bookshelves she was able to handle. The boxes containing the books, games and knick-knacks were nearby, so she started to fill the shelves and organize things. She opened a box containing photos and paused at the picture of her parents. At her townhome, she had a little spot set up for this photo where she could see it every day, and a candle she could light in remembrance. Pulling them both out, she glanced around to look for a spot that would work here. Her eyes landed on the fireplace with its mantle in the corner, and she made her way over.

She tenderly sat the photo down, placing the candle next to it. The space felt too big, too empty, like something was missing, and she realized what it was. If

Nate was comfortable with it, she wanted to include a photo of Angela here. To her, this was a sacred space, and Angela deserved to be honored right along with her parents. She would be sure to ask Nate about it tonight after the others left.

A few hours later, they were done for the day. They offered Nash and Natalie the traditional pizza and beer in thanks for helping out.

"You know, this was always an acceptable form of payment for helping people move when we were like twenty, but the older we get, the worse my back feels the next day," Nat said as they sat around the dining table eating. Nate and Nash both laughed.

Nash crumpled a napkin and threw it at her. "Oh please, you barely lifted a finger."

"Besides, I've moved you how many times exactly?" Nate gave her a pointed look.

"I'm just saying, a gift card for a massage is always welcome." Nat threw the napkin back towards them.

"Oh, I've got your massage, right here," Nash said before racing around the table with his hands held out.

"Don't you dare. You have greasy pizza fingers, you slob." Natalie tried to scoot her chair back in an attempt to escape.

She had failed to see that Nate had also left his spot at the table to sneak up behind her and pin her to her seat. He held her in place as Nash seized the opportunity to tickle her sides relentlessly. She shrieked in laughter, struggling fruitlessly against Nate's iron grip.

"Stop, stop!" She wheezed out between laughs, and Melody couldn't help but join in with the laughter. She had not grown up with siblings, and sometimes watching these three was fascinating. Other times like this, it was just plain entertaining.

They finally relented and let Natalie catch her breath, at which point she told them, "I hate you both," as she wiped the tears from her cheeks.

The boys leaned down in unison to hug her from either side, Nash kissing her cheek and saying, "No," followed by Nate kissing the top of her head and finishing, "You love us."

As they made their ways back to their chairs, Nate added on, "And you're stuck with us." He flashed her a devious smile to which she rolled her eyes.

"God help me, I do love you assholes."

"We know." They answered as one.

Melody laughed again, even as her heart tugged slightly. She was glad that Nate had these two. All three of them were very different people, but if you spent any amount of time with them, you couldn't help but feel the bond between them. Melody was thankful that he had that kind of unconditional support.

Nate walked them out to their cars once they were finished eating, and Melody took care of clearing the table and tossing out the empty pizza boxes. He had a small smile playing on his lips as he came back inside, stopping to look around at their progress so far.

"We still have a lot to do, but they definitely helped cut down several hours of work for me today. Or Nash did anyway." He chuckled.

"Nat carried a couple of boxes. Honestly though, her keeping Fredrick out the way probably was more helpful than we realized too."

"True." He crouched down to rub the dog in question's ears. "You most definitely have the knack of being in exactly the wrong place at the wrong time my man."

"It's a talent," Melody said.

"Thanks for getting some stuff unpacked. Having a functional kitchen is huge."

"No problem. After a certain point, there were only things that were too heavy for me on my own, so I figured that I might as well make the most of my time. Oh, that reminds me –"

She pulled him over to the fireplace and gestured to the photo of her parents on the mantle. "I always have a little memorial spot set up for my parents wherever I live. I was thinking, if it's okay with you, I'd like to put a photo of Angela here too."

Nate was so quiet that she turned to look at him. He had a pained expression on his face, and she quickly said, "We don't have to if you're not comfortable with it –"

" – No, it's a great idea. Thank you. I just, uh, I haven't really had any photos of her set out in a long time. It was too hard to see them at first. But I think it's a good idea. I think I'm ready now." Without saying anything further, he turned and headed down the hall.

Not knowing whether to follow him or not, Melody waited where she was and heard his steps coming back towards her shortly.

He had a frame in hand, and tentatively placed it up on the mantle, mirroring her parent's photo on the other side of the candle. It was a portrait of Angela in her wedding dress, bouquet of lilies in hand and a huge smile on her face.

"She's beautiful," Melody said.

"Yes, she was. Inside and out."

Melody laced her fingers through Nate's and squeezed. "Thank you."

"For what?"

"For sharing her memory with me."

He paused for a moment before answering. "Thank you for caring about something like that."

"Of course."

They worked on getting their room set up enough for them to use that night. Once things were in some sort of order and clean sheets were on the bed, they settled in, the hard day's work sinking into their bones and exhaustion weighing them down. Melody knew she would fall asleep quickly, and her eyes were already getting heavy as soon as they turned the lights off.

Nate leaned over and gave her a quick kiss goodnight and then curled up around her as they had grown used to sleeping these last few weeks. She had just about dozed off when she heard him mumble, "Oh yeah, Nat wants us to go to the karaoke bar with them next weekend. Fair warning." His breathing shifted, and she could tell he had already fallen asleep before she could respond.

Karaoke.

Well, that should be interesting.

She gave into the pull of unconsciousness.

Chapter 12

Nate

Nate was having one of those days. A heavy day. A dark day. There wasn't a day that passed where Angela didn't cross his mind at some point, but every once in a while, for whatever reason, the grief was just *louder*. The ache refused to be ignored; his memories flooded his mind, and there would be no distraction.

He found it best to isolate on these days. Pouring himself into his work was the only thing that gave him any solace. Channeling his pain at least gave him some sense of purpose. Thanks to the spacious garage out back of their new place, he didn't have to go far for privacy. This was one of the first areas he had made sure to set up once they started moving in.

Stopping to scribble a quick note on the kitchen counter to tell Mel he had gone out to work in the shed, he took his headphones and shut himself inside. Pulling up his playlist, he hit play. As Burial Plot by Dayseeker began, he knew if anyone else knew about this playlist, they might call him a glutton for punishment. This playlist was a collection of songs that either reminded him of Angela – her life, her illness, her death - or were songs that they had enjoyed together. Listening to them would always hurt. But that was the point.

These days often also left him feeling numb. Sinking into the music and his work allowed him to at least feel something. The only thing worse than the sharp pain of losing Angela was the dull ache of acceptance that time had given him.

He pulled out a hunk of wood and began to carve it down mindlessly, not exactly sure what he was working towards yet but trusting the process. The wood always told him what it was meant to be if he just listened. The tools moved, the wood wore down, and he wasn't sure how much time had passed when a form started to take shape.

Nate realized it was a woman. She was curled onto her side with fabric pooled around her body. It was Angela. Angela, after she found out she was sick. She had tried so hard to stay positive and to never let on how much of a toll it was taking on her body, but sometimes she would slip. He remembered this day in particular. It was an especially brutal round of chemo, and in the aftermath, she'd had no energy to pretend that things were fine. When he had gotten her home, all she could do was lie there, trying not to vomit with a vacant look on her face.

That was the day he realized that things really might not end okay. He had been so busy trying to play the role of the supportive husband that he had jumped straight into denial and planning how to help her get better, and he had not let himself consider that she might not. He had never felt so helpless in his life.

More memories floated through his mind: their first date, their wedding, birthdays, holidays, random Tuesday nights spent at home doing nothing, the day they learned she was sick, the rapid decline that followed, the day that the scent of her finally abandoned her favorite sweater and he knew he could never get it back.

He tenderly and painstakingly carved the details of her face, recalling the slope of her nose, the shape of her lips. Something dripped off the tip of his nose onto the worktable and he realized with a start that tears had joined the sweat running down his face at some point. He kept carving.

Sometime later, it was finished. Exhaustion settled over him and he finally registered the cramp in his shoulders from being hunched over for so long. Removing his safety glasses, he made his way over to the chair located at the side of the room next to a small side table, and saw something had been set upon the tabletop.

Melody must have poked her head in at some point, but he was so focused that he hadn't even noticed. She had left him some bottled water, a protein bar and a short note that just said, *"Don't forget to stay hydrated"* with a small heart drawn hastily underneath.

It was as if the sight of water reminded his body that it had been many hours since he had taken a drink. He drank about half of the water before checking his phone and finding that the day was gone. It would be time for dinner shortly. The thought was followed by a loud rumble of his stomach, though he didn't feel much like eating. He still had that hollowed out feeling in his chest. Wiping his face on the hem of his t-shirt with a sigh, he headed inside to take a shower.

Melody had been busy today. He had made sure to help haul boxes to the various rooms and do the heavy lifting these past few days, but she had made quite a dent at unpacking those boxes. The empty house was slowly but surely starting to feel like a home. Furniture was pushed into place, shelves were filled, and art was hung in various spots. She had been sure to snap photos of them together the last few weeks, and she must have gotten them printed at some point. Various frames held an assortment of candid photos and shots from their wedding. He glanced at them without really seeing any one in particular.

Following the sound of music playing, he found her in the room that they had designated to be her studio space. Fredrick was laying directly in the doorway and thumped his tail lazily in greeting rather than moving out of the way, so Nate leaned over him to peer inside. She had made good progress here as well. A drying rack was in one corner, filled with her various unfinished projects; a desk in the other corner of the room and a standing easel in between.

She was in the process of hanging various items on a large cork board that she had mounted above her desk. Photos and little drawings littered the surface of the desk while she arranged and rearranged where they would go. Not wanting to startle her since she clearly had not heard him approach, he knocked lightly on the doorframe and said, "Hey."

Melody still jumped slightly, but turned to him with a smile. "Hey stranger. I hope I didn't intrude, but I just wanted to check on you since you'd been out there for so long. You were lost in your work, so I didn't want to interrupt. All done for the day?"

Nate nodded tiredly. "You're fine. I didn't hear you at all actually, sorry. I was going to go get cleaned up now."

She studied him for a moment before asking, "Are you alright?"

Not wanting to get into it all, he said, "Yeah, I'm fine." His voice sounded flat even to his own ears though, and he knew she was not going to be convinced by that performance.

She paused for a moment. "It's okay if you're not. You don't have to pretend with me. I might not carry exactly what you have to, but I do know what it's like to continue loving someone that is gone. Everyone seems to think that just because enough time has passed for you to have some good days," she punctuated the words 'good days' with air quotes, "that means you're all better. But it's never *better*. Just different. You just adjust the best you can to a life that will never look the same again. And it's exhausting. I don't want to keep rambling, and I will not force you to talk if you don't feel like it, but please don't feel like you have to lie on my account. Feel your pain. Honor your loss. There's no judgement here. And if you do ever need to talk about it, I'm happy to listen."

Nate managed to say, "Thank you," around a lump in his throat. He didn't think he could say much else and decided it was not necessary anyway. She was right, it was exhausting. With a small nod, he turned towards their room and headed down the hall to take a shower.

The steam helped clear his head a little, and he felt slightly more put together by the time he was clean. Throwing some clothes on, he went to find Melody again. She had finished up for the day in her studio, and had settled with Fredrick on the couch, scrolling through her phone.

He braced his arms on the back of the couch to lean over her and asked, "Are you hungry?"

She tipped her head back to meet his gaze and said, "Yeah. Anything in particular sound good to you?"

He hesitated for a second. "Chinese was Angela's favorite." He cleared his throat. "There's a little cheap place nearby that she always chose when we would have a date night. You'd think there was some master chef working there, the way she would go on and on about the place." His face lifted into a small smile. "I was thinking we could order take-out if that's okay."

"That sounds perfect." Melody reached over to squeeze his hand softly.

After ordering a big batch of all of Angela's favorites, they settled into their shared meal on the couch and watched TV in comfortable silence.

Chapter 13

Melody

Mel had spent longer than she'd like to admit getting ready for karaoke. This was the first time they'd all really gone out together, and that felt intimidating. Like she would be under a microscope waiting to be picked apart if she let any hint of their deception show. The thought of going out on a double date like a regular couple also gave her butterflies in her stomach.

She shouldn't care so much what he would think about her appearance. Their friendship was growing every day, and they were clearly attracted to each other, so the nerves were unexpected on that front. She finally settled on a short black dress with a delicate print of violets. Paired with her leather jacket and her favorite boots, she decided it was good enough. She applied her dark red lipstick and went to meet him where he was waiting.

When he turned to look at her, his gaze grew heated as he took her in. From where her short skirt kissed her thighs, to the dip that revealed her cleavage, she could feel his eyes like a physical caress. She took the opportunity to appreciate his appearance as well. In his white button-down shirt and mussed hair, he made her heart race. It didn't help that she knew exactly what she would find if she were to unbutton each of those little buttons down the front of his shirt. How his warm skin felt under her fingertips. Where his tattoos were hidden and how they tasted. They should probably get out of here before they become very late.

As if realizing this himself, Nate said, "You look incredible. Are you ready to go?"

Mel nodded and smiled, not trusting her voice at the moment. They went out to his truck, where he opened her door for her and handed her up to make sure she was settled before going around and getting in himself.

This was the only karaoke joint in town. In a town like this that could not truly be deemed a "small town" but also was no sprawling metropolis, certain spots were a little more crowded than others. Tonight, it felt like everyone had the same idea.

Heading inside, they spotted Natalie already at a table where she was occupied by the man sitting with her. Nate took her hand and led her over, but she could see his shoulders tense just slightly as they arrived at the table.

Natalie turned and greeted them with a "Hey," before gesturing to the man to introduce him. "This is Brandon. Brandon, this is my brother Nate and his wife, Melody. Fair warning now, this evening is about all of us getting shit faced and getting up there to make an ass out of ourselves. There will be singing." She gave Nate a pointed look.

"You will definitely have to get me drunk before I will ever willingly go up there," Nate said.

"Challenge accepted." Melody laughed. Natalie nodded approvingly at her in response.

"I'm down for a good time," Brandon said.

"I bet you are," Nate grumbled under his breath, low enough that only Melody caught it. She threw him a confused glance, but he was still fixing Brandon with a hard stare.

"Okay, let's get this party started," Natalie said. "We need drinks."

"I'll go." Brandon tilted his chin. "What does everyone want?"

Nate started to answer when Natalie spoke over him, pointing an indignant finger at him. "No to whatever you were about to say. We are doing shots. Brandon, a round of Tequila if you please." She batted her eyelashes up at him.

"You got it," he said and headed over to the bar.

"Keep them coming," she yelled after him.

Nate watched him walk away and scoffed before turning back to Natalie. "Nice. So how long is this one going to last?"

"Hopefully at least a couple more hours. I have a few more plans for him this evening before I send him on his way." She smiled mischievously, but there was a hardened look in her eyes to betray the lightness of her answer.

Melody got the impression that this was a conversation they'd had many times and a topic they did not see eye to eye on, so she tried to steer them in another direction. She asked Natalie, "So, you aren't nervous about singing in front of a crowd?"

"Absolutely not. I don't give two shits what anyone might think. Besides, I'm hot and don't sound half bad. Definitely better than anyone of those drunk bitches from the bachelorette party that just walked in will sound like once they get started." Natalie laughed.

Melody glanced over her shoulder and saw the group Natalie was referring to. They had settled in over the next couple of tables and were already getting loud. It seemed like they had already been drinking and came here to end the night. "Why? Do you get stage fright or something?" Natalie asked.

"Nah. I won't be making albums anytime soon, but I can hold my own," Mel said. Nate raised an eyebrow at that but didn't comment.

"Glad to hear it. We need someone else around to make Nate come out of his shell and try new things." Natalie smiled.

Nate gave her a flat look before saying, "I do plenty."

"You will shortly," she said as Brandon arrived at the table with a tray of shot glasses.

Everyone but Nate reached for one, and so Melody lifted hers to his lips, stretching up to whisper in his ear, "Oh, c'mon. Don't be a party pooper. Let's have some fun. We told her we'd join them, so we might as well make the most of it." She gave him the puppy dog eyes, and he relented, letting her tip the shot glass into his mouth. She quickly grabbed another and finished it herself.

"Hell yes!" Natalie shouted.

The next thirty minutes passed in a blur of shots and some drinking game that Natalie seems to have invented. Melody was not sure if the rules are unclear, or if it is just the pure volume of alcohol it forced you to ingest, that was making things hard to track. By the time Natalie was up to sing, even Nate was red faced and grinning.

Brandon teetered after Natalie to get a closer spot by the stage while she sang, and Nate leaned over to tell Mel that he was going to get some water from the bar for them both. Since he was already a little unsteady, his lips brushed the shell of her ear, sending a delicious shiver down her spine.

As he made his way over to the bar, the bachelorette party, which had only gotten louder and more boisterous as the evening went on, spotted him in the crowd. The next thing she knew, a flock of drunk and screaming women had surrounded Nate. Melody wasn't sure whether to be concerned or to laugh.

The group slowly dissipated, most of them stumbling back over to their table for their drinks, but one petite blonde woman remained. From the familiarity she was showing Nate, they clearly knew each other. It was too far to hear anything they were saying, but the way she kept her hand on his forearm and batted a hand against his chest as she laughed made Melody's stomach twist in discomfort. She tried to shake it off. She refused to be one of those petty women that held a man's past against him. They both knew plenty of people from before their time together, and she'd had lovers in the past. There was nothing to get upset about.

The woman finally released him and made her way back over to her table while he pushed on towards the bar as originally intended. Natalie's song had finally started, and she joined the music, singing a rendition of "Stuck in the Middle With You." She was right, her voice was not bad.

Once the blonde made it back to the table, the party broke out in loud voices all talking over each other and the music.

"Karen –"

"How do you know him?"

"I need to know everything. Now –"

Melody wanted to tune them out, to not be that person eavesdropping on whatever this was. But she just couldn't help herself.

The woman, Karen apparently, said, "That is Nathaniel Blackwell. He's that hot carpenter that did some projects at my house a couple of summers ago." She paused for dramatic effect. "And let's just say, I got an up close and personal taste at just how talented those hands are." She laughed deviously as the drunk women exchanged open mouth glances and hoots of encouragement. "I was there to help pick up the pieces when his poor, dear wife died." Her voice took on a cold edge, and Mel tried to indiscreetly glance over to see what was happening. Karen was looking right at her as she said, "And I plan to be there again as soon as he is done with his latest mistake. It's just a matter of time."

Melody jerked her attention back to Natalie on the stage, her heart racing. She tried to calm down, to control her breathing but it wasn't working. She didn't want Nate to see her like this. How would she even explain it? She didn't even fully understand her reaction herself. Of course, the alcohol certainly wasn't helping with thinking clearly either.

Before Nate could return with the drinks, she decided to stop by the restroom so she could collect herself. As she splashed cold water on her cheeks, she told herself to pull it together.

Why am I reacting so strongly to this? I know I don't have an issue with the fact that he has been with other women before me. I mean, he was married for God's sake.

Then it hit her.

That's the difference. That was real, it was deep, it was pure. I can tell in the way he talks about her and that look he gets in his eye when he is lost in memory. Karen, however, is nothing in comparison. She just feels like some kind of cheap distraction. But what does that make me exactly? I'm nothing more than a fabrication. A lie to everyone who loves him. How long before he realizes that this won't work long term and I'm not worth his time and effort?

Her breathing stalled. She didn't know when her thinking had shifted, and it started mattering to her like this. She could feel herself spiraling as she closed her eyes.

I'm falling for him. The one thing I knew I could not, should not do. But my stupid heart just couldn't stay out of it.

She was up next to sing, so she tried to pull herself together as best she could before she headed back out. Nate had made it to the table by then and was waiting for her. She plastered on a too bright smile and could tell that her face was off. He gave her a concerned look as he asked, "Everything okay?"

"Of course." She knew her tone was too cheery, her eyes too wide to be natural. To distract them both, she picked up another unclaimed tequila shot from the table and threw it back, right as her name was called for her turn to sing. She had forgotten what song she meant to pick out, but another had come to mind and was screaming in the back of her head.

She made her way to the man in charge of playing the music and told him to pull up The One That Got Away by The Civil Wars. As she took the mic and made her way up onto the stage, the tequila worked its magic, loosening her limbs and her tongue.

She closed her eyes as the guitar started strumming and let herself become one with the music. She started to sing and poured all of her confusing emotions into the lyrics. Oh, how true they were: She never meant for things to get this deep; she never meant for them to mean a thing. The music rose to its crescendo, her voice rising with it and weaving the melody into the air.

She finished to a round of applause and cheers, and Nate was up next, but she couldn't meet his eye as she passed him on the way back to their table.

Natalie leaned over and hugged her when she got there. "Girl! You are good! Like good! You did so good!" Her words slurred as the evidence of her evening so far reared its head. Loud laughter from the table next to theirs drew her attention though. Rolling her eyes, she said a bit too loudly, "God, I always hated that bitch. I'm so glad my brother never actually dated her."

"What?" Melody asked. "That's not how she made it sound to her friends earlier."

Natalie snorted indelicately. "She would. That desperate ho-bag wanted to get her hooks into Nate so bad. She got him to agree to coffee once, and that was it. He couldn't stand any more of her company." She then broke down into full laughter, eyes watering.

Melody wasn't sure what to do with this information. She felt relieved, but it also didn't change anything. She had never been truly upset about Karen. Karen was just the catalyst that had made her stop to think.

Music started playing and she looked up at the stage to find Nate staring at her intently. She could feel her face flushing as she held eye contact. He started singing and she felt her mouth drop open.

Holy Shit.

Why had he been so against doing this? He sounded amazing. His voice was so warm and husky and hot. If she sounded like that, she would never shut up.

He held her eye as he continued, singing about how she blew into his life, how he wanted to be her man, her friend. The chorus of "Oh, I'm with you" repeating.

She sat there captivated and ensnared in his eyes. As he finished to raucous applause, she saw the title of the song on the screen: Love Song 1 by The White Buffalo.

He came up to the table and wordlessly took her hand, pulling her after him outside. She could hear Natalie hooting and laughing hysterically behind them as they made their way out.

Chapter 14

Nate

The cool night air was good. Hopefully it would help clear both of their heads. He led her towards his truck, not breaking the silence. She didn't say anything either.

Once they made it to the truck, he leaned against the passenger door, pulling her closer to him and tucking a stray strand of hair behind her ear.

"Are you okay? You seemed...off when I got back from the bar." Even in the dim lighting, he could see a blush creep over her face, and she tried to duck her head to avoid his gaze. He gently gripped her chin and pulled her eyes back up to his. "You can tell me anything," he said.

She looked as if she was going to resist before letting out a rush of breath. "I don't know what I'm doing. I know what I signed up for, and I enjoy being your friend. This last month has honestly been incredible. As crazy as this all is and how it all started, I can't imagine my life any other way now. But that's just it. I'm already getting too invested. I've done my best to stay as detached as possible, but it doesn't help. I care about you. You make it impossible not to. Every day, I find myself wanting to learn more about you, to let you learn more about me. I keep wanting more, even though I know I can't have it. My heart won't accept what my brain knows. And I'm terrified that by even telling you all of this, that I'm going to lose what we already have." She wrung her hands together.

At a loss for words, he leaned forward and placed a soft kiss against her forehead, giving himself a moment to process.

He finally pulled back and looked at her. "I'm not going anywhere." A half smile pulled on his lips as he added "I'm with you." A reminder of the song he chose.

He hadn't intended to climb on stage and serenade her in front of everyone. Between the alcohol and that vulnerable look on her face as she finished up her own song, he had just done it without thinking. He couldn't look too closely at that decision, though. He wasn't ready to admit what he was starting to understand deep down. That possibility was too terrifying, so he would avoid it as long as possible.

Instead, he closed the distance and kissed her.

As was becoming a usual occurrence for them, the kiss quickly grew heated. Melody pressed her body against him as she wound her arms around his neck. He gripped her hips through the fabric of her dress, sealing them together fully and feeling her soft curves under his hands.

Breaking their kiss, he trailed his lips down her jaw and neck, scraping his teeth over sensitive areas and causing her to shiver against him. The scent of lavender wafted off the silky strands of her hair. "Fuck, you always taste so sweet," he murmured against her skin as his lips travelled.

"God, I need you."

"Well, come on then," he said. He stepped away from the door of the truck before opening it and climbing inside. She looked confused for a second before he pulled her inside with him, lying flat on the bench seat and settling her on top of him.

A surprised "Oh" escaped her, and he sealed their mouths for another kiss. He released her briefly so she could shimmy out of her jacket and undo the buttons on his shirt. He let out a groan as she licked her way back up his abdomen and chest, to place another kiss on his lips.

She pulled back slightly to look at him. "Are we really doing this here? Anyone could walk by."

"I don't think I can help myself. Waiting the entire drive home to touch you just might kill me." Nate skated the back of his knuckles up the outside of her thigh. He felt her breath hitch as he slid his hand around towards the inside of her thigh. "If you want me to stop, tell me."

"Don't stop."

That was all he needed. Tangling his hand in her hair, he watched her face as he reached between them, teasing her over the fabric of her panties. He could feel how wet she already was for him. She began to rock over his hand, desperate for more friction.

He used his hold on her hair to angle her head back, giving himself better access to her neck. As he suckled and nipped her neck, he worked her panties aside, lightly tracing her. She let out a moan as he set to work in a rhythm he knew she loved. Before long, he could feel her thighs begin to quake, a telltale sign that she was close. He shifted, sliding two fingers inside of her and using his thumb to continue working her clit. The dam burst and he felt her tighten around his fingers, milking them greedily.

As she caught her breath, he sat them up and pivoted so that he was sitting upright in the seat. He wanted to be buried deep inside of her, and so he needed her to have plenty of room to open those pretty thighs around him. He leaned her back against the dash with a kiss to her collar bone as he worked his belt open and his pants down enough to release his cock.

Impatient as always, she reached for him, giving him a firm stroke before shifting forward to bear down on him with her dress bunched up around her hips and her panties pushed to the side. Sliding into her was always perfection. Once he was deep inside, they began to move together in what had become a well-known frenzy. It was a little more clumsy and unrestrained, thanks to their slightly inebriated state, but they didn't slow.

"More." Melody gasped.

He was more than happy to oblige her, gliding a hand up her torso to palm her breast under her dress. His other hand squeezed her ass, helping to pull her down onto him firmly with each thrust of their hips.

Her next orgasm ignited his own, and they laid there panting to catch their breath in the aftermath. He was rubbing soothing circles across her back when a knock on the window startled them both.

Glancing over, he made out the shape of his brother through the condensation on the windows. At least he was facing away from them.

"It's Nash," he said quietly, helping her slide off his lap and straighten her clothes as he tucked himself away and fastened his pants. "I'll be right back." Scooting over to the driver's side, Nate got out and shut the door behind him.

Nash said, "You guys know that you have, like, a house to go do that in, right? That is not what I planned on coming here to see tonight."

"You're the one peeping in car windows like some kind of perv, dude," Nate said.

Nash chuckled as he ran his hand down his face and shook his head. "Hey, I'm happy for you man. Seeing you lose even an ounce of restraint these days is a fucking miracle. And if I had voluntarily become celibate for years, I would probably be getting it on anywhere humanly possible too."

He tried to shift away before Nate's fist connected with his bicep, but he wasn't quite fast enough. Nate barked a laugh. "First off, fuck you. I'm fine. And I was never celibate. I just don't flit from person to person constantly like you two assholes I call siblings do."

"Woah man. You know Nat flits. I just...float. I'm not in any big hurry. I just haven't found a reason to stick around long term is all."

"You know, you may have to give it more than a couple of weeks to find that reason. You know, get to know a person?"

Before they could continue, the window of the truck rolled down behind them. "Um, everything okay out here?" Mel asked. Nate could tell that her face was still beat red even in the dark. "It looked like you guys were fighting."

With a wide grin, Nash said, "Everything is great. I just can't pass up on the opportunity to bust Nate's balls. I was heading inside and uh," he cleared his throat, "Caught a glimpse of the show. Not that I saw anything specifically –" he added when he saw Nate's face turn murderous.

"Okay, well...good. I'm just gonna..." She gestured vaguely behind her and quickly rolled the window back up.

After a pause, Nate looked away from the window and back to Nash. "What are you doing here anyway? Nat didn't say anything about you joining us."

"Oh, uh, she mentioned you all were going to be here, and I said I might drop by if I had time. So, it wasn't really a set thing. I just finished up work early and said fuck it." Nash shrugged.

"Well, Natalie and her latest coin operated boy are still inside, so feel free to join them. I think I should probably get Mel home now," Nate said.

Nash laughed again. "Oh yeah, I bet she wore you out real good. Best get to bed old man." He was successful in dodging the punch this time, darting towards the bar with a wave over his shoulder.

Nate stood there for a moment, staring after him before climbing back inside and starting the truck up. Thankfully, enough time had passed that his head had cleared enough to drive home. Buckling in, he looked over to make sure Mel was buckled as well. "Are you alright? I'm sorry about that."

"I'm fine," she said. "I'm just glad I still had my dress on. Otherwise, that would have been even more awkward."

"Little brothers live to torment their older siblings. But when it comes down to it, I don't ever think he would intentionally do something to disrespect or embarrass you too bad. You were probably right about this being too public. But I just can't bring myself to regret it, because it was also fucking hot."

Melody bit her lip and gave him a sultry look as she whispered back, "It was."

Nate rested his hand on her thigh as he drove away. They rode home in silence and got ready for bed, exchanging small smiles but not talking about everything that happened this evening.

Nate knew at some point he was going to have to unpack all of these feelings brewing inside instead of just stuffing them down. He didn't know how many details either of them would remember tomorrow, but as he pulled her close and drifted off to sleep, he drowsily thought that maybe they could stay in this bubble for a little while longer.

Chapter 15

Melody

The morning sun shining through the window woke Melody up with a stabbing pain behind her eyes. She was very warm and realized that she had been using Nate's chest as a pillow. He was still sound asleep, so she gently disentangled herself and tried not to jostle him. Her head spun slightly as she got up, so she made her way to the ensuite, looking for some painkillers.

After using the restroom, brushing her teeth and taking the pills, she crept back out to leave a few on Nate's bedside table as well. He was sure to feel as shitty as she did once he woke up.

Heading back into the bathroom, she decided a nice soak in the tub was just what she needed. Lighting one of the several candles they had set around the room, she shut the bathroom door quietly and started the water. She added in some lavender oil and a tiny bit of Epsom salt to help with the tension. She quickly threw her hair up in a messy bun to keep it out of the way.

Once that was done, she slipped out of her nightgown, tossing it in the hamper, before grabbing a washcloth to douse in cold water to make a compress for her eyes. She could count on one hand how many times in her life she'd had a hangover, and she was not a fan.

Settling into the hot water and starting the jets, she let herself sink against the edge of the tub with the cool cloth over her eyes. Bits and pieces of the night before began to resurface in her brain and much to her dismay, she found she seemingly remembered all of what happened. A flush spread across her face and ears as she remembered all that she had admitted, and the song she had drunkenly sang at him.

A different kind of heat flashed through her as she remembered his song and all that came after in his truck. She hoped that Nate would remember less than she did. Either way, she was not going to bring it up.

She wasn't sure how long she laid like that before she heard the door quietly open and Nate's soft footsteps in the space. After the sounds of his toothbrush ceased, she felt his hands gently on her shoulders, beginning to knead out some of the knots.

He brushed his lips against her temple as he said, "Good morning."

"Good morning. How are you feeling?"

"Last night is a bit hazy and I feel a little like I got run over by a truck, but it could be worse. Thank you for the painkillers, by the way. How are you?"

She let out a small groan. "Eh, about the same. This is helping though."

"Good." He continued massaging her shoulders quietly for a few minutes before asking, "Do you mind if I join you?"

She grinned. “Please do.” She shifted forward, so he had room to slide in, but felt him gently take her washcloth for a moment, applying more cold water to it and giving it back. Then he quickly chucked his boxers in the hamper before climbing in behind her, his thighs bracketing her own. Pulling her back against his chest, he wound his arms around her ribcage, and they settled into the soothing heat of the water.

After a while, the timer on the jets reached its end and they turned off. The water had cooled as well, but she was not ready to get out yet. As if he could read her mind, he set about adding more hot water and restarting the jets. The surge of heat in the water felt amazing, and she sighed contentedly.

They laid there quietly for a bit longer, just enjoying the bath and each other’s company.

“I should probably wash up before I end up falling asleep.” Melody slowly sat up and placed her compress on the edge of the tub. She reached for her loofah and soaped it, washing her body and face. As she reached behind her, Nate gently took it from her and helped wash her back.

Once he finished, he quietly instructed her to tip her head back as he undid her messy bun and released her hair down her spine. She felt warm water trickle down her scalp and then he softly worked shampoo through the long strands while massaging her scalp.

She let out a satisfied groan as more of the tension in her head slipped away. He repeated the process with conditioner and let it set for a few minutes while he took care of cleaning himself. The softer floral scent of her soap contrasted with the deeper spicy tones of his own. Once he was done, he rinsed the conditioner out as well, and she scooted back into his embrace once more. This time, she could feel him hard and ready against her lower back. She felt her nipples harden in response and squirmed against him, drawing a hiss from his lips.

With a husky chuckle, she said, "I'm a little surprised you feel like it this morning after all of the alcohol last night."

"I can't help it. I want you all the time. Seems like the perfect hangover remedy to me." His hands skated up her sides as he began to tease her breasts. His lips left a trail of kisses down the side of her neck before pausing briefly with a surprised laugh. "Oops. I guess I got a little carried away last night and left you a small souvenir."

"What?" she asked. With his hands still wandering, it was hard to focus.

"It looks like I gave you a hickey here." He kissed the spot in question.

"Oh." She laughed. "That's okay."

"I kind of like that you have my mark on you. The world can see that you're mine."

Before she could think too much about that statement, she was distracted by his right hand drifting its way down her stomach, towards where she was aching for him. Her breath caught as she felt him at her entrance, and his other hand kept up the delicious torture on her taut nipple.

He kept a leisurely pace, as if they had all the time in the world, and her climax built and built until she broke sweetly on his fingers. Withdrawing his hands, he wound his arms around her again to give her a moment to catch her breath.

"Should we get out now so we can continue this elsewhere?" Melody asked.

"Sounds good to me." He stopped the jets and drained the tub as she stood up and leaned over to grab them towels. She felt him shift behind her and say "God, I love your ass." To her surprise she felt his lips brush the curve before he bit down softly, causing her to let out an involuntary moan. He gave her a small clap on the ass as well, and she could tell she was even wetter than before.

With a blush on her face, she turned back to where he was kneeling and handed him a towel. "You do look good on your knees." She felt him follow her out of the tub, hounding her steps. She started to head back towards their bedroom when she felt him pull her to a stop. "Did you not want to –" she gestured towards the bed.

"In a minute. I think you need to enjoy the view of me on my knees a bit longer first." He pulled her towards the counter before lifting her up and scooting her ass to the edge. He dropped his towel on the ground before kneeling on it and draping her thighs over both of his shoulders.

She didn't have time to prepare before he descended on her, holding her legs right where he wanted them and bearing her to him. Between his mouth and hand, she was lost quickly again. Instead of slowing though, he kept his rhythm straight through her orgasm and she could feel it building into an even more intense release as he kept up the pace. The pressure built up in the base of her spine, and she trembled as she tried to wiggle away to get some relief from the onslaught. He was relentless though and held her firm. When she came this time, she saw stars and felt her limbs go slack.

He placed a sweet kiss against the inside of her knee. "Now we can go." He scooped her into his arms and walked them over to the bed, setting her down on her feet beside it. Since she was a little unsteady, he held her upper arms for support with a small smile. "What would you like now, baby?"

"I don't have the capacity to answer that after that last orgasm." She laughed.

"Hmm. Well, there is one thing I've wanted to try." He backed her up to the bed. She climbed on, scooting back to the middle as he crawled after her and then up her body, lifting one of her legs over his shoulder and settling himself between her parted thighs. With a hard thrust, he filled her completely. They simultaneously let out appreciative moans.

With her leg up as it was, this angle was hitting that perfect spot deep inside. He set a ruthless pace, and they lost themselves in each other. As his release barreled through him, it sparked a final rush through her as well. While they caught their breath, he lowered her leg back onto the bed and wound his arms around her, resting his head on her breast. She stroked his hair idly as they came down from the high.

Eventually though, he untangled himself and told her to stay put for a second. He went into the bathroom and came back out with a damp and warm washcloth, which he used to gently clean her off. Once he was done, he headed back into the bathroom, presumably to clean himself as well.

He walked back out a couple of minutes later wearing only a pair of grey sweatpants. Melody rolled her eyes with a smile. "We've talked about this. You know exactly what you're doing right now."

He threw her a wink over his shoulder. "You're welcome. I'm going to go make us some hangover breakfast." As he opened the door, she saw a blur of fluff burst through right as Nate said, "Incoming!"

Fredrick pounced on the bed, staring straight at Mel with an indignant huff. "Sir. That was rude. You have an automatic feeder now, so I know you got breakfast, and you have a fancy new doggy door that we showed you how to use, so you don't need to be let out. Please dial back the dramatics." He shook his head and sneezed in response, letting out a small grumble.

"Fine, fine," she grumbled back, begrudgingly getting out of bed. She fished out a new set of pajamas from her drawer; a short and tank top set this time before quickly brushing her hair. Coming back from the bathroom, she heard Nate's phone dinging with a notification where he had left it on his nightstand. She picked it up to take down to him as she headed down to join him for breakfast with Fredrick in tow.

Chapter 16

Nate

Nate glanced over his shoulder as he heard Mel pad into the kitchen behind him and the clicking of Fredrick's nails on the floor. She had on a silky and black little pajama set, which made his eyes trail over her hungrily again. "Food is almost done," he called over.

She walked over, holding something out to him. "Smells good. Here's your phone by the way, it was going off so I brought it down in case it was anything important."

"Thanks." He took it and checked the notifications. There were several from Natalie – mostly messages from last night after they had left, one from her this morning, followed by a text from Nash last night and one this morning as well. He didn't have the energy to deal with them right now, so he decided to leave it until after breakfast.

He handed her a mug of coffee and then plated up the French toast, eggs and bacon before he joined her at the breakfast bar. She breathed in the steam from her coffee and sighed. "This looks absolutely amazing. Thank you."

He nodded in welcome.

Nate resigned himself to checking his messages while they tucked into their food. He opened the text thread from Natalie first, seeing she had started with a video which was clearly of Mel singing last night. He scrolled down past it to read the rest and almost choked on his bite of egg.

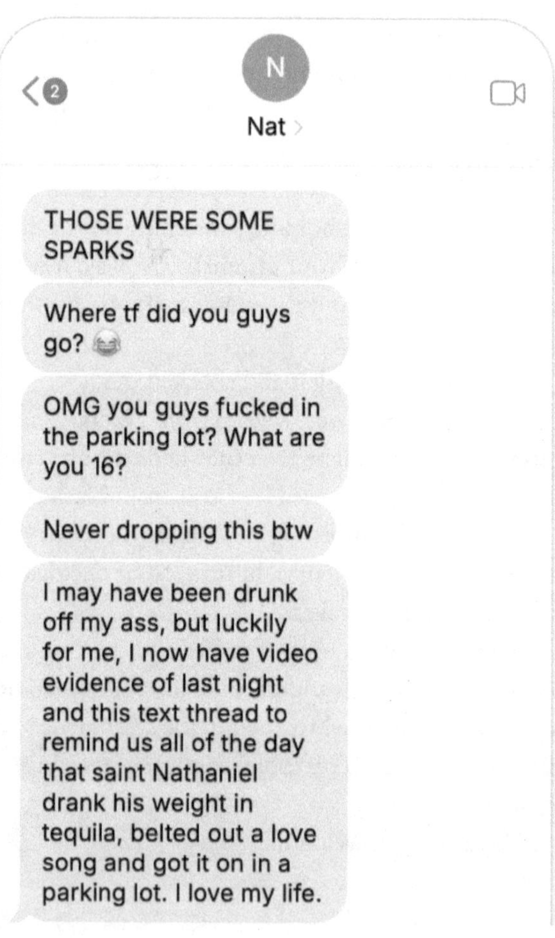

He jabbed at the screen as he typed out a reply.

He rolled his eyes and checked Nash's texts.

He set his phone down with a drawn-out sigh and massaged his temples.

"What's wrong?" Melody asked.

"With all the booze last night, I totally forgot we were having my mom and everyone over here tomorrow. Do you still feel up for it? If so, I guess I'll run to the store after this and grab everything we are going to need." He studied her face.

“Of course. I’ll tidy up around here after I take Fredrick for a walk.” She smiled.

“Thanks, I appreciate it.” He gave her a soft kiss on the cheek and gathered up their empty plates to load into the dishwasher. Once he was finished, he ran back upstairs to get dressed for the store.

After throwing on a t-shirt, his shoes and a baseball cap, he gave Mel a quick kiss and told her, “Be back soon.” As he drove to the store, he tried to think of what they would need for the next day, but his mind kept drifting back to the unopened video from Nat. He hadn’t wanted to play it with Mel nearby, but now that he was alone, his phone was burning a hole in his pocket.

Finding a parking spot and turning his truck off, he pulled the text back up and hit play. The night before came rushing back as her voice drifted through the speaker. He was surprised by the camera shifting to him partway through though. He remembered how he had felt listening to her the intense desire to convince her that this was not a mistake, the unexpected fear of losing her – but he was not prepared to see all of that written across his face for the world to see.

Nate closed his eyes and ran a hand down his face as the song ended. The emotion in her voice still resounded in his mind, and he said, “This is getting out of hand. It’s only been a month. Pull it together, man.”

He headed into the grocery store and gathered up ingredients, but he couldn’t help but hum along to the sound of her singing in his mind.

Chapter 17

Melody

After Nate took off, Mel got changed into some running shorts and a tank top. As soon as she asked Fredrick if he wanted to go for a walk, the fur hurricane started. Once she had wrangled him into his harness, she put on her headphones and set out.

They hadn't developed a regular route in the new neighborhood quite yet, but she was happy to explore. She pulled out her phone and was trying to decide whether to play some music or a podcast when she saw she had a text from Natalie from the night before.

Opening it, she saw a video with a quick message that said, *"I know he will kill me if he ever finds out I took this video and then kill me again for sending it to you, but if I were in your shoes, I would want to keep it forever. You're welcome."*

Mel's breath caught as she played the video and realized it was Nate's song from last night. Her face flushed and a shiver went down her spine as she listened to his voice. She had half wondered if her mind had exaggerated the experience due to the alcohol, but no. If anything, watching him with a clearer mind only made it more intense.

The video ended and she decided to look up music by The White Buffalo. Mel remembered him mentioning them as one of his favorite bands a few weeks ago, but she had forgotten to check them out. She found the album with Nate's song and set it playing as they wound their way through the neighborhood.

Listening to the lyrics did not help her put the night out of her mind, but she resolved to keep up the pretense of not remembering the details. She had already said too much, and she wasn't going to risk ruining things. Hopefully things were fuzzier for him.

The new neighborhood was peaceful, and they made a wide loop around before heading home. Nate was still gone when she got there, so she decided to start with taking some storage boxes up to the attic to get them out of her way before cleaning.

She pulled the rope and the stairs unfolded before her. Picking up the boxes, they slid precariously, and she considered just making two trips.

Stubbornness set in though, and she started climbing the stairs with her arms full. She made it to the top and a couple steps into the attic itself when she knocked into a stack of boxes that she had not seen in the dark.

The pile spilled over, and her top box fell onto the heap as well. She hoped nothing breakable was inside. Reaching blindly for the string that would turn on the single lightbulb overhead, she finally found it above her head. Light illuminated the space, and she saw with dismay that one of Nate's boxes had popped open and spilled across the attic floor.

She set her boxes off to the side and put his unopened boxes back in their places before kneeling to pick up the contents that had fallen out of the last box. Melody paused when she saw that the label on the box read "Angela". It felt intrusive to look at anything in this box without Nate's permission, but she couldn't just leave it sprawled across the floor to be trampled on.

Most of what had spilled out seemed to be photo albums. Curiosity got the better of her, and she flipped open the cover of one. Nate and Angela as teenagers filled the first pages, their eyes full of light and laughter. The rest were filled with snapshots of their life together, prom, graduation, silly shots of them as young adults dating.

The next album was full of wedding photos. The next was clearly the years that followed, their faces aging slightly and the scenery changing – their first home, vacations, family gatherings, Christmas. There was so much joy shining on Nate's face. She didn't think she'd ever seen that expression from him since she'd known him. It made her sad to think that life had stolen it from him.

She ran her finger over that look on his face, and she gently tucked the album back in the box with the others. The last item was a smaller leather-bound book. It was too small to be another photo album, and when she opened it, she realized with a start that it was a journal. Angela's journal. She knew she had absolutely no business reading this, and it would be a gross invasion of privacy to do so.

She started to place it back in the box too when a loose photo floated out from between the pages. It was of Nate and Angela again, but much later. This must have been not too long before she died. They were seated on a bench in what looked to be some kind of garden.

Angela was ghastly thin and had lost her hair, her bald head discreetly covered by a hat. She rested her head on Nate's shoulder as he held her, his arm around her as if he could shield her from the world. Though he was smiling, it did not reach his eyes. Her breath caught at the raw pain shining there that he was trying to hide behind that smile. The transformation from laughing, carefree Nate in the previous photos was stark and made her heart ache for him.

She tucked the photo back into the journal, noticing that there were more odds and ends tucked throughout and glanced at the date on the last entry. Angela must have kept journaling as long as possible. As wrong as she knew it was, Melody felt the need to read the journal. To get to know Angela, and to see Nate through her eyes.

Without allowing herself to second guess the decision, she closed up the box and returned it to the stack, taking the journal with her as she made her way back down into the house.

She didn't have the nerve to read it right now, so she decided to tuck it into a drawer in her studio. She would figure the rest out later. Needing a distraction from the guilt, she got back to cleaning and turned music on over the Bluetooth speakers around the house.

Melody had gotten quite a bit done and had stopped for a dance break as her music shuffled onto a metal song. Naturally, Nate arrived home with an arm full of groceries to find her using the Swiffer as a microphone and whipping her hair around.

He cleared his throat. "Whatcha listening to?"

Swiping her hair out of her face, she smiled unabashedly and told him, "Bloodywood," continuing to dance without a care.

Nate set the grocery bags on the kitchen counter and hesitated for a moment before shrugging and starting to dance as well. She had never seen him cut loose like this before, and neither of them danced particularly well, but she couldn't help but smile.

The song shifted to Pony by Ginuwine and she heard Nate laugh as he pressed up behind her. Hands on her hips, he rolled his in time with the beat and her own movements. She wound an arm back around his neck and ground her ass back into him like she was in high school again.

The song changed again to a slower song, the opening notes of Haunted House by Noah Gundersen playing. Nate turned her in his arms, and she laced her hands behind his neck as they slow danced in the kitchen.

"Noah Gundersen?" he asked her.

She nodded. "He was on your list of favorite artists a few weeks ago, so I downloaded some of his music to listen to."

He smiled. "I do like him."

Melody laid her head against his chest as they slowly spun in place until the song ended. Once it was over, they parted and she bent to pick up the abandoned Swiffer while he got to work putting the groceries away.

"Thank you for cleaning. I appreciate it."

"No problem. Thanks for knocking out the shopping. Need me to do anything else for tomorrow?"

"I don't think so. I'm going to do a little food prep tonight so it's faster in the morning, but everybody usually brings stuff, so there shouldn't be anything crazy left to do."

"Cool. I think the place is ready, so we should be all set. I've never hosted something like this though. I'm a little nervous."

"Don't be. It'll be just like the last one, except that we don't have to drop any crazy news on them this time. Mom will be excited to see the new house and other than that, we'll eat and shoot the shit and then they'll go home. Easy peasy."

"Easy peasy," Melody repeated with a nod.

He came over and placed a kiss on her nose. "Seriously, it'll be fine. I promise."

"You're right. Plus, I'm pretty sure I've won Natalie over, so that's a win."

Nate let out a groan. "Oh, god. You and Nat teaming up is slightly terrifying if I'm honest. I can't even imagine the chaos that could ensue."

She jabbed him in the side in response. "Watch it or you'll find out."

With a snort, he said, "No, no, I know it's a good thing. She doesn't trust people easily, so it definitely is a win."

Melody's stomach felt like a leaden weight had been dropped inside, guilt at lying to Natalie rising. She tried to mentally shake it off. Their lies were necessary. Everyone would just be hurt if they found out the truth. But the thought of being one more reason that Natalie had trust issues bothered Melody more than it had a few weeks ago. Getting close to people made lying to them harder. She had started caring about Nate's family as if it were her own. She hoped that she never gave them a reason to not look at her that way in return, so she knew she needed to keep their secret no matter what.

Chapter 18

Nate

The next morning, he rose early to get started on some baking and did his best to not wake Melody as he gently untangled himself from her arms. He pressed a soft kiss to her hand as he laid it back down on the sheets and pulled the covers up over her.

Creeping out, he closed the door softly behind him and hoped that Fredrick would stay quiet. He found him on the couch, lazily wagging his tail at Nate's approach.

"Hey buddy." He ruffled the fur on his side and Fredrick yawned but made no move to get up. Nate headed into the kitchen and quickly washed his hands before pulling out what he would need for muffins.

A bit later, he heard Melody's soft footsteps, and he turned to see her coming down the hall wearing one of his flannel shirts and nothing else. Her lovely legs were on display once again, and he gave himself a moment to let his gaze roam before returning his attention to her face. Her hair was thrown up in a messy bun, and she let out a small yawn, which made him smile.

"Good morning, sleepy head." He pulled her in for a quick kiss. She stretched up on her toes to meet him, and he heard her let out a contented sigh.

Breaking away, she smiled up at him. "Good morning. You should have woken me up when you got up though. What can I help with?"

He waved her off. "I just wanted to get a head start on the muffins, but I got most everything else ready last night."

"I guess I didn't realize that you baked too."

"Yeah. I made that banana bread for the last brunch, remember?"

"I remember us taking it, but at the time I didn't think too much about it and just assumed you picked it up."

"Nah. Mine's better." He winked.

"It was delicious," she said as she wandered over to the coffee pot and poured herself a mug. "What time will everyone be here?"

"Around eleven." He glanced at the clock and saw it was almost ten already. "I've got this under control, but you can set the table if you want."

"Can do." She gave him a salute before gathering up plates, napkins, and utensils. Once she had laid everything out, she said, "I should go hop in the shower real quick. Are you still in the middle of anything, or can you come keep me company?" She flashed him a saucy smile.

He tossed the towel he had been using to dry his hands onto the counter and followed her down the hall. "I can spare a few minutes."

His mom arrived first as usual and handed him a round casserole dish. "I made quiche Florentine." He kissed her on the cheek and showed her into the house.

"Oh my, this place is beautiful," Naomi said.

"Thank you," Melody said and accepted a hug from her. "Let me show you around."

They disappeared further into the house as Nate took the quiche to the table and placed it with the rest of the food he had prepared. He heard the front door open again and Nash appeared with a grocery bag in hand.

"Hey man. I brought juice," Nash said.

"Thanks. You can put it on the bar," Nate said. "Mom is here; Mel is showing her around."

Nash nodded. "Place looks good. You guys got a lot done."

"You helping me move the heavy stuff definitely sped up that process, so thank you again."

Nash just waved him off without replying. They both turned at the sound of Natalie arriving, and she promptly sat down to shower Fredrick with affection, abandoning her grocery bag and purse on the floor.

"Hello to you too." Nash snorted.

"Best boys get the most attention, Nash. I don't make the rules," Natalie said. "Isn't that right, Fredrick? You are the bestest boy. Yes, you are."

Nate gathered up the bags from the floor, depositing her purse on their coat rack and taking the other to the kitchen. "What did you bring?"

"Uh, grapes. I always bring grapes. Duh," Nat said with a smirk.

"Right, of course." Nate chuckled. He quickly rinsed them and added them to the table too.

He went to see where his mom and Melody had gotten to and found them in her studio. Mel was showing her a work in progress that he had not seen yet.

It was full of golden browns, creams and all the shades in between, giving him a warm feeling inside. It reminded him of his own work, of the grains of wood and lines of timber he used to bring life to his projects.

"That's amazing," he said over her shoulder.

She glanced up at him with a bright smile. "Thank you. Your woodworking kind of inspired it, actually."

"You can say no if you want, but can I have this when you're done? I would love to hang it up in my shop," he asked.

"Of course. I would love that," Melody said.

"That's a wonderful idea," Naomi nodded.

He hugged them both around the shoulders. "Well, everyone is here and the food is ready. You guys about ready to eat?"

"Yes." His mom clapped her hands.

He took Mel's hand and led them back out, everyone taking their seats around the table.

"You guys have done a wonderful job setting up the house," Naomi said as the food was passed and plates were filled.

Melody said, "Thank You," as Nate said, "That's all Mel." They exchanged small smiles and Natalie rolled her eyes halfheartedly.

Nate listened as his family chattered and ate, a familiar warm feeling in his chest at having them near.

"So, children, next month's brunch will be Easter. I was going to invite Shirley and Sean. Melody, I wanted to see what you thought about us inviting your aunt to join us too?"

"Oh, um, that's so nice. If it's okay, let me talk to her about it and get back to you," Melody said.

"Of course, dear. We would be happy to have her though," his mom said.

Nate hadn't met Beatrice yet either. He would ask Melody how she felt about that later, but he didn't want to pressure her into it before she was ready. They would have to face her at some point though.

Chapter 19

Melody

The bell above the door jingled as Melody went into Nate's shop. She was greeted by Sean who was working the front counter and assisting none other than Karen. "Hey Mel. How's it going?" he asked.

"Hey Sean, what's up? Is Nate here?" Mel asked him while studiously ignoring Karen.

"Yeah, he's in the back." He nodded before yelling, "Nate, your wife is here!"

Karen, who had been sipping a latte, choked at the word *wife,* sputtering a cough.

"Thanks Sean." Melody laughed and headed around the counter. Nate met her at the doorway leading to the back where his office was located. "Hey. Are you busy?" She held up the bag of food she brought him.

"For you? Never." He placed a lingering kiss on her lips. She turned to wave over her shoulder towards Sean and caught the sour look on Karen's face as Nate drew her into the hallway by her hips.

"I thought I would bring you some lunch," she said. "I also have that painting you wanted to display here in my Jeep."

He gestured for her to go first into his office, shutting the door behind them with a click. "Mmm, sounds good," he said, sounding distracted. Setting the food down and looking over her shoulder, she caught him checking out her ass. "Or here me out. I've got another idea." He wound his arms around her from behind, pulling her back against him.

She laughed, "Your food is going to get cold."

"We have a microwave," he murmured against her neck.

"People are right outside, they'll hear."

He released her briefly to reach for a knob near the door, and she could hear the music out front get louder before he backed her up and braced his hands on either side of her body. He skated his lips back up her neck and lightly scraped his teeth over her earlobe. "No one will hear a thing. As far as I'm concerned, they don't exist. I'd much rather talk about whether you'd like me to fuck you on my desk or up against this wall."

"God, that mouth of yours. I swear." She whimpered as he flicked his tongue over the sensitive spot below her ear.

Nate let out a thoughtful hum. "Well maybe we can start with me putting that mouth to good use on the desk and then once your legs refuse to hold you up, I can pin you to this wall and have my way with you." He placed another kiss on her collarbone. "Say yes. You know you want to."

She gathered her bearings enough to breathe, "Yes."

He wasted no time, shoving a stack of papers off his desk and turning them, so she was perched on the edge. Nate gripped her chin and angled her face up to steal a kiss. Melody opened for him, and he deepened the kiss, sweeping his tongue in to dance with hers.

With a groan, she ran her hands up his shirt, unbuttoning as she went so she could feel his skin against hers. He responded by tangling one of his hands in her hair, tugging slightly in the way he knew she loved.

Their kisses turned urgent, shedding clothes as they went. Eventually Nate pulled back to look at her. "I need to taste you."

Melody thought she might combust as he resumed his trail of kisses down her body. When he reached where she needed him most, he gave her no reprieve, chasing her orgasm greedily. Soon, she came on his tongue with a cry of ecstasy.

He had been right about one thing, her legs felt like jelly, and she had doubts that she could stand up on her own at the moment. She felt him place a gentle kiss on her inner thigh and heard the sound of his pants hitting the floor as she worked to slow her breathing. Propping herself up on her elbows, she enjoyed the view until he picked her up to make good on his promise.

Melody wound her legs around his waist and could feel him primed and ready at her entrance as he walked them over to the wall. With a few slow thrusts, he seated himself fully inside her before stilling. She raked her nails over his back gently and groaned. "Please."

With a wicked chuckle, he said, "Patience, baby," and planted her with a filthy kiss. She could taste herself on his tongue and thought she might go insane if he didn't start moving.

He tightened his grip on her hips and finally began, thrusting hard and deep with each jerk of his hips. Running her hands through his hair, she moved with him, matching him thrust for thrust. When she felt herself coming again, he increased his pace to draw it out as long as possible. She could tell he was close, and he did not slow. Taking a page from his book, she bit down on the spot where his neck met his shoulder and with that, felt him tip over the edge, taking her with him one more time.

They remained intertwined for a minute, and she just stroked her fingers through his hair as he held her. Eventually though, he gently set her down before turning to a gym bag on the floor that she hadn't noticed. "I was planning on swinging by the gym later, so I've got a couple of clean towels in here," he said before coming back over to her. He tenderly cleaned her off and before caring for himself.

Once they were put to rights and dressed again, Melody asked, "Do you think they noticed anything?" She watched him crack the door open and peer out. From where she was standing, she couldn't hear anything beyond the music playing overhead.

Nate started down the hall and Melody quietly followed him, only to find the front of the store darkened, and the open sign flipped to close. He picked up a note from the front counter and read, "*Yeah, the music didn't quite cut it, so I figured I'd take my lunch now and just put up the "Be Back Soon" sign. Hopefully an hour is enough for you guys. -Sean. P.S. Nice.*" He chuckled.

"Oh my god." Melody groaned and covered her face with her hands. "I'm never going to be able to look Sean in the face ever again."

Laughing again, he pulled her hands away so he could look her in the eye. "Sean is a twenty year old dude-bro. He probably will give me one of those chin tilts or fist bumps or whatever the hell people his age do now, but I'm a guy. It's a lot easier to joke and stuff with me. I can't see him bringing it up with you. He'll probably just be business as usual when talking to you. And hey, if he does decide to be a dumbass, I have a trump card. Shirley is his grandma, and will absolutely not hesitate to rip him a new one if he is disrespectful to you." He flashed an evil grin.

She grimaced. "I would not want to be on the receiving end of Shirley's disapproval."

Nate nodded, switching gears to ask, "So are you hungry now?" and heading back down the hall.

"I could eat." She followed him.

After heating the food up in the breakroom, Nate took a seat at the table and pulled her down to sit sideways on his lap. He playfully held a French fry up to her lips with a teasing look, so she took it from him with a laugh. "This is not a very conventional way to eat."

"I don't care." He scoffed. "I like it and my store, my rules." He gave her a wink.

They finished up their meal, chatting about their days so far and what they had left to do. Once they were done, Nate showed her his workshop in the next room. She didn't know where to look first. All around the room were beautiful pieces of furniture in a variety of colors, from warm honey to cool ash. The care poured into each piece was evident as she brushed her fingers along the edge of a large dining room table.

"You're very talented," Melody said.

"This was one of the only things I ever actually felt good at." He shrugged. "I was never the best student back in school, but I did alright working with my hands. Once I got to try out woodshop, I realized that not only was this something I could excel in, but I also enjoyed it. I've worked to hone my skills ever since. The business side of things became easier too once I had something that was my own to care about."

"It's very impressive. Do you strictly work on furniture here at the store or do you also sell your sculptures from here?" She glanced around the room but did not see any of those pieces.

"I stick to furniture and more traditional carpentry work like cabinets, bannisters and the like out of the store. Whenever I make sculptures that I'm comfortable parting with, I typically set up a booth down at the local farmer's market."

Her face lit up at that. "I sometimes sign up there too! I wonder if we were ever there selling at the same time."

"Maybe," Nate said with a smile. "It's a small world."

They heard the bell above the door chime again, and Nate checked his watch. "I guess it's been an hour. Oh shit, I forgot I have a client consult soon. I have to go to their house and get some measurements. Can I get the painting out of your truck real quick and meet you at home later?"

"Of course. Let me grab my keys out of your office."

Fishing them out of her purse, they passed Sean, who was back at the front counter on their way out to her Jeep. She felt her face flame a bright red, but Nate was right; Sean made no comment.

Once she had unlocked the doors, Nate opened the back hatch, pulling the painting out and looking it over.

"This is gorgeous. It's exactly what I was hoping for." He pulled her closer and gave her a quick kiss. "Thank you. I already have the nail hung where I want it in the lobby."

He led her back inside and showed her the spot he had picked out. Sean came up as he straightened it on the wall and said, "That's awesome. It's like trees, but not. Did you make it?" he asked Mel.

"Yes, thank you," she said, still not quite able to meet his eyes.

"Nice," Sean said and headed back up front.

They went to his office where Mel collected her purse, and Nate grabbed the paperwork he would need and stuffed it into a compartment of a clipboard. "I'm going to go knock out this meeting and then hit the gym, then I'll be home for dinner," he told her, pulling her in for one last lingering kiss.

"Mmm, one second," Mel said when they parted. She reached into her purse and pulled out a stick of gum, handing it to him. "You, um, have *me* on your breath. Which is hot from where I'm standing, but I have a feeling your clients will find it less endearing." She laughed with a grimace.

Nate threw his head back and laughed, taking the gum from her outstretched hand. "Thanks. Good call. It's my favorite flavor, but not exactly professional to flaunt."

"Exactly." Nate picked up his gym bag and led them out of his office, shutting the lights off as he exited. "Oh, can I use your restroom real quick?"

"Yeah, totally. It's that door right there." He pointed. "I really have to get going though, so I'll see you later, okay?" He gave her one more peck on the cheek and headed out.

Once she was done, she made her way back up front and Sean said, "Oh hey! Nate said he needed to take this spokeshave home for a project he was working on at your place, but he forgot it on his way out. Do you mind taking it with you?"

"No problem. Thanks."

She had no idea what this contraption did, but at least it wasn't very heavy. Sean waved goodbye as the door swung shut behind her, and she gave him a smile, returning the wave.

On the drive home, her thoughts turned to her aunt. While she had continued their tradition of talking on the phone each Sunday night, and she had indicated that she was seeing Nate, she hadn't exactly broken the news that they had gotten married. Melody knew she needed to, and that waiting any longer would only end in disaster, but she was terrified of her aunt's reaction.

Aunt Bea was great. Melody admired her so much for her strength, independence and ability to speak her mind. But that was also what made her so intimidating. Aunt Bea would not hold back. She would tell Melody exactly what she thought of this decision, and she would probably be right.

The thought of disappointing her in any way made Melody want to crawl under a rock and not come back out. This woman had held her together after the loss of her parents and had taught her how to be an adult. She owed her the world, and if she ended up not approving of their marriage, Melody didn't know what she would do.

If she was being honest with herself, it was more than that too. Against all her better judgement, she was falling for him. Every day with him put another chink in her armor, every considerate gesture, every fleeting touch, every spark of passion. As much as she knew she was running the risk of getting her heart crushed if he never grew to feel the same, she had no defense against this.

Loving Nate was starting to feel as inevitable as gravity. He drew her in like she had never experienced with anyone else, and even if things stayed just as they were now, well, at least she'd have a piece of him. This little slice of paradise they'd carved out would have to be enough. She needed Aunt Bea to be okay with this, because she couldn't bear to let this go now.

Steeling her nerves, she resolved to get it over with this afternoon. Nate would be out for a while, and so she would have the house to herself as she paced and babbled her way through what was sure to be a difficult phone call.

When she got home, she took the tool out back to Nate's workshop, forgetting what Sean had even said it had been called. She punched the access code into the keypad to let herself inside and flipped on the lights. Not sure where this would go exactly, she decided to just leave it in the middle of his worktable where he couldn't miss it.

He had a project there, covered with a cloth. Her nosiness got the better of her, and she decided to peek and see what he was currently working on. She had never seen anything like it. The base looked like a canvas or an easel, and rising from it a paintbrush, gripped in a slender hand. With a jolt, Melody held her hand up next to the carving and realized that it was *her* hand. An exact replica of her hand, the details breathtaking. She had never seen something so intricate made from wood. The fact that Nate had studied her so closely to know each intimate detail of her like this made her breath catch and yet another blush rise to her face.

She replaced the cover and quickly went back inside where she splashed some cold water over her cheeks to calm herself. Melody had never considered herself to be someone who blushed easily, but ever since Nate had come into her life, she felt like she couldn't stop. She found it slightly infuriating. But she needed to put this out of her mind for now.

Fredrick followed her to the bedroom, hopping onto the bed to await attention. She changed into her pajamas since she had nowhere else to go today and sat down to oblige him. Burying her face into the fur of his neck, she hugged him. "How am I supposed to tell Aunt Bea that I got married without her?"

He let out a huff and a grumble as if he understood and knew exactly what she should do, wasn't it obvious? Silly human.

She let herself stay with him for a few more minutes to gather her courage and then picked up her phone. As the sound of the phone rang in her ear, she began to walk through the house, hoping to burn off some nervous energy.

Aunt Bea answered after several rings. "Melody. Child, what is wrong?"

"What? Nothing, Aunt Bea. Why would you ask that?"

"It's a weekday. You never call during the week. We talk on Sundays. So, what's wrong?"

Melody let out a sigh, not having thought about that. "Nothing is wrong, I promise. I just wanted to talk to you."

"Uh-huh. Okay then. I'm always happy to hear from you. And when you work up to whatever it is you're about to tell me, I'll be happy to hear that too."

Bea knew her too well. She tried to skirt the topic for just a little longer. "How are you doing today?"

Aunt Bea snorted on the other end of the phone. "I'm just peachy. Nothing too exciting has happened since I talked to you a couple of days ago. I washed my hair. I made a trip to the library. Found a good sale on some strawberries at the supermarket. Now will you please tell me why you're calling me, babydoll? You know you can tell me anything. You of all people know that my bark is worse than my bite, so out with it."

"Okay, uh, you remember the guy I was seeing?"

"Nate, wasn't it?"

"Yes. Well, um, we decided to take things to the next level."

"Next level? What does that mean? You sleep with him?"

Aunt Bea was very open-minded when it came to a woman's sexuality, but Melody had never inherited that ease in talking about things like that. "No, I mean, yes, we've had sex but that's not what I meant. I meant like the next milestone in a relationship." She could tell that she was blundering this badly.

"I'm still not sure what that means child. You're moving in with him? You get engaged? Tell it to me plain."

"Umm kind of. I did move in, we actually got a new place together, because we...got married." She held her breath as she waited for her response.

"Excuse me? What do you mean you *got married*?"

"I'm sorry. I know I should have told you sooner, and I never wanted to hurt you by going behind your back. It's just that we didn't want to make it a whole thing, and we didn't want to wait. Nate's been married before and his wife passed away, and I don't have any family besides you, so it just didn't make sense to have a big ol' ceremony or anything...please don't hate me." She felt her throat tightening.

"Melody, you know I could never hate you. You are the only family I have too, you know. I'm not going to lie, it hurts that you didn't invite me. You're the closest thing I've ever had to a child of my own, and to learn that I missed something like that in your life is heartbreaking. That is something we will never get back. So, I'm not going to just let you off the hook and pretend that it was okay. I understand not wanting to have a big ceremony, but shit, I would've come to the courthouse with you. In a heartbeat. But nevermind that now. When do I get to meet this mysterious Nathaniel that you ran off and married like a shotgun wedding? I'll reserve judgement on all of this until I spend some time with him."

"I hadn't made plans or anything yet, I just couldn't go any longer without telling you. I'm so sorry that I hurt you. I wish that I would've just told you and had you there. The whole thing was just such a whirlwind, and then we were house hunting and moving right after. We just got settled in and –"

"Good, I'll come down for the weekend then."

"Oh, Aunt Bea, you don't have to come all the way here. I'm sure we can find time to come up and visit sometime soon –"

"Are you going somewhere out of town this weekend?"

"No."

"Then that's that. I won't hear any further argument. I'm going to come and stay with you for a couple days and see this man for myself. I think you owe me that much."

Aunt Bea had always been the queen of guilt trips. With a sigh, Melody gave in. "Okay. We both work on Friday, but if you want to be here by dinner time, we'd be happy to have you."

"Very good. I'll see you in a couple of days then. Don't do anything else crazy before then. And Melody?"

"Yes?" she whispered.

"I love you. Please don't forget that."

"I love you too, Aunt Bea."

After hanging up, she flopped down on the couch to stare at the ceiling. That had been about as harsh as she had expected, but a surprise visit had not been on her radar. She made a mental checklist of everything she would need to do now before Friday and was still laying there dejected when Nate got home from the gym.

Unused to seeing her laying in one spot and doing nothing, Nate leaned over the couch to look at her. "Everything okay?"

Her voice was flat as she said, "I called my Aunt Bea and told her that we got married. She's apparently coming to stay with us for the weekend."

Nate grimaced. "She didn't take it well, I'm guessing? Are you okay with her visit? I'm happy to have her if you want her here, but I'm not about to let her bully you into it if you don't want to see her."

Melody sat up and reached a hand over to rest on Nate's. "She took it about as expected honestly. She's always had a sharp tongue, and she's not perfect, but I know she means well. I've never doubted that she loves me and wants what's best for me. You just have to get past the prickly exterior to find the gooey center with her. Her visiting is...unexpected. It does make me a little nervous, just like meeting your family made me nervous. But at the same time, it's been a long time since we've been together and I miss her, so part of me is glad she is coming. She is very perceptive though, so I am freaking out a little about being under her microscope. It's all just a lot."

He nodded, lost in thought for a moment. "I think it'll be good. We've got this. And hey, our families will need to meet at some point, so why don't I see if everyone is free Saturday night, and we can all have dinner? That would take some of the attention off us directly and give her more people to focus on. I know Mom would be ecstatic to meet her, and Natalie is always distracting. I'll be sure to tell her to be on her best behavior."

"That sounds perfect actually." She snorted a laugh. "And don't bother saying anything to Nat. I have a feeling that she and Aunt Bea will get along just fine."

"Should I be worried?"

"Maybe a little."

"Well, it sounds like we have a game plan. A weekend with Aunt Bea. Bring it on."

Chapter 20

Nate

Nate was not as confident about this weekend as he had implied when talking to Melody. Actually, the thought of being under Beatrice's watchful eyes for a full forty-eight hours sounded like a special kind of hell. He knew that the nerves Melody had experienced around his family were legitimate, but he couldn't help but think that the short visits she had endured would be quite a bit easier than this. Though, he had to admit that she was required to see his family far more often than he was sure to see her aunt. Shaking his head to clear the racing thoughts, he got back to the task at hand.

The week had of course gone quickly as soon as he heard the news, and here they were on Friday afternoon. All he needed to do was finish up his paperwork for the week and he could be on his way.

Pushing through, he signed the last order form and added it to the stack. He stood up and stretched, trying to work out the tension his bad posture had seeped into his muscles as he hunched over the endless papers for the last hour or so. His back popped and he let out a groan as he turned off his lights and headed out.

"Have a good weekend." He waved to Sean as he passed. "You too. Good luck with the aunt thing."

On his way home, he stopped by the grocery store and picked up odds and ends that he would need for dinner tonight and the rest of the weekend. He had decided to make a chicken alfredo for tonight, and he always insisted on making his sauce from scratch, so he was hoping this would earn him a few brownie points with Beatrice. Brownies may not hurt either actually.

Melody had assured her that Aunt Bea did not have any food allergies and wasn't particularly picky aside from the fact that she hated fish. He could work with that. He quickly made his way through the checkout and drove home. Melody was already home, and when he walked in the house smelled like cinnamon baked goods.

"Mel?" he called. "Are you cooking?"

He heard her laugh before he saw her in the kitchen. "Definitely not. I am capable of lighting a candle though." She pointed to the source of the scent, lit on the mantle.

"Ah, that tracks. I thought maybe I had slipped into some weird alternate universe or something." He laughed as he gave her a playful smack on the butt.

"I should be insulted by your utter lack of confidence in me, but I can't even deny it." She shook her head in mock sorrow.

Nate pulled her back against his chest and told her, "That's okay. You have many *other* talents."

She laughed again and asked, "Why do you make it sound so dirty?"

"I wasn't. Well, I mean, that's also true. But for once, that is not what I was implying. Though, if you wanted to demonstrate some of *those* talents for me real quick, you would have my rapt attention." He nipped her earlobe, feeling her ass squirm against him.

"We do not have time for that right now." She bit back a smile and worked to extract herself from his arms. "Aunt Bea will be here in like thirty minutes."

"Shit, I need to get the food going. But I plan to continue this conversation later."

"Yes, sir." She gave him a mock salute.

"Now get out of here before I change my mind." He used a kitchen towel to shoo her out of the kitchen.

She headed off into the guest bedroom as he set some water boiling and prepped the meat. Fredrick watched him closely, just waiting for him to slip up and drop something so that he could snatch it. "Sorry buddy, not tonight. It's all business for us."

Fredrick let out a grumbling whine as he rested his head on his paws, but his attention did not waver.

A bit later, Melody came back into the living room, straightening the pillows on the couch each time she paced back and forth. Her nerves were clearly getting the better of her and so he pulled out his phone and set some music by Japanese Breakfast playing.

She leaned over the breakfast bar to peer in at him in the kitchen. "You started listening to my music?"

He mentally patted himself on the back for distracting her. "Yeah. You reminded me that we had sent those lists, so I decided to check out your bands like you did mine."

"And? What do you think?"

"They're good. I've been enjoying them quite a bit actually." He stirred his sauce, making sure it kept the right consistency.

"Damn right." She smirked. The doorbell rang then, and Fredrick charged over, bellowing to announce their visitor. "I got it."

He worked to finish things up, pouring the sauce over the noodles and turning the burner down to keep it warm until they were ready. The chicken breasts in the oven had a few more minutes to go, so they would be okay if he stepped away for a moment.

He heard Melody greeting her aunt as he made his way to the entryway to join them. Beatrice was a tiny woman, shorter even than Melody's five and a half feet, and dwarfed by his six-foot three frame. Short hair framed a face containing eyes the same shade as her niece's. She was addressing the dog as he rounded the corner.

"Fredrick, still as loud as ever my boy." She gave him an affectionate pat on the side as he leaned against her legs with his tail thumping happily.

"Aunt Bea, this is Nate." Melody laid a hand against his chest. "Nate, this is my Aunt Beatrice."

He held out his hand for a handshake and said, "It's a pleasure to meet you, ma'am."

Beatrice snorted a laugh as she shook his hand in return. "Ma'am, he says. You can call me Bea, child. Everyone else does."

"Bea it is," he said. "Can I take your bag to your room for you?" He reached for her suitcase, and she let him take it from her with a nod.

"Let me show you around," Mel said.

Bea nodded again. "Please."

Nate took her bag into the guestroom, setting it on the edge of the bed and headed back into the kitchen to check on the oven. The sound of their voices carried through the space as they continued walking around. He glanced over and could see that they had paused by the fireplace and were talking quietly with their attention on the memorial photos Melody had set up. The candle was still lit and the flames cast a soft glow on the faces of their loved ones.

He tried not to eavesdrop on what was clearly a private moment. It hadn't really hit home until then that when Melody had lost her parents, Beatrice had lost her only sister as well.

They stayed there for a few minutes before continuing their way through the house, stopping by the kitchen next as he pulled the chicken out of the oven.

"Well that certainly smells good," Bea said.

"Thank you. Hopefully it tastes good too." Nate smiled over his shoulder.

"So, you found a man that cooks. That's definitely a point in his favor," Bea said to Melody.

Nate and Melody locked eyes, both of them remembering her little joke about a point system and the vastly different meaning it held to them, as they did their best to keep straight faces.

Melody cleared her throat and looked away. "Yeah, it's great. I haven't eaten this good since I moved out of your place. Here, let me show you the rest of the house."

They were gone for a few more minutes during which time Nate set the table and placed the food. He was opening a bottle of wine when they arrived back at the table, and Melody showed Bea to her seat.

"Wine?"

"Please," Mel said with a smile in his direction.

"That would be lovely," Bea said.

He poured them each a glass and took his place, passing the first dish of food to Bea.

They were quiet for a few bites before Bea said, "This is quite good. I'm impressed, young man."

"Thank you. I helped my mom with the cooking pretty often growing up, so I learned a thing or two." He smiled.

"So, Melody tells me that you are a carpenter."

"Mmm, yes," Melody said once she swallowed her bite. She patted the table. "He made this dining set actually. Isn't it gorgeous?"

Aunt Bea cast a critical eye over the table and ran her hand over the surface. "This is a very nice piece indeed. Clearly you do well for yourself, if you can afford a place like this between the two of you." She gestured around to the house.

"I do alright," Nate said. "Melody has been quite successful herself too." He smiled.

"I've had a string of good luck recently. A bunch of local businesses have had an interest in buying pieces to display, so that has been a bit of a whirlwind," Melody said.

"It's not luck, Mel. You're extremely talented and hardworking. Your success is all you. Give yourself credit where credit is due. You are absolutely amazing," Nate said.

"He's completely right, Melody. You have always been so dedicated to your art and your efforts are paying off. Don't let anyone tell you differently, not even yourself. You have built your business from the ground up and that is something to be proud of. I'm sure as hell proud of you," Bea said.

Melody ducked her head with a sheepish smile. "Thank you."

"Things keep going like this, and you might need a gallery before too long," Nate said. Melody raised her eyebrows as if the thought had never occurred to her before, but she didn't reply.

They finished their dinner, Beatrice catching up with Melody and asking Nate questions here and there. He cleared the plates and came back out with brownies for dessert, at which Bea's eyes lit up with excitement. She took a bite, and hummed her appreciation. "I love me some chocolate.

Melody laughed and took a bite of her own. "They are very good."

"These are unfortunately just out of a box since I didn't have enough time after work to make them from scratch, but I got stuff to make us scones for breakfast tomorrow," Nate said.

"Melody Parker! You did not tell me that this man not only cooks, but also bakes."

Melody grimaced. "For one, I didn't realize at first. And two...it's actually officially Melody *Blackwell* now." She cleared her throat and took a drink of her wine, as if she was looking for anything else to focus on besides the narrowed eyes of her aunt.

"Since when?" Bea asked.

"As of today actually. My paperwork came back and my new driver's license just got here in the mail today." She held Nate's gaze as she spoke. This was new information to him as well.

"Any other news you'd like to share?" Bea asked, her tone slightly mocking.

"My family was excited to meet you too, so we planned for us all to go out to dinner together tomorrow night," Nate said, hoping to take some of the heat off of Melody.

Beatrice relaxed back into her chair, letting out a sigh. "That sounds very nice," she said and then paused. "I'm sorry for being cross. This has all just been a bit of a shock and I'm still trying to wrap my head around it. But I thank you for welcoming me into your home. I think I'm going to call it a night, but I look forward to getting to know you better tomorrow, Nate. And to continue catching up with you, my dear." She started to rise, and Melody took her hand.

"I'm sorry I waited to tell you, Aunt Bea. But I'm glad you're here. I love you."

Beatrice rose and bent to brush a kiss on the top of Melody's head. "I love you too, babydoll. Goodnight."

She headed to the guest room, closing the door quietly behind her and they worked on cleaning up the table and kitchen before heading to their own room.

Once the door was closed behind them, Melody flopped onto the bed as if she was exhausted. Nate sat next to her and said, "I think that went okay. Definitely could've gone worse."

Melody sighed. "That's true. I just wish I knew what to say to make her feel better. I never meant to hurt her."

Nate stroked the hair back from her face. "I'm sorry. I feel like this is all my fault. All of this was my idea in the first place."

She placed her hand over his, trapping his palm to her cheek. "I knew what I was getting myself into. You were very up front from the beginning and I agreed to the terms. And I knew that this would hurt her, and I did it anyway. I don't regret marrying you. Not for a second. But I do regret that she was hurt by it. I don't know how I could've done anything differently though."

It was Nate's turn to sigh. "I don't know either. But this is where we are and we'll find a way through."

She nodded thoughtfully and then checked the time on her phone. "It's not very late yet. I forgot she goes to bed so early. What do you want to do now?"

"Well, I can think of one thing. I'm still most interested in an up close and personal display of your many *talents.*"

She let out a laugh. "Now? With Aunt Bea right next door? She'll hear."

"Well, then you better do your best to be quiet then." Nate rolled over her and snared her lips in a kiss. He felt her melt under him as he nipped at her bottom lip and teased the sting away with his tongue. She opened for him, and he leisurely mapped her mouth with his own, content to take his time tonight.

She tugged on his shirt, and he broke away long enough for her to pull it over his head. He watched as she frantically tossed her own shirt aside and struggled with the clasp on her bra; fingers moving too quickly to gain purchase.

He drew her close, pressing a searing kiss to her shoulder as he reached around and undid the clasp for her. "We have all night, baby," he said softly.

Nate claimed another kiss before she could answer and eased her back down to the bed. His hands roamed, palming her breasts, and he swallowed her moans as she rolled her hips against him.

After a while, he helped them shed their pants and settled back into the cradle of her thighs. A few rolling thrusts, and he could feel her stretching around him, until he was buried deep inside of her.

He kept his rhythm slow and deep, watching her face as she took him inch by inch, always ready for more. Finally, when he felt her winding tighter and tighter beneath him, he eased a hand between them to swirl his fingers over her clit and devoured the sound of her climax with a kiss. A few more thrusts and he found his release as well.

After he had gotten them cleaned up, he settled back into bed and pulled her into the curve of his body. He breathed in the scent of her and allowed the satisfied exhaustion in his body to lull him to sleep.

Chapter 21

Melody

Melody felt Nate ease out of bed the next morning, but she hunkered down into the blankets, not ready to leave her warm cocoon quite yet. She buried her face into her pillow, attempting to block out the sunlight and steal a few more minutes of sleep before facing the day.

She wasn't sure how much time had passed when she heard the click of the door opening and felt the bed dip down right before the covers were pulled away from her, and her aunt said in a much too chipper voice, "Wakey, wakey, sleeping beauty! That man of yours is out there cooking already. You can get that tush of yours up and join me for some morning yoga." She gave Mel a pat on said tush in emphasis.

Melody let out a grumble of protest, finding words still beyond her. How quickly she had gotten used to sleeping in thanks to Nate spoiling her this past month or so. She cleared her head enough to wave Aunt Bea away with a vague noise of agreement and headed into the bathroom to get her day started.

Once she was done, she joined her in the living room. The mouthwatering scent of baked goods wafted through the space, and for a moment she wished they could skip the yoga and just sit to enjoy a warm pastry with some coffee instead. But that was not Aunt Bea's style.

"Come on, girl. The morning is calling," Bea called as she opened the back door, her mat tucked under her arm. With a sigh of longing, Melody picked up her own mat and followed her outside.

"Have you kept up with your practice?" Aunt Bea asked. She arranged her mat on the back patio, leaving room for Melody to lay her own next to it.

"Yes. Though, I lean more towards afternoons once I have finished up my painting for the day rather than early mornings these days," Melody said.

"Mmm. Well, thank you for greeting the day with me." Bea raised her arms, reaching towards the sky with a deep inhale.

They settled into a familiar flow, their bodies remembering the poses and stretches with little direction. When she had lived with Aunt Bea, this had been a regular part of their routine, and Melody found that falling back into their old ways was comforting. It felt like they were getting back on even footing after being out of sync with all of her recent life changes.

They finished their routine, ending in Savasana to rest their limbs and calm their breathing once more.

"Thank you for dragging me out of bed. That was really nice."

"Anytime, dear. Now, let's go get some of that good smelling breakfast inside." Aunt Bea rose to her feet and offered a hand to pull Melody up as well.

The aroma of coffee had joined the air inside, and Nate wordlessly held out a mug of coffee to Melody as she came into the kitchen.

"Bless you." She took a big gulp.

He handed one to Beatrice, too, who laughed. "I didn't think it was possible for you to become less of a morning person, but here we are."

Melody chose to ignore the comment in favor of the plate filled with golden scones, which was clearly the source of the other delicious smell. "What did you make?" she asked Nate instead.

He smirked at her dodging Beatrice's observation. "These are cranberry orange scones, and these are blueberry." He held the plate out between the two women, gesturing for them to try one.

They each took one, letting out appreciative murmurs as they took a bite.

"Is there anything you can't do?" Bea asked.

"Whistle." His face was completely serious.

Melody laughed. "You never told me that!'

"It's my secret shame." He nodded.

"I'll take it to my grave." Melody etched a cross over her heart.

A brief flinch passed over Nate's face, and she realized her blunder. He recovered quickly, but she knew she had chosen her words poorly. She also knew he would not appreciate her drawing attention to it with Bea sitting right there, so she made a mental note to be more careful in the future.

He changed the topic, suggesting they have lunch at Rudy's and then show Bea his shop. Everyone agreed and with a game plan in mind, Beatrice said, "Thank you for breakfast. I think I'll go get a shower real quick now."

Once she was out of earshot, Melody turned to Nate and placed a hand on his forearm. "I'm sorry. That comment I made was callous and I didn't even stop to think before I said it."

His expression softened. "It's okay. There are a million little things we get used to saying that never used to make me think twice, but now they just hit differently. I've gotten a lot better about shrugging them off, because no one ever means anything by them, but once in a while one slips past my defenses. Please don't feel like you need to walk around on eggshells for me though."

"I don't. It's not that. I just understand where you're coming from. I've been there, and I guess it's just been long enough that I've started to slip back into the old habit. I just want you to know that I am sorry and I don't take death lightly."

"I think I've gotten to know you well enough to realize that. Really, it's okay." He placed a soft kiss on her forehead. She wound her arms around his waist for a hug and buried her face into his chest.

Rudy's was a hit, and Bea had been most impressed by the shop as well. Melody's painting hanging in the lobby did not hurt either.

They arrived back at the house in the late afternoon to freshen up and change before meeting Nate's family for dinner. The restaurant they had chosen was slightly upscale, so Melody dressed in a short black dress and Nate chose a slate gray button-down shirt, which he rolled the sleeves of back to expose his muscular forearms.

Melody mentally chastised herself for being so distracted by that simple action, knowing that her aunt was likely waiting for her in the living room already and there was no time to get carried away now. She quickly exited their bedroom before Nate could see the effect he had on her and found Aunt Bea standing in front of the wall containing photos that she had hung once they moved in. There was another wall with family photos, but this wall in particular was just photos of her and Nate. Photos she'd snapped while they were "dating", photos from their wedding. It was one of the latter that Bea was studying when she reached her side.

"You looked so beautiful," Aunt Bea said.

Melody took her hand and squeezed gently. "Thank you."

"I had my reservations about all of this, and I came here ready to kick your ass and take you back home if I needed to, but I can't deny it. Seeing how he is with you, how you both are together, and seeing the love shining in both of your eyes in these photos – I understand now. And I'm happy for you."

It was as if a weight had been lifted, and Melody felt the tension melt away from her. It didn't matter that Aunt Bea was clearly reading more into things than was really there, Melody's own confusing feelings aside, they needed everyone to see them this way. She turned to hug Beatrice, drawing her aunt's small frame against her and breathing in her familiar, comforting scent of peppermint. "You have no idea how much that means to me," she said into her hair.

Beatrice pulled back to look her in the face, cupping her cheeks in her palms. "Child, I know I'm hard on you. But I hope you know how damn proud of you I am. You have grown up to be a wise, patient and compassionate woman despite all that life has thrown your way. I miss your mama every day, just like I know you do, but I just know that her and your daddy are smiling down on you and are just as proud as I am." A couple of stray tears made a path down Melody's cheeks and Aunt Bea wiped them away.

"I love you, Aunt Bea. And I do miss them. So much. Every day."

"Me too, babydoll. Me too."

Melody released her enough to raise her left hand between them. "I didn't show you my ring yet, but it reminds me of hers."

Beatrice took her hand and inspected the ring closely. "It does look very similar. She would love it."

They heard the sound of footsteps shortly before Nate came into view. "I hate to interrupt," he said, "but we need to get going if we are going to be on time for dinner."

They both laughed nervously, wiping their cheeks and seeking to right themselves after the display of emotions. "We'll be right there," Melody said.

With a nod, he headed down the hall, and they could hear him talking to Fredrick in the distance.

"I think you'll really like his family," she said, "Especially his sister Natalie. She's spunky like you."

Bea chuckled. "Well, this should be fun then."

Twenty minutes later, they pulled up at L'Autre Endroit in town, and Nate helped Aunt Bea down from his truck. Inside, a waitress led them to a table where everyone else was seated.

Introductions were made, and Melody bit back a smile at her aunt's stiff surprise to Naomi's warm hug of welcome. As she released Beatrice, Naomi said, "It's so wonderful to meet you!"

They took their seats and browsed the menu until the waitress came back for drink orders. Once the drinks arrived, the alcohol seemed to help take the edge off and conversation picked up.

"So, what do you kids do?" Aunt Bea asked Natalie and Nash.

"I'm the VP of Marketing at McConnell and Associates," Natalie said with a proud tilt of her chin.

"Very impressive." Aunt Bea nodded. "That sounds like a competitive field."

Natalie brushed her hair over her shoulder. "They try, but most of the boys just can't keep up."

Bea chuckled and turned to Nash.

Nash said, "I'm a Cybersecurity Analyst."

"Is that something to do with computers?" Aunt Bea asked.

Nash chuckled. "Yes. Basically, I get paid to go around testing the security of different company's websites and systems."

"Uh-huh. Well, no need to say more. I can barely work my cell phone, so any further explanation would surely be wasted on me," Bea said.

Nash laughed again. "Fair enough."

Refills were poured, and the conversation turned to Beatrice's life. Having just finished her second glass of wine, Naomi asked her, "So Bea, anyone special in your life?"

Beatrice, who was also working on her second glass of wine, snorted. "Girl, absolutely not. There's never been anything I needed a man for that I can't get done with a strong pack of batteries."

Naomi held up her glass and said, "Amen, sister!" while Natalie also saluted her drink with a cry of "Here, here!" The women all burst into laughter while Nate and Nash exchanged uncomfortable glances of panic. Their mother and sister participating in this topic was clearly an unwelcome thought. Melody couldn't particularly blame them for the discomfort.

Thankfully for those two, the food arrived then, and they all settled into eating. The rest of the meal passed with less colorful conversation, but Melody was pleased to see that Aunt Bea was fitting right in.

As they said their goodbyes outside, Naomi told Beatrice, "We have to get together again sometime. I haven't laughed that hard in ages."

"I would like that. I had a good time too." Bea said. They exchanged phone numbers as Nate and Nash chatted off to the side and Natalie came up to Melody.

"I kind of love your aunt. I want to be her when I grow up," Nat said.

"I know right? She's got the whole *independent, take no shit* thing down. I've been lucky to have her in my life."

Natalie glanced around at her family, studying their faces for a moment before she said, "Well, I think we're all lucky to have you both in our lives now."

She refused to meet Melody's gaze, and Mel couldn't resist teasing her just a bit. "Oh, Natalie, that is the sweetest thing you've ever said to me." She threw her arms around her.

As expected, Natalie balked at the affection, immediately trying to extract herself from the hug and saying, "Agh, okay, okay! We really don't need to do this. This is a bit much."

The boys, never ones to miss out on an opportunity to pester their sister, ran over to close in from the other side and trap Natalie in a group hug.

A muffled, "You're all freaks!" came from where Natalie was smothered beneath several arms.

They eventually released her, and she shoved away, sputtering and trying to smooth her hair back into place. Melody exchanged a wide grin with Nate, who was still chuckling. She looked over to where her aunt and Naomi still stood, finding them watching the commotion with amusement.

Finally bidding everyone a goodnight, they went their separate ways. Beatrice reached out and wove her fingers through Melody's on their way to Nate's truck. "I know being part of a bigger family again will take some getting used to, but I'm happy to see you being drawn into the fold. These are good people; I can feel it."

"Me too, Aunt Bea." She squeezed her hand.

Beatrice headed for home the next morning, with promises to come back to visit soon.

She gave Nate a hug. "Thank you for taking care of my baby girl. I'm trusting you with her, so don't let me down."

"No, ma'am. I will do my best," he said.

She laughed and shot him a mock scowl. "What did I say about calling me ma'am?"

"Sorry – Bea."

She nodded and gave him a soft pat on the cheek before turning to Melody and drawing her in for a hug.

"Thank you for having me, child. It was so good to spend some time with you. If you ever need anything, don't hesitate to call me, you hear?"

"I will. Thank you for everything, Aunt Bea. I love you."

"I love you too."

They waved as she pulled out of the driveway and watched from the porch as she drove away. Melody wrapped an arm around his waist and said, "I didn't realize how much I needed that. For her to know and be okay with everything. I feel like I can breathe easier now. You were incredible – thank you for all that you did this weekend."

Nate looked down at her. "I'm glad it went well, but I barely did anything. You're the one who knocked it out of the park this weekend. All I did was cook really."

"It was more than that. I wouldn't have made it through without your support. Though, the scones definitely didn't hurt."

He laughed. "I'm glad you enjoyed them." Then he leaned down to kiss her.

Chapter 22

Nate

A few days later, Melody called him at work.

"Hey babe, what's up?" he said as he answered the phone.

"Hey, so my friend Emily really wants us to go on a double date with her and her husband, Patrick. Would you be okay with us meeting them for dinner at Joe's tonight?"

"Yeah, sure."

"Thank you. She's the last person in my life that I've needed to break the news to, and as soon as she found out, she was just dying to meet you."

"I'm sure it feels good to have everything out in the open finally."

"It really does. We've been friends since college, and I hated keeping this from her. But I'll let you get back to it. See you at home?"

"Of course. I'll be home a little after five. Talk to you later."

"Bye."

When he arrived home after work, Melody was in their room getting ready with Fredrick monitoring her progress from the bathroom floor. She was wearing a short black skirt and top that had one shoulder strap, leaving her other shoulder bare. The olive-green shirt brought out the flecks in her hazel eyes, which she was currently applying eyeliner to.

"You look sexy as fuck." He came up to stand behind her in the mirror and ran his lips over the exposed curve of her shoulder. His fingers tangled in the ends of her hair, and he felt a shudder pass down her spine.

She turned to him with a palm on his chest. "You're sweet, but we need to get going soon, so focus. You need to get changed too." She flashed him a smile.

With a dramatic sigh, he said "Fine," but gripped her chin for a brief kiss before turning away.

He shed his work clothes and threw on some jeans and a black t-shirt since Joe's was just a sports bar type place.

As he drove, Melody said, "So, I've not heard you mention any friends really these last few weeks. Is there anyone else in your life we still need to tell?"

He paused before answering, trying to find the words. "No, not really. I just haven't really had anyone I've been close to other than my family for a long time. You know, Angela was my best friend. She was my person. So, she was who I spent my time with. I didn't ever really think about it or care to do things without her or to go out and make friends. It just never really occurred to me that I should bother. I was content with what I had. And by the time she was gone and I realized that I hadn't really nurtured any other friendships, I didn't care to try and rekindle any of the surface level relationships I may have had in passing, and I definitely didn't have it in me to go make new ones. So, I just spent time with my family when I needed company, and that was that."

He was afraid he would see pity in her eyes when he glanced over at her, but he didn't. She simply said, "If I'd had siblings, I probably would've been the same way. I'm more of an introvert by nature, but as it was, Emily just kind of adopted me in college. She's the only person I have other than Aunt Bea. Sometimes when you find the right person, they really are all you need."

"Exactly." He found a parking spot and turned the truck off.

"Thank you for coming with me."

"Anytime."

As they headed into the dimly lit bar, they were greeted with the sound of music playing overhead and pool balls clanking from across the room. They saw her friend waving from a booth table they had claimed.

Emily stood to hug Melody while Patrick shook Nate's hand and made a quick introduction. "It's so nice to finally meet you," she said to Nate once she released Mel.

"You too," he said, letting Melody slide into the booth first and settling beside her. He draped his arm over her shoulder, and she rested a hand on his thigh under the table. He tried to not focus on the way he could feel the heat of her through his jeans, otherwise this would be a long night.

The usual questions came and thanks to all their practice, they were like a well-oiled machine now. He could pick up where she left off; she could chime in with endearing details about their time together, and together they weaved their story with ease.

Once the food was gone, Patrick invited Nate to join him for a game of pool. He gave Mel a peck on the cheek and followed him across the bar to claim an empty billiard table. While queuing up the pool balls and getting the game underway, they talked about their work and life as a newlywed.

Nate said, "I may have been married before, but marriage to Melody is a different beast entirely. No two women are alike, and where I had been used to Angela going right, Melody goes left. It's been an amusing ride to say the least." He chuckled.

Patrick joined in with a laugh too. "I don't know that any woman can be predicted, man. Whenever I think I know how Em is going to react, I'm dead wrong. But it keeps things interesting. And it's in the best way possible – she just always finds ways to surprise me."

"I know what you mean. I honestly didn't really expect to feel the same sense of being a newlywed all over again, and it's been both easier and harder at the same time this time around."

"I bet it's more complicated in your situation for sure, man. For us it's like this weird mixture of nerves, trying to get used to the new dynamic and being together twenty-four-seven now, but then there's still that honeymoon infatuation that helps distract and takes some of the tension out of all that. The real trick will be keeping up the spark once we're out of that honeymoon phase. But I'm not too worried about it. Em's the best person I know, and she keeps me on my toes. I can't see that changing."

Nate smiled as he lined up his next shot. "I think that's the important part anyway. Being aware that it won't always be like this, and you'll have to actively work at it for the rest of your lives. And knowing that it's work worth doing."

"Exactly. Shit, I guess we left our beers at the table." Patrick noticed now that they'd played a couple of turns.

"I'll grab them." Nate headed back to their booth and saw that Melody had moved to sit beside Emily facing away from him. As he got closer, he heard his name and paused just out of their sight.

"– just to check on Nate because he'd been in his shop for so long, but he was so intensely focused that he didn't even see or hear me. And *oh my god*, Emily. I have never been so turned on just by looking at a man in my life. The laser focus, the way his shirt clung to his muscles as they bunched and rolled as he worked with his body, the fucking bead of sweat that went rolling down his bicep like it was begging me to lick him...part of me felt like I was intruding on something sacred and the other part of me wanted to pull up a chair and watch all day. Or just melt in a puddle at his feet and beg him to touch me." She buried her face in her hands with a nervous giggle as Emily hooted with raised eyebrows.

With a dark chuckle to himself, Nate closed the distance and braced a hand on the table next to Melody, bracketing her in her seat with his body. He said next to her ear, “I’m glad you enjoy the view. No need to beg though.”

She jumped and turned to look at him with wide eyes, her face turning beat red. He tossed her a wink and placed a lingering kiss against her cheek before straightening. “Forgot our beers.” He picked up the two bottles and headed back to Patrick, girlish whispers of “Oh my god,” and laughter sounding behind him.

A bit later, they saw the girls head to the small area set aside for dancing, hands intertwined and arms waving to whatever song was playing. Nate smiled, and Patrick said, “I’m glad they have each other. I know Emily thinks the world of Melody.”

Nate nodded his agreement, but his attention snared on the two men approaching behind the girls. A muscle in his jaw ticked, but as long as they were respectful and were welcome, he wouldn’t spoil Melody’s fun. He could tell by Melody’s body language that was not the case pretty quickly though. He was tossing down his pool stick and stalking across the bar before he realized it. Patrick followed closely behind.

He watched as the more aggressive of the two men gripped Melody’s wrist and her face hardened as tension bracketed her shoulders. The other man, clearly the wingman of the two, hovered around Emily a little farther back with a stupid grin on his face, but kept his hands to himself. As they drew up behind the men, he heard Melody say in a hard voice, "I said, no. Let go of me."

"You heard the lady," Nate said, using the few inches of height he had on the man to tower over him. "I suggest you get your hands off of my wife."

The man turned with an incredulous look, but once he saw Nate's large frame dwarfing him, it quickly morphed to fear. He released his grip on Melody and raised his hands, feigning innocence. Nate pulled her around behind him, shielding her with his body as the douchebag said, "Hey man, I didn't know. You know how it is; women always play hard to get."

Nate took a threatening step towards him but stopped when he felt Mel's hand on his arm. "When a woman says no, you fucking *listen*, you piece of shit. Now get out of here before I kick your ass."

His friend pulled on his arm, and they stumbled away with one last, "Whatever man," tossed over their shoulder.

Nate turned to Mel, running his hands down her arms and looking her over for any sign of injury. "Are you alright?"

"I'm fine. He was just a pushy asshole. Thank you for getting rid of him. My next step would have been a knee to the balls, but you never know how pricks like that will react when things get physical."

“Not that I don’t want you to stand up for yourself, but I would always rather step in for you than risk you getting hurt.”

“I guess I’m still getting used to that being an option.” Her lips pulled up in a half smile.

He glanced over to Patrick, who nodded to reassure him that Emily was fine too. The tension in his shoulders relaxed, and he squeezed Melody’s arms where he still had a hold of her.

The music changed, and everyone around them paired up to dance slowly. He saw Patrick and Emily follow suit a few feet away. “Dance with me?” Nate asked as he recognized the song.

Melody smiled shyly and wound her arms around his neck as he settled his hands on her hips, drawing her flush against him and turning them slowly in a circle and she rested her head against his chest.

The lyrics to Home Is In Your Arms played overhead, the gruff voice of the lead singer from the White Buffalo familiar to Nate. He was starting to realize that it was true. Maybe home was in Melody’s arms.

Chapter 23

Melody

Easter morning dawned, sunny and warm. It had been three weeks since her aunt's visit, and she was excited to see her again today. Aunt Bea had hit it off with Naomi pretty well, and she had been invited to stay with her last night before the holiday. The thought was both encouraging and nerve-wracking.

Melody had chosen a short black dress that from a distance looked like it had polka dots, but if you looked closely, they were actually tiny rabbits. It felt fitting given the occasion, and it just made her smile.

Nate was buttoning up a green shirt which complimented his eyes, and Melody let herself track the movements of his fingers up the buttons as she did the clasps on her sandals.

"You about ready?" he asked, drawing her gaze back to his face where a small smirk was sitting.

She cleared her throat. "Yeah. You're sure it'll be okay to bring Fredrick with so many people though?"

"Eh, it'll be fine. He's a good boy."

Melody smiled, still grateful that he doted on Fredrick as much as she did. They gathered him up, along with their contribution to the meal then drove the couple of blocks to Naomi's.

Like last time, Nate let them inside, calling out, "Hey, we're here."

Nash and Sean rose from where they were in the living room, and they could hear feminine voices coming from the kitchen.

"Hey," Nash greeted them as he leaned down to pet Fredrick who was keen to explore his new surroundings and check out everyone there.

The door opened behind them as Natalie arrived, and they waved towards her as the guys continued chatting.

"Here, I'll take the food in with Nat." Melody reached for the bag Nate still had a hold of.

"Thanks, babe." He smiled.

"How are you?" she asked Natalie once she finished showering Fredrick with attention.

"I'm good. I found these grapes that are supposed to taste like cotton candy, so that's pretty exciting," Natalie said.

Melody snorted. "Well, you look amazing by the way." The baby pink dress she had on gave her a softness that she didn't usually emit. Natalie always looked gorgeous; put together and fierce, but often it felt like battle armor. Something about her today felt more at ease.

"Thank you, lovely. You look stunning as always, and I'm digging the bunnies." The smile she gave felt like it was about more than this conversation though.

"Good week?" Melody asked, unable to help being a little nosy as to what had her in such a good mood.

"You could say that." Natalie shrugged.

They reached the kitchen before she could pry further, and the three women inside started calling out in welcome. The sight of her aunt was a welcome one, and Melody quickly went to embrace her.

"Aunt Bea, I'm so glad to see you." She squeezed her tightly.

"You too, child. This is so nice." Beatrice gestured around to the gathering.

Naomi came up to claim her turn for a hug, and Shirley waved from across the counter. "Hello Melody, good to see you. Happy Easter!"

Naomi released Mel and said, "Yes, happy Easter! I'm so glad to have everyone today."

"Is there anything I can help with?" Melody asked.

Aunt Bea laughed and swatted her with a potholder. "*Please*. We have enough cooks in the kitchen as it is, and I love you, but we both know this is not your strong suit. Everything is about ready anyway. Why don't you and Natalie go take a seat and you can help with cleaning up later?"

She gave her aunt a playful salute. "Yes, ma'am."

They made their way back to the living room and found that the men had gone out to the backyard to play catch while they waited for the meal to start. Fredrick ran back and forth, chasing the ball, sure that he would steal it the next time.

"Should we join them outside or hang out in here?" she asked Natalie.

“Mmm, normally I would love to go out and commentate on their ball handling skills, but I’m not feeling getting bug bites today,” Natalie said.

Melody laughed. “Fair enough. So, what happened that made this week such a good one?”

They took a seat on the couch, curling their legs up beneath them. “I got invited to this marketing expo that’s coming up in a few months, and they asked me to speak on one of the panels. I’ve been before, but never as a panelist, and it’s kind of a big deal. I’m pretty flattered, actually.”

“That’s amazing! I’m so happy for you.”

“Thank you. A lot of the firms around here tend to be boy's clubs, so I’m excited to add some feminine perspective,” Natalie said.

“You’re going to kick ass.” Melody grinned.

“Hell yeah, I am.”

From the dining room, they heard someone shout, “Food is ready. Call the boys inside, please.”

Melody went to the back door and stuck her head out. “Time for lunch.” Fredrick led the charge, nose in the air as he smelled the food inside.

They all settled around the table, and the addition of Shirley, Sean, and Fredrick added to the chaos that was their monthly brunch, bringing a smile to Melody’s face. As much as she had worried that family gatherings would be difficult to navigate, they were turning out to be something she cherished.

Listening to the cheerful voices, the laughter, the teasing, she felt like she belonged. It was both a wonderful feeling, and also made her chest tighten as she wished again that her parents could be there too.

She exchanged a knowing look with Aunt Bea. They would always miss them, and no one would ever be able to take their place. But this family was drawing them in, and if they let them, she knew that they could be a part of something new and wonderful.

Chapter 24

Nate

Nightmares chased Nate from sleep, and he blindly reached for Angela in a panic, needing to make sure she was safe. His mind was still hazed from sleep and instead of Angela's blonde hair, he found dark locks on the pillow next to his. He sat up, anxiety bubbling in his chest as he fought to clear the cobwebs from his mind.

Slowly, reality crept back in and he remembered. Angela was gone. She had been gone a long time now. It was Melody's sleeping form lying next to him. Inhaling deeply, he focused on trying to regulate his breathing.

Hold the breath in. Release. Again.

It had been a long time since he'd had one of these vivid nightmares. In the beginning, they plagued his sleep constantly, but over time they had faded. They always ended the same, with the hopeless feeling that Angela was lost and that no matter what he did, he couldn't save her. His imagination was cruel and changed the why and the how often enough, but the result was always the same. They left him drained and exhausted every time.

He was thankful that he hadn't woken Melody, not wanting to disturb her sleep and also not really wanting to dissect his dream. She was always ready to listen, but he wasn't always ready to talk.

He needed some air, so he quietly used the restroom and headed to the backyard. Fredrick followed him outside, and he found he was grateful for the gentle presence. At least with Fredrick, he wouldn't have to answer any questions. He sat down in a patio chair, absentmindedly petting the dog as he tried to think about why he had another dream now after all this time.

They'd been married for several weeks now and had settled into a familiar routine. In all honesty, a lot of their routines had not changed, just adapted around each other slightly. They both worked, and he would hit the gym afterwards a few times a week. Melody started using that time to make her volunteer visits to the animal shelter, and then they'd meet at home.

He had expected it to be harder to get used to living with her than it was. Neither of them were particularly high maintenance or confrontational people, they both kept things pretty neat by nature outside of their artistic spaces, and he wouldn't lie, he let himself get distracted by his attraction to her and their natural chemistry enough to overlook a lot of what could have otherwise been growing pains or moments of awkwardness.

Maybe that's why his subconscious dredged the dream up. Maybe things were just a little too easy, and he needed to be reminded that this was all a fragile illusion, to make sure he didn't get too comfortable and take things for granted again.

"Or maybe, I'm just fucked in the head," he said to Fredrick.

Fredrick rested his head on Nate's knee, peering up at him as if to say, *"Well, you are either talking to yourself or a dog like he's your therapist, so yeah, maybe."*

He'd been out here a while, so he pulled out his phone to check the time. It was getting to be late morning, and Melody normally would be up by now, so he decided to put aside all of these thoughts and go check on her.

Closing the door to keep Fredrick from pouncing on her, he found their room still dark. While he didn't mind if she wanted to sleep in late, it wasn't like her to stay in bed all morning. He quietly crept to her side of the bed and saw that she had rolled onto her back. Beads of sweat had collected on her temple and chest, and he reached out a tentative hand to her forehead. She was burning up.

Cracking an eye open at his touch, she said in a scratchy voice, "Nate? I don't feel so good." As soon as the words were out, she lurched, reaching for the small trash can kept by her bedside table. Nate did his best to hold her hair back as she retched.

"You've got a fever. We need to get you to the doctor as soon as possible."

Once she was done emptying the contents of her stomach, she wiped her mouth and collapsed back down on the bed. "I probably just caught that flu that is going around. I'll be fine."

"Melody, your health is not something to mess around with. I'm taking you to get checked out and that's final."

He was vaguely aware that his behavior might not totally be rational, but he didn't care. Fevers were bad. Fevers meant that something was not right. Ignoring fevers was like ignoring the check engine light in the car. In hindsight, he and Angela had ignored so many little signs that there had been something seriously wrong, and he would never make that mistake again.

Walking over to their chest of drawers, he pulled out some clothes for her with shaking hands and helped her into them before scooping her up and carrying her to the car.

"Nate, I'll let them check me out, but really, I think all I need is some fluids and rest."

"We'll let them tell us if that's all you need."

He drove her to the urgent care, knowing at least that taking her to the Emergency Room was a bit extreme. He carried her inside here too, refusing to let her walk on her own. The nurse at the front counter looked up in alarm at the sight, and at the sound of his loud voice. "We need help, she's sick."

Melody, trying to calm the poor woman, said, "I'm fine, I'm just dealing with a fever and some vomiting. I'm guessing it's the flu, but he wanted to make sure."

The nurse looked between them and slid a clipboard across the counter. "I'll just need you to fill these out and then take a seat. We'll call you back as soon as it's your turn."

Nate was about to protest, but Melody interrupted, "No problem, thank you." She took the clipboard and squirmed as if wanting to be let down.

Still not wanting her to risk walking in case she should get dizzy and fall, Nate walked over to the waiting area and deposited her in a chair.

Once she was finished filling out the form, he took it back up to the front counter for her. "How long until we can see a doctor?"

"It should be just a few minutes, sir." With a reluctant nod, he went back to sit next to Melody and wait.

She reached over and gripped his arm. "I promise, I'm fine. Everything will be okay, Nate."

"You can't promise that." He tried to keep his voice even and keep the hysteria out, but it was proving difficult. Being back in a hospital-like environment was harder than he had expected. It was the smell mostly. That sterile, almost bitter scent trying to cover up the underlying smell of decay. That smell featured in so many of his worst memories.

Melody's hand tightened on his arm, and another nurse opened a side door calling out, "Melody Blackwell?"

He scooped her up again with relief, following directions back to the exam room. It was as if muscle memory took over from there, and he helped her down to stand on the scale so they could take her weight, and then settled her on the cushioned chair inside, taking the vacant seat against the wall to stay out of the doctor's way.

The exam was quick, taking her temperature, looking at her throat, and in her ears. Within a few minutes, the elderly man said, "Yep, looks like that nasty flu that is getting passed around. With viruses like this, unfortunately the only thing you can do is wait it out. Get lots of rest and fluids. If your fevers get too high, take some over the counter painkillers to help bring it down."

Nate knew he was being a little unreasonable, but he couldn't help it. "That's it? You're not going to run any other tests to make sure nothing else is going on? No blood tests or anything?"

The doctor gave him a confused frown. "No, this is a pretty clear-cut case of the flu, son. Are there any underlying health concerns we should know about that would indicate further testing is needed?" he asked Melody.

"No, sir. I get my regular checkups and screenings, and I'm fine." She looked at Nate, holding his eye. "There's no reason for concern."

Nate let out a breath, his shoulders slumping, and he nodded. The doctor made his way to the door and said, "Very good then. If you need anything, don't hesitate to call our nurse's line. The number will be on your discharge papers."

When the door closed behind him, Melody held a hand out to Nate and said, "Come here."

He took her hand and rested his forehead on her shoulder. "I'm sorry. I shouldn't have freaked out."

Melody wrapped her other arm around his neck, cradling the back of his head as she answered, "I understand why you panicked. But I'm fine. I'll be right as rain after a few days of rest."

Against her protests, he closed the shop for the next few days so that he could stay home with her. He forced down all the water, hot tea and soup she could handle, making sure she was constantly bundled up in blankets and always had an anime playing in the background.

He breathed easier once she showed signs of improvement and felt his anxiety slowly settle once more. He didn't know what he would do now if anything ever happened to Melody. And that terrified him.

Chapter 25

Melody

For the first time in over two months, Melody woke up alone and with no sign of Nate. The bed sheets were cool on his side, so he had been gone a while. She hadn't heard him stir or get ready for the day. Blinking away her sleepy confusion, she checked her phone and found it was still early. No missed calls or texts.

Don't panic.

He probably left a note on the counter. Maybe he had a breakfast meeting he forgot to mention, or a pipe could have burst down at the shop. He might even just be out back working. It could be anything, and there was no reason to worry yet.

She padded her way over to use the restroom, brushing her teeth and washing her face once she was done to help her wake up a little more. Nate had left one of his hoodies draped over the chair in their room, and she pulled it on as she passed. His scent of lumber, citrus, and spice eased her nerves a bit.

In the living room, Fredrick perked up from his spot on the couch to watch her as she checked the kitchen counters for a piece of paper. There was no note.

Don't panic.

She headed to the backdoor to check his workshop, and Fredrick joined her outside. The door to the garage was locked, and she started to knock before remembering he always worked in headphones and wouldn't even hear her knocking if she tried. She punched the access code into the keypad and let herself inside once she heard the lock click. The space was dark and Nate was nowhere to be found.

Don't panic.

Pulling out her phone, she shot him a quick text: *Hey, just checking in. Everything okay?*

To help distract herself while she waited for a reply, she went in and fixed herself some coffee. Five minutes passed, and then ten. She tried calling instead. The line went straight to voicemail, and she hung up without leaving a message.

Don't panic.

It was getting harder to listen to her mantra. With trembling fingers, she tried calling once more, only to get the same result.

She could feel her heart racing and her breathing turning erratic. Despite her best intentions, she *was* panicking. Before she could spiral too far, she decided to call Natalie.

"Hey, what's up?" Natalie answered.

"Hey. Nate was gone when I woke up and he's normally really good about leaving a note or letting me know when he'll be gone, but I have no idea where he is and I can't get ahold of him. I'm getting a little worried. Have you heard from him today?"

"Oh. Umm..." Natalie paused and let out a sigh as she said under her breath, "Dammit. Typical Nathaniel." Her voice softened on the other end of the phone. "Well, Angela passed away on May 7th. So today is the anniversary. Every year on this day, Nate closes up the shop, shuts off his phone and tends to fall off the grid. I'm sorry he didn't warn you. I know he has a hard time talking about it all, being Mr. Stoic "I'm Fine" Guy all the time. But his usual tradition is to start the day visiting her grave. She's in the cemetery over off Elm. He is usually there for quite a while, so I'd bet that's where you would find him right about now."

Melody sank onto the couch as she listened, absorbing this information. "He told me it happened in May, but never the specific day...thank you. I, uh, well, after my parent's accident, I tend to freak out a little when people are missing or I can't get ahold of them. I'm sorry."

"No need to apologize. He's your husband; he should have communicated with you. He's my brother and I love him, but he has got to learn to open up a little. For his sake and for everyone else's. I think he is starting to with you, but clearly, it's a learning process. He just...I mean, I think you know the piece of shit that passes for our father walked out when we were little. Nate was about ten at the time, and I was seven. Nash was only three, so he doesn't even really remember the guy. But Nate does. And as we got older, he tried to fill his shoes so that we never had to feel like we were lacking anything. It was too much pressure for a kid. And he just stuffed everything down. Like he didn't want us to see him struggle or admit that it bothered him how unfair life was sometimes. I don't know that he ever grew out of that. And then everything with Angela...I know he loves us, but it's like talking to a wall sometimes. We've all tried to get him to open up to us, to just tell us anything at all, but he just shrugs us off. We worry about him, but seeing him with you gives us hope. I think you're getting through to him, a little at a time. You know though, it would probably be good for you to share that people not answering their phone is a trigger for you as well...not to butt in or anything."

"You're probably right. It's just been so long, honestly, I thought maybe I had gotten over it. But I guess it was more that I just hadn't had to deal with it in a long time instead. Thank you for talking me down. And for telling me about today."

"Anytime."

They hung up and Melody sat there for a few minutes, thinking things over. Making her decision, she quickly got dressed and tossed Fredrick a treat on her way out. She pulled out her bike and headed towards the cemetery, stopping at the flower shop on the way and placing a bouquet of lilies in her basket.

As she rounded the entrance of the cemetery, she followed the path until she spotted Nate's truck. Quietly, she pedaled up and parked her bike next to it. She could see Nate in the distance, sitting next to a grave with his back to her, and she softly lowered the tailgate on his truck, hopping up to sit down and wait.

After another thirty minutes or so, he slowly rose and turned to head her way. She saw him briefly hesitate when he spotted her, but then he started walking once again.

His face was dry, but his eyes were red as he approached and said "Hey," in a gruff voice.

"Hi. I got worried and called Nat; she told me where you might be. I wanted to be here for you, but I didn't want to intrude."

She saw when he noticed the bouquet and he asked, "How did you know that lilies were her favorite?"

"Well, they were the flowers in your wedding photos. Generally, women pick their favorites for a big day like that, so I just kind of assumed," she told him with a small smile. "Is it okay if I take them to her?"

He nodded and leaned against his truck, his gaze turned down to his boots as she walked away. Melody walked gingerly across the grass, trying to be respectful of the surrounding graves. As she got closer, she saw a wooden statue resting against the headstone. It was a beautiful and simple rendering of a man and woman embracing. It was clearly Nate's work.

She knelt on the grass, gently laying the flowers down. "Hey Angela. I'm Melody. It's nice to meet you. I just wanted to say thank you. I can tell from how Nate talks about you that you loved him so, so much. I can hear it in his voice, I can see it in the old photos of you two. He misses you. Every day. I hope you know, I will never replace you. I don't want to. I'm so sorry that you can't still be here with him. I promise I'll do my best to take care of him for you though. I hope you're at peace. And if you happen to see my folks around up there, give them a hug for me please."

Melody rose and gently ran a hand over the tombstone, then turned away. Nate had loaded up her bicycle into the back of his truck, and was sitting at the steering wheel, just staring blankly ahead. She climbed in the passenger side, but didn't say anything, letting Nate speak when he was ready.

Without turning to look at her, he said, "It's been five years. *Five years*, and it still feels like I just lost her. It's like I lost a limb, and I'm just stumbling around, trying to figure out how to make do without a part of myself. Most days, I can push it down and make it through the day because at the same time, it's like this hole has always been a part of me. Like this ache in my soul is just a permanent piece of me. I don't remember what it feels like to be happy without that happiness carrying an undercurrent of guilt or sorrow. Were there really days back then when things were that simple? I don't even feel like that man anymore. He took everything for granted. He didn't appreciate the time he had enough. And I kind of hate him for it. If I'd known, maybe I could have done more. Maybe things could have turned out different. Or maybe there never would have been any changing things. I know that playing the "What If" game will only drive you crazy, but sometimes I just can't help myself. Days like this, I feel crazy anyway, so what does it matter? Every year, I visit her. It never really gets easier, talking to dirt and stone instead of her smiling face. But it's all I've got now. I visit, and then I do the things she can't. I eat her favorite foods, I visit her favorite places. It doesn't make me feel any better, but it does make me feel a little closer to her." He ran a hand down his face. "I'm sure I sound insane."

"You don't. Grief is...chaos. It's bloody and brutal, there's not really a rhyme or reason, and often it leaves you feeling like a walking contradiction. But it *is* all of those things. It's anger and fear and sorrow and guilt and exhaustion and love. It's unbearable, and yet, it's the last link to the person you love and so letting it go is terrifying. It feels like you're letting *them* go if you start to feel "better". The days that joy does creep back in feel repulsive. How can you possibly feel joy when they're dead? Talk about feeling crazy, I remember the first time I tried to ride in a car after my parent's accident. I hyperventilated and ended up on the curb with my head between my knees. That was the year that I got into bicycling. And there are still times when I'm in a crowd of people and I could swear I saw one of their faces. Everyone always says shit like, "They'd want you to be happy" or "They're in a better place" as if that fucking helps, but it doesn't. That's just their way of pushing you back into the box of their comfort zone. It's so much easier to deal with if they don't actually have to deal with it. I know you don't talk much about all this. It's been drummed into us by society that it's too much, too messy to tell anyone. But that's not real. *This* is real. And I'm here for you. Whatever you need from me. Whether that's talking, sitting here in silence, or just meeting you at home later when you're ready."

Nate took her hand and squeezed it. "I'm honestly not sure what I need. For now, do you want to go with me?"

"Always."

Chapter 26

Nate

After Angela's death anniversary, Nate realized he had two options. He could let himself feel self-conscious about everything Melody had learned and witnessed, or he could give in, just a little more, to this ease and understanding that existed between them. He could let her have this piece of him, this part that he didn't let anyone else see, and take comfort in her.

This was the part of him born from losing Angela, and so it felt like less of a betrayal to let Melody soothe these broken pieces. He could compartmentalize – he'd been doing it for years. Angela still had his heart, but he never knew it could be such a relief to let someone else bear witness to his grief so fully and just be there with him. No trying to fix it, to fix him. No trying to downplay it or distract from it.

Even though her own loss was vastly different, there were just some fundamentally universal experiences in grief. She found the common ground where she could, and she respected the differences where she couldn't. It was like a knot that had been tangled in his chest for the past few years was slowly starting to unravel as she gently tugged on a thread here or there. It would never take away the loss, but it made him realize that he didn't want to be totally isolated in this anymore.

Voices sounded from the front of the shop, making him realize that he had zoned out, lost in thought. He just needed to finish up his paperwork, and he could call it early today. Then, instead of sitting here thinking about Melody, he could go see her. He didn't know if she was done for the day or what she was up to, but he wanted to surprise her.

Pushing through, he finally reached the end of the stack and breathed a sigh of relief as he straightened his desk again. He eyed his gym bag on the floor, deciding to leave it and skip the work out today too. He just wanted to go home.

He walked through the shop and spotted Sean crouched behind the front counter, getting another stack of order forms out of a box below.

"Hey bud, I'm ducking out early. Feel free to close up whenever. It's too nice to be stuck indoors today," Nate said.

"Thanks man. Big plans tonight?" Sean asked.

"Not really, just one of those days that feels criminal to sit inside and do something like paperwork." Nate shrugged.

"And that's why you're the best boss." Sean laughed.

Nate sketched a bow. "I try. Anyway, see you later."

He sang along with Johnny Cash as he drove home, enjoying the light feeling that felt so rare ever since he lost Angela. Maybe they could go out tonight and do something fun. Honestly, whatever Melody wanted to do was fine with him as long as they were together.

Nate pulled into the garage and turned his truck off, assuming that the noise of the garage door would alert Melody that he was home. However, loud music greeted him inside and as he peered into her studio room, it was clear she hadn't heard him at all.

She was lost in a painting as a song played over the speakers, talking about darkness and joy being dangerous. Melody still hadn't noticed him hovering in the doorway, and Fredrick was fast asleep, so he took a moment and let himself just watch and take her in. He pulled out his phone to look up the song. The search results told him that this was In the Darkness by mxmtoon, and he saved the information for later.

She was so focused, and he watched the way her fingers gripped the paintbrush, remembering the sculpture that had come to life as a result of seeing her work like this. It was one of those times where he wasn't sure what he was carving until it emerged, like it had been waiting for him the whole time beneath the layers of wood. He hadn't had the guts to tell her about it or show her, slightly unnerved by the detailed accuracy he had been able to produce after such a short time together.

His attention paused on what she was painting, and something about it snagged in his mind. It felt familiar, though he couldn't tell why...it was another abstract piece like she normally worked on, but something about it felt personal for some reason.

The shades of green swirled and melded across the canvas, an array of that particular shade. His eyes widened as it dawned on him. *His eyes*. It was the shade of his eyes. It was the *exact* shade of his eyes.

His gaze traveled over the canvas with new understanding. She must have been studying him just as much as he had studied her. She had managed to capture it all, how his eyes appeared in the sun, how they darkened with rage or desire, the way they grew flat with depression; it was all there for the world to see. He had never felt so exposed and so seen.

Nate remembered the conversation he had overheard between her and Emily, and suddenly he understood that too. It felt like he was intruding on something sacred here. If she had walked in on him when he was carving her hands, he would have felt utterly mortified, and he didn't want to make her feel that way either, so he quietly backed away.

He waited in his truck for a few minutes before heading back inside, being sure to loudly slam the door and call out this time. "Hey, Melody, I'm home!"

The volume of the music lowered, and he heard her moving about in the studio before she appeared in the hallway. She had a smudge of paint on her cheek and a slight flush to her skin.

"Hey, you're home early." She smiled.

"Yeah, it was slow at the store, and I felt antsy to get out of there. I thought we could go to dinner maybe?" he said, reaching forward to brush away the streak of paint with a grin.

She blushed harder at the gesture. "Sorry, I'm kind of a mess when I work. But dinner sounds great, just let me get cleaned up."

His hand snaked from her cheek to the nape of her neck, and he pulled her to him, wrapping his other arm around her waist as he kissed her. She softened against him and gripped the front of his shirt in her hands, opening for him as he swept his tongue in.

Nate peppered kisses down her jawline and spoke into her ear. "Want help with that? I could use a shower too."

"Yes, please."

He wasted no time, scooping her up and walking them to their room. She reached out a hand to fling the door shut behind them. When they reached the bathroom, he perched her on the counter and paused to capture her mouth again.

She kept her legs wound around him, molding their bodies together as he nipped her lip, and she flicked her tongue. He groaned, wanting to convey all the emotions her painting had stirred in him with his body. He wouldn't tell her that he'd seen it, but maybe he could release some of these feelings. If he could make her feel an ounce of what he felt right now, he would be satisfied.

Pulling back, he helped her peel off her clothes and tossed them in the hamper. He pressed another kiss to her mouth and said, "Wait right there."

He reached in to start the water running in the shower and made quick work of shedding his own clothes next. When he turned back, Melody's eyes were raking over him slowly and he felt his cock stiffen further in response. If she didn't touch him soon, it would grow unbearable. He held her eye as he gave himself one firm stroke to ease a little bit of the tension, and she drew her bottom lip between her teeth as she watched.

The water was hot now, the steam softly billowing out to fill the air between them. He held a hand out towards her. "Ready?"

She nodded and hopped off the counter, brushing against him as she slipped into the shower. They quietly took care of washing themselves quickly, wanting to be rid of any paint or sawdust they might have on them from their workday, but when Melody went to wash her hair, Nate took over for her. It was becoming a habit when they showered together, and she leaned back against him as he worked his fingers against her scalp, eliciting a happy sigh.

With the last of her conditioner rinsed out, she turned in his arms, running her lips across his chest and trailing a hand down his torso. The light touch sent goosebumps erupting across his skin, and the ache for her grew tortuous. He ran a finger down her spine, and felt her peaked nipples brush against his flesh as she arched into him.

His hand drifted down to the base of her spine, and he cupped her ass so he could grind her against his hardness. She let out a muffled moan onto his chest and drifted her own hands to cling to his hips as she stretched up to steal a kiss.

Nate let her set the pace, opening when her tongue teased his lips and following her lead as they moved together. He felt her hands sliding over his wet skin, working their way up his sides, his arms, his chest to finally tangle in his hair as she clung to him.

A moan escaped him as she tugged his head back, her lips tracing down his throat and her teeth scraping the column of his neck. "Fuck." He gasped as she flicked her tongue on a particularly sensitive spot, his grip that was still on her ass, tightening.

He started walking them back towards the bench in the back of the shower and pulled her down to straddle him once he was seated. She kept her grip on his hair as she kissed him again and began to grind on his lap. He could feel his cock sliding through her wetness and he wasn't sure how much longer he could last before he would break and bury himself inside of her.

Her breath on his lips was growing ragged, and the roll of her hips was growing more and more frantic as she chased her release. Rolling one of her taut nipples between his fingers sent her over the edge, and her back bowed, her thighs locked around him, and her head tipped back as a loud moan filled the bathroom.

Taking advantage of the way her breasts were thrust towards him, he caught the other nipple with his mouth, wanting to send her spiraling again as soon as possible. He worked a hand between them, circling a finger over her sensitized clit and she let out a harsh breath.

"Nate, please. I need you inside of me. Now," she managed to gasp out.

He hummed against her breast, letting the sound rumble through her before releasing her, but did not stop the movement of his hand. "Well, since you asked so nicely."

Letting her pull back for a moment, she gripped him as she lined herself up and with one rolling thrust, she took him fully inside. They let out satisfied moans at the feeling of her stretching around his length.

He resumed the steady torment on her clit as she began to move over him. She had her eyes closed as she focused on the sensations wracking her body, and he was content to watch her face as she came undone again. Some of the tension left her body now, and she rested her head against his shoulder, letting him guide their thrusts now.

Breathing in her lavender shampoo, he moved his hands to grip both her hips as he directed her movements. He thrust up as he pulled her down onto him, grinding their pelvises together with a swirl before repeating the motion. Melody's fingers dug into his biceps as she held on, her moans of encouragement stifled by his shoulder, but he could feel the tension mounting in her once more each time he hit that spot deep inside of her.

The need to go faster, deeper, harder took over, and he gave himself over to it. Her moans got louder as he pounded into her, until finally he broke. He sealed them together as he held himself deep inside her and felt the tension in her snap as well, both of them pulsing and fluttering around one another.

He let himself lean back against the wall of the shower, keeping her tucked in his arms as he ran a hand up and down her back.

"I like when you get home early," she said.

Nate smiled and pressed a kiss to her temple. "Me too, baby. This definitely beats work any day."

Melody laughed. "Well, I would certainly hope so. If not, I'm clearly doing something wrong."

"Oh, you're doing all the right things." Nate chuckled. He grew serious as he drew her face up to look at him. "You're perfect." His lips skated over hers in a gentle caress.

Yes, he might not ever be able to give her all of him, but maybe he could give her a little more than he'd originally thought. He could give her all his broken bits and pieces without his heart. He could do this.

Chapter 27

Melody

It had been a while since Melody had found the journal when they first moved in. She still hadn't worked up the nerve to read it. One afternoon while Nate was still at work though, she finished up painting for the day and saw it in her drawer.

With a sigh, she said, "You either need to get this over with or put it back..."

She checked the time, and knew she probably still had two to three hours before Nate would normally get home. Steeling her resolve, she picked it up and sat in the oversized armchair they had placed next to her desk.

Flipping it open, she saw that the entries dated back years ago and were fairly sporadic at first. The further in she went, the closer the dates between entries became.

She chose one at random, unsure how far back to go or if she would eventually read them all anyway. Angela's neat and swirling handwriting scrawled across the page. Melody ran her finger over the letters, admiring the shape of the words before starting to read.

June 20th

The weather was gorgeous today. I made sure to get out and do some gardening. The vegetables are coming along nicely. Nate worked on his project on the patio, and I did my best to sneak peeks without being obvious. I wish we had a better space for him to work, but someday...he is so immensely talented, and I just know that if we can find a way for him to open a shop, there'll be no stopping him. I love watching the way his eyes light up when he thinks of a new design, and his enthusiasm is infectious when he tells me all about it. I never want that to go away.

The entry cut off, and she began thumbing through the pages, stopping to read others here and there.

January 3rd

Winter has well and truly settled in. I don't mind it so much, but I know Nate gets stir crazy. I think it helps that we've started using the garage as an indoor workspace for him now. We've begun to seriously look around for a retail space where we can finally open a shop. We've scrimped and saved and planned, and it's finally starting to take shape. There's still a lot to figure out, and once we find a space, we'll have to meet with the bank to see what our options are, but I have hope. I just know he's going to do amazing things. When we aren't busy with all of that, I take advantage of all the downtime winter brings. Nate has always been affectionate and attentive, but he also has always been extremely motivated. There's always something for him to work on, something for him to do. In winter, that list is considerably narrowed down and it's much easier to keep him to myself. It may be selfish, but I don't really care. I'll take as much of this man as I can get. After all these years, I still crave his arms around me, his hands on my skin just as much as I did when I was seventeen. His eyes undo me. Someday, when we have children, I hope they get his vividly green eyes. Until then, I'll keep savoring my time with him and his undivided attention.

August 5th

Today is the grand opening of the shop. The last couple of months have been crazy, all of the things to do and details to get in place, but I've never seen Nate so determined. He can't hide his nerves from me entirely, but when I see them rear their head, I do what I can to soothe them. I remind him of who he is and how I see him. He can do this. <u>We</u> can do this. Last night when we made love, I watched it all fade away until it was just us, and he let himself get swept away. I could feel all of his hope, his desire and his love for me in every touch. I did my best to pour all of my love for him right back. Today, we'll start a new chapter, and I can't wait to see where it takes us.

July 29th

I can't believe it's been almost three years since I last wrote. I always have such good intentions, but then life happens I'm too busy living it to record it. I know that's not really a bad thing, but I just want something to look back on, when I'm old and gray and my memory is fading. I want to be able to go back and read and see my life again. I want to laugh at little things I forgot, or smile at something sweet Nate did on a typical Thursday night. I want to remember every little thing about our life together for as long as I can. So much has changed over the years, and I've loved every minute of it. The shop took off, the kids all chipped in to buy a lakeside home for Naomi, and we spend lazy weekends down by the water once in a while. There are countless moments over the years where it takes my breath away to realize that I'm living the dream. I met the man of my dreams as a child, and he has spent the last decade loving me like a fairytale. Sure, we've had our ups and downs. We are human after all. But there has never been a second where I doubted his love. Today is his birthday. A small part of me had hoped that I could tell him that we would be expecting our first baby today. I pictured it, wrapping up the positive pregnancy test and giving it to him this morning. In my mind's eye, I saw his eyes widen, I saw his wide smile split his face, and maybe a tear or two spilling. Then he'd pick me up and spin me in a circle as he laughed, only to promptly put me back down in a panic, worried he would hurt the baby. Because that's the kind of father he will be. He will always do everything he can to protect them. I know it. But none of that will happen today. The negative result stares back at me once again, and I can't help but feel disappointed. I won't say anything to him. I won't spoil his birthday. He deserves all the happiness in the world, and today is the day that he was brought into this life, so it is worth celebrating. He is worth celebrating. I know what he would say anyway. He would hold me, and tell me that it's okay – it'll happen when it happens. Every time this has happened, he is so sweet and does his best to make me feel better. I know it's not the same for him though, it's not his body that is failing here. And as much as I try to push it down, it does feel like a failure sometimes. I'm doing my best to keep my chin up, to be grateful for all that I still have. The love of a good man, a beautiful home, a loving family. I can be content. Even if it's not in the cards for us and we never end up having a child, at least I still have Nate. I don't know what I would do without him. The family will be here soon for his party, and I need to go help get things ready. Today will be a good day.

October 12th

I've made a decision. I'm going to go to the doctor, just to get checked out. I know I should have probably been doing this for years, but I wasn't raised to do things like that. It just never really occurred to me. But month after month of little red lines on pregnancy tests has me worried. I've been feeling poorly more often too...I get tired so easily and I get sick to my stomach easily. It's a cruel irony – every time is a guessing game of, is it morning sickness or am I just sick? <u>I need answers</u>. I haven't told Nate yet, I'm a little scared to. I don't want to make him worry for no reason. I also never wanted him to know just how much it has hurt, not being able to get pregnant by now. It's not his fault and I know that he would feel like he has let me down. I don't know how I know, but I just have this feeling that I'm the problem here, not him. But I'm getting ahead of myself. I'll go to this appointment and see what they have to say, and I'll go from there. I think I'll wait to tell Nate until after this first visit. Once I have more concrete information, then I'll talk to him about it. No sense in worrying him before I know anything. He'll have a million questions, and I want to be able to answer them. We'll be fine.

Melody's stomach clenched. She wasn't sure Nate ever really knew the depths of Angela's struggle with wanting children. It made sense, being pregnant was such a personal thing, feeling a life growing within your own body, versus the distance it held for men. Even the men who deeply wanted children, it was not the same as being the one to bear them. Melody had no personal experience, but just from the way Nate talked and the words Angela had written, it was clearly very different for them both. When you're expecting it to just happen, there's probably not a lot of reason to talk about it much. And when you're young, it's easy to just go along with the flow of life, always expecting the best. Ignorance is bliss, as they say.

She closed her eyes and let out a deep breath through her nose, trying to brace herself for what she knew would come next. The rest of the entries were sure to be devastating. Again, she felt guilt tug at her chest, and she considered putting the journal away. But she just couldn't do it.

October 26th

They did a bunch of tests and said they'd call when the results were in.

They called me at the end of last week and said that I needed to come in today to discuss what they found. They advised that I bring my husband. I've never been more scared. I held the phone in my grip as my hands trembled, and I struggled to keep hold of it. I could feel cold sweat bead on my spine and I had the urge to vomit at the tone in her voice. I remember scratching down the date and time I had to be there on a notepad, and then I just stared at my phone, wondering how I was going to tell Nate. He would have to close the shop. I was about to disrupt his life, and I hadn't even told him that I was worried. I should have told him I had gone to the first appointment, prepared him just a little. But it was too late now, and he would be blindsided by whatever news they were about to give me. I couldn't do this without him, and he would never let me go alone anyway, but I hated everything about it. This weekend I sat him down and told him that I'd been keeping track of my cycle, that I'd been taking pregnancy tests, how negative after negative greeted me every month. How I had decided to get checked out, just to be safe and they want us to come in to discuss the results. I thought I'd seen every side of Nate, but turns out, I've never seen him truly scared before. The look in his eyes will haunt me. Being Nate, he tried to push it down and comfort me instead. God help me, I let him. I let myself take comfort in his arms and I let myself believe that it would be fine, whatever they found could be dealt with. Now, he's in the shower and we are preparing to go hear the news and the confidence I had felt is slipping. I'm terrified again.

Cancer…I have cancer. I have to write it out because I still can't believe it. It doesn't feel real. Cancer is something that people older than me have to worry about. It's something that happens when you smoke all your life. How is that possible? Epithelial ovarian carcinomas they said. As if that should help explain. As if that will help me make sense of this. I have to go to see an oncologist now and do more testing to see where all it has spread and what my options are. From what my doctor could tell me about my reproductive organs though, it has already spread significantly. They said I should prepare myself for needing a total hysterectomy with salpingo-oophorectomy, which means they'll cut out all of my reproductive organs in an attempt to save my life. It was stated as if it was a foregone conclusion, no possible hope that I could avoid that fate. And I don't know how she expects me to prepare for something like that. I know she was doing her best to comfort and inform me, but I just sat there in shock, totally overwhelmed. Nate took over asking questions and taking notes. I couldn't look at him. I knew if I did, I would lose what little composure I was holding on to. I could see his posture change when he heard the words though. He steeled his spine, tension bracketed his body and he went fully into problem solving mode, as if this is some challenge to be tackled and he could make it go away if he just tries hard enough. I love him for that. Because I don't have it in me right now. I know I'll have to fight for my life, literally, but for right now, all I want to do is curl up and mourn my dreams. I'll let him be strong for me until I can do it.

October 28th

The last couple of days have been a special kind of hell. Nate has been doing his best to act normal and take care of things for me. We haven't really talked about everything since we first got the news, and neither of us knew what to say. He tells me that I'll get through this and promises that he'll be here every step of the way. I know he will, but I can't stop my spiraling thoughts. How will this change us? I know he will do anything and everything I could possibly need, but will caring for me like this change how he sees me? Will it change how I see him? Will I start to grow bitter and jaded at some point throughout all of this? I already feel the anger simmering...I just wanted to live my life, loving my husband, and raising our babies. Why is this the hand I've been dealt? I can't let myself dwell here. If

I do, I'll drown. But what if I don't get better? What will Nate do then? I feel like we need to talk about it, but I know that he won't. I can already tell that he has rejected the possibility that I might die. And I might. I hope to God that I get better, but I don't know. I don't know if I have it in me to talk about it yet either, I just know that at some point we do <u>need</u> to. For now though, I'll try to be strong. I'll pretend that Nate is right, and it's just a matter of fighting for it. My oncologist appointment is in a couple of weeks and we will know more then. For now, I'll cling to the remains of my old life for just a little longer.

November 13th

This appointment was even more overwhelming than the last. So many statistics and medical terms and things for me to sign and consider. The term "Treatment Plan" was repeated over and over. Treatment Plan. Treatment Plan. Treatment Plan. Nate held onto that like a lifeline. I just heard all of the ways they're going to chop up and poison my body, hoping to kill the cells that are trying to kill me. It's an unsettling feeling, knowing that your body has betrayed you. They told me not to look up things online about my condition, but I couldn't help myself. Oh, the irony that not having children can increase your likelihood of getting ovarian cancer. It's like a sick cosmic joke. That is all I wanted, and maybe it would have saved me. I'm already exhausted, and my "Treatment Plan" hasn't even started. They scheduled my first surgery for after Thanksgiving. So I guess I get one more holiday to be whole. After that, they're going to start me on chemo as well, hoping to keep it from spreading to any other parts of my body. If I'm lucky, those measures will work. We need to tell the family. I don't know how. I don't know whether we should do it before the holiday or to let them have one last normal Thanksgiving. There's no good answer.

December 5th

They tell me that the surgery was a success. All I know is that every inch of me hurts. It's like I can feel the missing organs with each breath, and all I hear is <u>barren</u>, <u>barren</u>, <u>barren</u>. I'm doing my best not to fall into the pit of self pity, after all, I know more than most that there are many ways to make a family. I grew up in foster care, and while I never found a loving family myself, I've always known I could be that for other kids going through the system. That selfish part of me just wanted to start out by having a couple of our own kids first. A tiny Nate running around to look out for his little brothers or sisters. But maybe, just maybe, if I get through this, we can explore those other options. There are so many children that need love. Need a home. For now though, I'll let myself grieve my dreams just a little. I'll focus on getting through chemo, on getting better. If I say it enough, it's got to be true eventually, right?

December 23rd

They said that we need to wait roughly six weeks after my surgery before chemo starts, so we are looking at mid-January. I'm relieved. Recovering from surgery has been rough and I was so afraid that I would spend Christmas sick from the treatments. I've been doing my best to keep my spirits up, and I want to make the most of this Christmas. I found the perfect gifts for everyone and I found dorky matching sweaters that I plan on guilting Nate into wearing with me. He's been Mr. Supportive, making sure I want for nothing these last weeks. If he could get away with carrying me literally everywhere, I think he would. We haven't been able to be intimate since the operation, but he hasn't shied away from me. I am grateful for any excuse for contact. He's always been physically affectionate, and I don't know what I would do without his tender reassurances now. Holding my hand, carrying me, just resting his hands on my arms or legs, it almost feels like he needs to feel me as much as I need to feel him, as if he needs to reassure himself that I'm still here. He still doesn't talk about his fear though. Only that I will get better.

January 19th

My first chemo treatment was today. They said that I will come in once every three weeks and that it is likely that the day after each treatment will be when I feel the worst. Today wasn't so bad. It burned some when they started pumping it through the IV, but I expected to feel more. It felt like it took forever though. Nate drove me, and sat there with me the whole time. I've been worrying about how much time he is missing at the store, but he assures me that he found someone to help out while we "get me better". I should probably insist he go in more, but I'm just so relieved to have him with me that I can't bring myself to say the words. I don't think I could do this on my own.

January 20th

They were right. I feel like absolute shit today. If I thought my bouts of nausea before chemo were bad, I had no idea. And I'm so very tired. I think I would sleep the day away if this need to purge my stomach would subside. I don't know how many times Nate has held my hair and emptied my trash can for me when I couldn't make it all the way to the bathroom. I can't believe I'm going to have to go through this every month for the foreseeable future. How has this become my life?

February 10th

My hair has started to fall out. The first bits that came out in my brush, all I could do was stare down at it, trying to make sense of what I was seeing. A large chunk came away in my hand as I ran my fingers through it next. I couldn't help it, I fell to the floor and cried. I know it's vain, and I know they told me it would happen, but I'm just so tired. I had to give up my uterus, my ovaries, the very core of being a woman and mother, and now this cancer is taking my hair. I know it will grow back, but I'm just so tired of losing things. I'm tired of not recognizing myself in the mirror. I look at her and I don't know her. I don't recognize that haunted look, those dark circles under my eyes, the way my cheekbones are already growing sharper as I involuntarily lose weight. I hadn't cried yet, not really. I shed a few tears after my surgery, but for the most part, I've tried to stay strong, to pretend that it hasn't affected me. But I know it's a lie. Nate found me after a bit. He held me as I cried on the bathroom floor, kissing away my tears as they fell down my cheeks. When he pressed his lips to mine, I tried to pull away, ashamed of the mess that I was. He held my face in his hands and made me look him in the eye as he told me that he still found me breathtaking. I couldn't accuse him of lying, because I could see the truth shining in his eyes. He was looking at me like he always had. Like I was the girl he fell in love with. I let him kiss me then, melting into his arms and letting myself forget it all, for just a second. But as I felt his hands trail down my body, resuming a natural journey that we have taken a thousand times now, I stiffened again. It was one thing to let him kiss me, it was another to let him see my body like this. This time when he looked at me, his eyes were just a little bit harder. He told me that if I didn't feel up to making love, then he understood and wouldn't push. But if it was just insecurity holding me back, that he wanted to try. To show me how much he still wanted me. How nothing would ever change that. My heart was in my throat, but I told him yes. He carried me back into our room and laid me on the bed reverently, and my body took over from there. His touch awoke all of those familiar sensations in me and I let myself fall into the feelings of love and safety. I could tell he was trying to be gentle at first, but I didn't want gentle. I didn't want him to treat me like I was breakable, so I showed him that I'm not. I made love to him like I used to and he met me, thrust for thrust, touch for touch. When we laid there in the quiet after, I listened to his heartbeat beneath my ear and I realized, it's just hair. This is what is important. Right here. Nate and me. I can handle the rest. So I think I'm going to shave my head. I'll take charge of this, and I'll do my treatments, and I <u>will</u> get better.

February 20th

If it's possible, this month feels even worse. I can tell Nate is worried even though he tries not to show it. I feel bad, I wish I could be stronger, to pretend that this isn't hell on my body. But all I can do is lay here. It takes all my energy not to puke on myself. I have a follow up appointment soon to see if the treatments are working. I don't know what I'm going to do if they aren't.

March 9th

It's not good. The test results show that the cancer has spread through my lymph nodes to my liver and my lungs. They are having me come back in to help drain off some of the fluid that is building up in the lining of my lungs. I hadn't really registered that it was getting harder to breathe. I've felt pretty miserable in general, so it seemed like just one more thing. I have to make a decision...I can keep doing the chemo and hope it buys me a few more months, or I can stop now and make the most of my remaining time. They say I have maybe nine months at best if I continue chemo. Worst case, I have two months. I don't know what to do, what to think. None of this feels real. I never thought I'd be sitting in some doctor's office, blinking under their fluorescent lights as they use words like "months" to describe my life expectancy. I know Nate wants me to keep fighting. I don't know what I want. I don't want to leave him, but I also don't want to spend the little time I have left feeling like this, like a shell and shadow of who I am. I have a lot to think about.

March 12th

Nate took me to the arboretum today. The sun on my skin felt amazing after being indoors so much. I tucked my beanie onto my head and let myself pretend we were on a date just like the good old days. A passerby even snapped a photo of us for me. Nate has gotten quieter in the last few days, as if he is afraid to bring it up, knowing what I might say. I understand, but at the same time, I wish we could have talked about this months ago. I let myself go along with his positive attitude, his can-do mentality. There were days when I wished I could just tell him how scared I was without him trying to reassure me that everything would be fine though. I know that is a normal thing to do, but sometimes you just need someone to look at the worst case scenario with you and acknowledge it's reality. Maybe we could have prepared, just a little. Probably not. I doubt there's any amount of talking that can prepare you for the horrors of cancer or losing your wife. I don't know what to say to help him. There's no guidebook to help us through this.

March 16th

I've been wrestling with this decision for a week now, and I've decided to quit chemo. I just want to be comfortable in my remaining days, to spend as much time as I can present with Nate and our family. No more tubes, no more surgeries. I have to tell Nate tonight. He went into the shop today, and I encouraged him to. He needs to get out of here for a bit, get some air and focus on something that isn't cancer or me dying. I know *he'll probably try to talk me into continuing treatment, and I know it comes from a place of love, but he's going to have to accept my decision. My next treatment is supposed to be in a few days, and I called and cancelled it an hour ago. If I'm going to die, I'm going to die as <u>me</u>. I hope that one day he will be okay. I won't be here to help him, but I hope he will find happiness again. That is my greatest wish as I stare my own death in the face.*

Tears blurred Melody's eyes as she finished the last entry in the journal. She wiped her eyes on her sleeve, the knowledge that Angela had passed about seven weeks or so after that date, stealing her breath. Her heart ached for Nate as she pictured him hearing the news of Angela's decision; of going through those final weeks; of finally losing Angela completely.

She wasn't sure what was worse, losing the one you loved suddenly and having no opportunity to say goodbye, or watching the person you love be ravaged by disease over time. They both presented such unique horrors and pains, but at least with the sudden death, the one you loved didn't have to suffer for long. The suffering came on your part, the lack of closure lingering like a specter. Comparing griefs didn't help anyone though. There were no answers to questions like this, and she knew that.

With some effort, she stood and closed the journal. She needed to collect herself before Nate got home. It wasn't fair of her to read this without permission, and it would be even less fair to bombard him with the things she had learned out of the blue.

Melody hastily shoved the journal beside the cushion of her armchair, settling a pillow over it to hide it. She would come back to this later and figure out what to do next. For now, she would go take a shower and get her head on straight before Nate joined her for dinner.

Chapter 28

Nate

Steering his truck down the winding road that was barely big enough for two cars, Nate could feel his grip on the wheel tighten. He always hated this part of the trip, and as much as Melody was trying to not let on that the sheer cliff face outside of her door was bothering her, he could tell by the strain in her voice and the way her fingers gripped the door handle.

Lake towns always seemed to have sections like this – just woods and hills and tight turns right before you got to your destination. Finally, the trees opened up around them, and he heard Melody's intake of breath as she took in the view. The lake stretched as far as the eye could see; the sun gleamed merrily off the gentle waves, and small boats dotted the surface. The weather was perfect for his family's annual Fourth of July weekend at the cabin.

"It's beautiful here," she said.

"It is. It's not like I hate coming out here, but it's just never made much sense to me. We aren't lake people. But suddenly once a year, we're all bougie and have to take a long weekend on the water?"

She laughed. "So why do you come then?"

He sighed. "You've never tried to tell my mom no. She just gets these big ol' eyes full of disappointment, like I just kicked a puppy or something. Plus, I mean, it's not like I have something against spending time with them...it's just been a little harder to go from bringing Angela every year, to coming out here alone and then having no privacy. It's like there's been some unspoken rule that since I didn't have a woman with me, that nothing counted as intruding on me. Or like they all felt like they were doing me a favor by not letting me have any time alone. At all. Like if they left me to my own devices for five seconds, I'd suddenly notice that Angela was missing and fall apart. I know they mean well, they always mean well. But it's been a bit exhausting the last few years. And then of course there's the unbearable lake housewives to contend with. I swear, if I get one more thinly veiled invitation to keep some lonely broad company while her husband goes fishing, I'm going to grow a beer gut just to spite them."

He smiled at the sound of Melody's laughter. She said, "I mean, I'll still be here if you did decide to do that, but I have to say that I'd miss all those pretty little dips and swells on your body that I love exploring." She shrugged when he glanced at her with a smirk. "Hopefully they'll ease up this time though."

"Who? My family or the lake wives?"

"Both." She snorted. "I'm guessing we won't really get much privacy from your family still, but hopefully they'll hover a little less? And I will be more than happy to drape myself all over you in public as an anti-lake wife repellant." She grinned.

"Oh, we will get some privacy. Even if I have to lock all of them out of the house for a few hours, we will have some time alone. There's no way I'm going to make it a whole weekend of you running around in some itty-bitty swimsuit and be able to keep my hands to myself. And for the love of god, yes, please drape yourself all over me as much as humanly possible. And then, when I do get you alone, I'll be sure to show you just how crazy it makes me."

She bit her lip and looked up at him from under her eyelashes. "Promises, promises."

They rounded the final turn, and he threw the truck into park in the gravel driveway before tossing his seatbelt off and closing in on her. He held her with a possessive grip on the nape of her neck and pulled her bottom lip between his teeth, nipping lightly. He drank in her soft whimper and teased her lips open with his tongue. He would never get enough of her. He loved the way she woke up under his touch, how she squirmed and wiggled as if she just couldn't get close enough, how she eagerly met him stroke for stroke. Common sense was quickly leaving his body as his blood all flowed south, and his other hand skated up to the hem of her shorts.

A sharp rap on the window caused them both to jump. He glanced over his shoulder to see his brother in running gear outside of the truck. Through the glass he heard him ask, "Really? Again guys? Can you ever just, like, keep it in your pants?"

Nate laid his head back against the headrest with a long sigh. "See? No privacy."

"I mean, we are kind of out in public. He has a point." Melody cringed.

"I can hear you. And yes, I do have a point. Though, by the looks of it, so do you man." Nash laughed. "Might want to...*sink the ship*...before you go see mom."

"Get out of here, dude," Nate grumbled.

Nash waved him off and jogged up the stairs, kicking his shoes off at the door.

"So, what should we do about that?" Melody glanced down at his lap with a pointed look.

"Just – give me a minute." He closed his eyes, trying to think about anything other than Melody. Work. Taxes. Lake wives. *Melody in a bikini*. Shit. "On second thought, I need out of this truck. You just...stay here for a second."

"Okay then." He could tell she was trying not to laugh, and he appreciated the effort.

Hopping out, he used the car door as a shield from the house as he adjusted his jeans and then he walked around to the back of the truck. He had tied down their bags in the truck bed, so maybe unloading everything would be a good distraction.

Thankfully, by the time he was done, all was clear. He went to the passenger door, helped Melody down, and carried their bags up the stairs. "The house is really cute," she said.

"My mom always wanted a place like this, but never had the means, being a single mom and all. She barely managed to hold on to her house in the city when my dad left, but she worked her ass off and made sure we got to stay in our home. So, once we were all grown and out on our own, we all started to do well in our careers, so we decided to pool our resources and do this for her. She comes here with girl friends, or we do family trips here and there, and the rest of the time she has neighbors keep an eye on the old place."

"So, you guys own lakeside property, but you're not lake people?"

"Exactly. There is a difference. It's like a culture honestly. Maybe it would be different if we'd grown up with this place, but since we only started doing this later in life, I always just kind of feel like I'm stepping into someone else's shoes while I'm here. But I can't complain too much. It's gorgeous, for the most part people are kind and there are way worse things in life than being forced to spend a weekend here. I know I'm kind of being an entitled asshole with all of this, so I try to watch it. But I think it'll be better this year since you're with me."

She held the screen door open for him and he went inside, calling out, "Hey, we're here!"

They didn't hear an answer, so he led her further inside. "They might be out back. Here, let me show you our room."

The room that had always been his was decorated in navy blues and white, the traditional, albeit tacky, sailing theme popular in homes like this. Touches of Nate were sprinkled throughout though – mostly in the woodwork. He had made sure all of his furniture passed his scrutiny, and the ones that did not had been replaced with some of his own creation. He also had a habit of whittling some trinket or another each year as they sat around the firepit in the evenings. Those odds and ends lined the windowsill overlooking the water.

Melody wandered over to them, and he watched as she lightly ran a finger over a small turtle on the end. "It looks like it could breathe at any moment. You made these, right?"

"Yes. It's hard for me to turn off the need to create something, even for a few days. It keeps my mind and hands busy while I'm not working."

"They're amazing." She inspected each with care; her brow furrowed in concentration.

He walked over and plucked up an owl. "This guy came to visit us every night a few years back. I was able to sit there and watch him as I worked, like he wanted to be immortalized. I'll never forget the feeling."

Glancing out the window, he saw his mom kneeling in her little garden behind the house with Nash sitting in a chair on the back deck and talking to her while she worked. "Looks like they're outside." He pointed. She followed his gaze and smiled at the sight.

"Should we go say hello?" she asked.

"In a minute. Why don't I show you the house while we have a few minutes of quiet?"

"Sure, whatever you want to do."

He murmured a thoughtful, "Hmmm," as he wrapped his arms around her waist and pulled her back towards the middle of the room. "Well, this," he said as he sat down on the bed and pulled her into his lap, "is the bed. I have all kinds of plans for later that involve it."

She swatted at his shoulder and tried to wiggle out of his hold on her. "You are terrible. We just got busted, and now Nash knows we are here. We have to make an appearance soon or it's going to be weird."

"If you keep squirming like that, we aren't going anywhere. I'll tell you that right now," he breathed in her ear.

She stopped struggling and turned to look him in the eye. "Nathaniel Blackwell, you are going to show me the rest of this house and then we are going to go greet your mother. We are going to show your family that we do indeed have some semblance of self-control."

"Self-control is no fun."

"Self-control now, fun later."

"Seal the deal with a kiss?" He raised an eyebrow. He held perfectly still as she leaned into him, ghosting her lips over his in a taunting caress.

"Let's go," she whispered.

Relenting, he let her stand and pull him up after her. They walked through the small home, and he pointed out who each room belonged to and where they kept things like board games. It wasn't much, but the place was cozy with its exposed wood beams, thick rugs, and stone fireplace.

The back door squeaked and swung shut with a bang behind them as they joined Nash on the deck. "Hey Mom," he said.

"I'm so glad you both made it," she said as she stood and dusted her hands off. Coming up the short steps, she pulled Nate in for a hug before turning to hug Mel too.

"Thank you for the invitation," Melody said.

"Of course, sweetie. You're family now. I want you to feel free to come up here anytime at all."

Melody gave her a warm smile in return.

"When is Nat supposed to get here?" he asked.

"Oh, she should be here anytime. I thought she might beat you, actually, so she may have gotten tied up at the office," Naomi said.

"Hmm. Well, want to see the fire pit, Mel?" He held out his hand.

She took it, winding her fingers through his with a smile. "Sure."

They walked down the little trail through the trees, finding the chairs that surrounded the circle of stones. From here, you could still see the house and hear the gentle lapping of the lake further down the path too.

"We usually end up down here after dinner most nights while we are here. Nat likes to drink and make s'mores, Nash sometimes will pull out his guitar and mess around on it, and Mom is a wild card. She may join in with either of them, or she could find something totally random to do each night. Sometimes Nat tries to make it a drinking game to predict what Mom will come up with this year." He chuckled.

Melody rolled her eyes, laughing. "Natalie and her drinking games..."

The telltale squeal of the backdoor sounded again, and in the distance, they saw that Natalie had arrived.

"Speak of the devil." He smirked.

"Sorry I'm late. That tool, Brad, was trying to sneak in a meeting with one of my clients before the holiday weekend, and there was no way I was going to let that weasel edge me out of the deal I spent weeks negotiating. Fucking Brad," they heard Natalie telling his mom and Nash in the distance.

"And where is my nephew?" Natalie yelled down at them as they made their way back up to the house.

"He's staying with my friend Emily for the weekend," Melody said once they were within speaking distance again. "He gets really freaked out by fireworks, and Nate said they shoot off a ton here. I figured it would be pretty traumatic for him, and Em's neighborhood doesn't allow them to be shot off there at all, so it seemed like the best option."

Natalie crossed her arms. "Well, I'm bummed I don't get to squish his cute little face, but I would hate for him to be miserable all weekend. I guess I'll just have to find other ways to entertain myself."

Nash leaned over to whisper in Nate's ear. "That sounds like we should be worried."

Nate kept his face studiously blank as Natalie glared between the two of them suspiciously.

"Oh! Mom, the Johnsons are here this year. I ran into Justin at the convenience store, and he invited us to join them on the boat to hang out on Sunday and watch the fireworks later that night," Nat said.

"That sounds delightful. Have you ever been on the water during fireworks, Melody?" Naomi asked.

"No, but I bet it's beautiful," Melody said.

"It is. As dark as it gets out here, they light up the sky and then reflect in the water, and it's like you're suspended inside them. I'm so glad you'll get to experience it for your first time out here." She squeezed Mel's hand.

"Mmm, I actually told Justin that I'd go out with him on the boat for a bit before dinner tonight. So, I'm going to go get changed and be back later, okay?" Natalie said over her shoulder, already heading inside without waiting for anyone to answer.

"And there it is," Nash said with pursed lips.

Nate let out a sigh and looked up at the canopy of trees, hoping he might find some patience for his sister's terrible dating practices in the sky, because he sure as hell had never found any inside.

"I'm guessing we don't like this Justin guy?" Melody tilted her head to the side.

"Justin is fine. The Johnsons are a nice family. It's just that Natalie...God love her, she just doesn't give any man much time before she's onto the next." Naomi grimaced. "It's probably thanks to me and her dad, but I've never been able to get her to talk to me about it."

Nate wrapped an arm around his mom's shoulders. "It's not your fault, Mom. *He* has plenty to answer for, but you're not the one who abandoned your family."

She sighed. "Still, I know it affected her. It affected all of you."

Nash came up and kissed his mom on the forehead. "We turned out alright. You're all we need."

"You boys are too good to me. I don't know what I'd do without you." She patted a hand against Nash's cheek.

Nate glanced over at Melody as his mom teared up, and saw that she was fighting tears as well, a sad smile playing across her lips. When he caught her eye, she swallowed visibly as if trying to collect herself. "Excuse me," she whispered and went inside.

"I'll be right back," he told his mom and Nash, giving her shoulders one more squeeze.

He found Melody in their room, sitting on the bed and looking out the window towards the lake. He knelt down in front of her and clasped her hands, noticing that they trembled slightly. "Are you okay?"

She gave him a teary smile. "It's the sweetest torture to see you with your family. You all love each other so much, and yeah, it's not perfect, but it's real. I just...I haven't been around family like this in a long time. Until you, I'd been on my own for the most part. Aunt Bea is always in my corner, but I haven't lived with her in years. I forgot how it feels to be in the middle of it all. It reminds me how much I miss my mom. My dad too."

He reached up and wiped the tears from her cheek. "I know you do. We can't replace them, but I know my family already considers you to be one of us. I hope we can help fill that gap, just a little." He rested his forehead against hers.

It didn't matter that he knew better than most that there was no erasing the pain of loss, it didn't stop him from wishing he could take it from her all the same. The deeper things got with Melody, the more her pain felt as reprehensible as his own. His chest caught at the thought, and he kissed her, needing to silence this rabbit trail his mind was taking him down.

She melted into his embrace, allowing him to distract her from her grief, at least for a little while.

Nate awoke while it was still dark outside. This was his favorite time of day out here. Melody was curled up to his side, her head resting on his chest, sound asleep.

He kissed the top of her head and whispered, "Mel, wake up. There's something I want to show you."

She let out a sleepy groan. "What time is it?"

"It's early, but I promise it's worth it. And I also promise, if you come with me, I won't wake you up this early for the whole rest of the trip." He ran his fingers through her sleep-tousled hair.

With a deep inhale, she said, "Okay, okay."

He kissed her head again before wiggling out from under her and getting up. He quickly threw some clothes and shoes on, hearing Melody stumble around to do the same behind him in her sleepy haze.

Heading into the living room, he grabbed a quilt and an afghan out of a basket and then went to the kitchen. Their trusty coffee pot was still set to his timer, and so a fresh batch was ready to go. He poured enough for them both into a thermos and pulled a flashlight out of the junk drawer.

Melody shuffled in behind him, and he smiled as he saw she had thrown on some leggings and one of his hoodies. Wrapping the afghan around her shoulders, he tucked the quilt under his arm and picked up the thermos. "C'mon. Follow me."

He quietly let them out the back door, making sure to catch it before it slammed and led her down the path for a short distance, before turning off the trail to head uphill through the woods.

"You woke me up before dawn to go on a hike?" Melody asked around a yawn.

"Yes and no. It's not much farther, you'll see when we get there." He used the flashlight to illuminate the ground, making sure she didn't trip in the dark.

As they crested the hill, the trees opened up and the landscape dropped off to reveal an uninterrupted view of the water. He stopped and laid out the quilt on the ground, taking a seat. Patting the space in front of him, he pulled Melody back against his chest and waited.

A couple of minutes later, the sky began to lighten, and he felt her spine straighten as she noticed. Dawn broke over the horizon, painting the trees and lake in a soft golden glow.

"This is unbelievable," she whispered.

"I found this place a few years ago. The first time I came here with everyone after Ang died was only a couple of months after it happened, and I was having a hard time sleeping. So, one morning I just got up and went for a walk. Everyone else was asleep still, and I was able to just be alone for a bit. It felt like this spot was made just for me. And then I could sneak back into bed before anyone ever knew I was gone. I knew you would love it too, so I had to share it with you."

"I want to paint it."

"Then you should." He pressed a kiss to her temple. "I brought coffee, it's got sweet cream like you like it." He handed her the thermos.

They sat like that for a while, passing the hot coffee between them until it was gone and just enjoying the view of the world waking up. Birds called in the trees and the hum of far-off fishing boat motors sounded as the first of the men ventured out onto the lake.

He felt Melody shiver from where she was seated between his thighs, and then she pulled the afghan off of her shoulders and draped it around him as well, enclosing him with her. He banded his arms back around her waist, letting the back of his knuckles brush against her breasts before finding her skin between her leggings and his hoodie. "Cold?" he murmured in her ear.

"Just a slight chill," she said with a hitch in her voice.

His hands itched to wander, to follow the trail of exposed skin he could feel beneath the blanket, and so he slowly traced a line up her stomach. He found only more smooth skin. "Mmm, no bra." He felt her intake of breath as he drew one of her peaked nipples between his thumb and finger, rolling it gently.

She drew a breath, "I didn't see the point since no one else was awake and we were trying to get going quickly."

"An excellent decision." He nipped her earlobe and let his other hand skim down to disappear beneath the soft waistband of her leggings. Continuing to toy with her breast, he slipped his hand into her panties. "Always so wet for me," he said as he traced a finger over her. Her back arched and he did it again.

"Nate." She gripped his thighs on either side of her as she let her own thighs fall open to give him better access.

He delved two fingers into her, letting his palm grind against her clit with each thrust of his hand. She was rocking in time with him, creating a maddening friction on his own lap, and he watched her face as she got lost in the sensations. Finally, he felt her tighten over his fingers and go limp in his arms with a cry.

He gently removed his hands from her clothes and couldn't resist drawing his fingers into his mouth, sucking off the taste of her. "You're so fucking sweet."

She let out a whimpering noise and said, "I want to feel you inside of me."

"Well, why don't we head back to the house and have some fun in the shower? Getting naked in the woods is a great recipe for getting ticks in bad places." He winked.

Melody grimaced. "Ew. Indoors it is."

Nate followed her as she stood, gathering up the quilt and thermos. Creeping in the backdoor, he made sure it closed quietly and listened for any sign that the others were awake yet. All was silent, so he set the thermos on the counter and tossed the quilt behind the couch before pulling Melody close and snaring her lips in a kiss.

They clumsily backed their way down the hall to the bathroom, bumping walls as they went but not pausing. He closed the door behind them, fumbling for the lock without looking and once he heard the click of the tumbler, he released her to pull his shirt over his head. He watched her do the same, joining his in a heap on the floor.

His gaze dropped to her full breasts on display, still peaked and rosy from her arousal. With some effort, he turned to the shower, wanting to get the water going. "Old pipes. Takes a minute to heat up," he said.

When he faced her again, she had disposed of the rest of her clothing and was fumbling with his waistband next as she dropped to her knees in front of him. Air hissed between his clenched teeth as he felt her run her tongue over the sensitive skin between his hip and pelvis, his abdomen tightening in response.

He kicked off his shoes and socks, helping her with his pants and his hard cock sprung free before her. She wasted no time, gripping him in her hand and swirling her tongue over his tip. He braced a hand on the wall over her head and watched her with hooded eyes. A few more teasing flicks of her tongue and then she was taking him in, slowly sinking her lips around him, inch by inch. He let out a groan as his back arched, and he tapped the back of her throat.

She started bobbing, repeating the motion over and over, encouraging him to move with her. Tangling his other hand in her hair, he did as she bid and watched her go. It was as if this was turning her on as much as it was him, and he felt the pressure building in the base of his spine. Her fingers dug into the skin of his ass, not willing to let him go and so he didn't fight her this time. He thrust again, stilling as he came, and he watched as she greedily sucked down every drop, eyes watering but blazing with heat.

She released him and stood, her tongue flicking out to lick her lips, and she reached a hand into the stream of water. "It's hot now."

This shower was not like theirs at home; this one was barely big enough for two and so as they washed, every movement caused their skin to brush and slide. Nate watched the beads of water running over her exposed flesh, feeling his cock stirring again already. He was glad – he wasn't done with her yet.

When she went to wash her hair, he took over. There was something about having his hands buried in her hair in any way, shape, or form that he craved. He massaged the shampoo, and then the conditioner into her scalp before rinsing out the locks. She sighed as her shoulders relaxed, and she leaned her head back onto his chest.

"There's not room to bend you over in this tiny shower, so I'll have to fuck you against the wall instead." He gripped her hips and rolled his against her ass.

"Yes, please." She turned in his arms, pulling his face down to hers and tracing her tongue over his bottom lip.

He gripped her thighs and lifted her, her legs winding around his waist and lining them up perfectly. She beared down on him as he pushed into her, rolling thrusts seating him deeper and deeper until he was buried inside her.

They kept a steady rhythm, her heels digging in as she moved with him. His tongue danced with hers, and he eventually felt her begin to squeeze him. The pressure sent him over the edge with her.

His hair fell over his eyes as he rested his forehead on hers, holding her gaze. "You're so perfect."

Before Melody could reply, there was a pounding on the door, followed by Natalie shouting, "Nathaniel!

Just because you have a sex life again does not mean you can use up all the fucking hot water, you dick!"

In the distance they could also hear Naomi, "Natalie! Language! You leave them be."

Lastly, a disgruntled Nash called out, "Why is everyone yelling? Some of us are trying to sleep."

Nate closed his eyes with a groan. "Oh my god. Like I said, no privacy."

Melody started shaking, and he opened his eyes to see that she was biting her lip and holding back laughter. Her control snapped when he met her eye, and she threw her head back as her laugh echoed through the bathroom. It was infectious and he couldn't help but laugh too.

He set her on her feet, starting to rinse them off again. "Nothing like my mom's voice to kill the mood."

Melody snorted. "Can't blame you there."

He wrapped her in a towel and quickly patted himself dry too, tucking his own around his waist. Melody gathered up their scattered clothing while he peaked out the bathroom door. The coast was clear, so they made a mad dash for their room, closing the door behind them.

Chapter 29

Melody

Unsure of the plans for the day, Melody dressed in a pair of shorts and a tank top. She was in the process of pulling her hair up into a ponytail when she glanced over at Nate who was pulling on his own clothes. She let herself be mesmerized by the way his muscles bunched and moved on his back as he pulled a shirt over his head, silently bidding his tattoo farewell for now.

"So, what do you think we'll do today?" she asked, trying to focus again.

"No idea. If I had to guess, probably hang out around here, maybe go grab some lunch at one of the places on the water. It'll probably be a laid-back day honestly."

"That sounds nice." She let out a sigh. "Do you think it's safe to go out there yet?"

He pressed an ear to the door for a second and then shrugged. "Natalie smells fear. Best to face it head on."

Squaring his shoulders, he opened the door and went out. Melody hesitantly followed behind him, listening for the others.

They found them at the kitchen table. Naomi was reading a newspaper, Nash was typing on his laptop, and Natalie was nursing a cup of coffee and scrolling on her phone. There were plates of toast and bacon in the center of the table, which they all seemed to be sharing.

Nate kept his face impassive as he walked through to the coffee pot and poured them both another mug. "Morning."

Natalie leveled a narrow-eyed look Nate's way while Nash glanced at him with raised eyebrows and pursed lips as if trying to decide how to react.

Naomi said, "Good Morning. Come, have some breakfast, please." She gestured to the open chairs across from her, and Melody quietly sat. Nate returned, placing a steaming cup of coffee in front of her and taking the next seat.

Apparently, everyone had decided to ignore the incident from this morning, and they made small talk instead. Melody felt the tension slowly leave her as she stopped anticipating the embarrassment she had been sure was coming and let herself enjoy their company instead.

They passed the morning lazily playing card games, snacking and laughing. The more time she spent with this family, and got to know each of them, the more they felt like hers. Like she held some small claim on them too.

After a particularly rowdy round of Bullshit, much to Naomi's chagrin over the language, Natalie said,

"Let's go get lunch at The Dock and then hit the beach after. I'll just need to throw on my swimsuit real quick."

The guys sounded their agreement before Nash said, "We can all fit in my truck."

A plan in mind; they all headed off to change. Considering how much quicker it is for men to tug on swim trunks, Nate was dressed well before Mel and told her he'd meet her outside. She looked through her swimsuit options, selecting a plum-colored strappy bikini that she knew Nate would both love and hate with other people around.

Once she had wiggled into the fabric and gotten it adjusted properly, she pulled her shorts and tank top back over it and headed out to the car. She climbed up into Nash's Toyota 4Runner, finding everyone, but Nat was ready to go.

After a minute, she came bounding out of the house and climbed in beside Mel. The winding drive up to The Dock was thankfully pretty short, and they all climbed out and were seated at an outdoor table that overlooked the water. This place was just filled with beautiful views everywhere you looked.

They watched people sailing by on various watercrafts as they ate – she saw fishing boats, jet skis, kayaks, you name it. The beach Natalie mentioned was just below too, and she could make out a volleyball area.

The doors leading inside the restaurant opened and a group came out, talking excitedly. Natalie waved. "Justin, hey!"

"Nat, hey I was going to call and see what you guys were up to. We were about to head down and play some volleyball, you guys in?" He looked between Nate and Nash.

The brothers exchanged a look and shrugged. "Sure. Why not?" Nash said.

"My mom is inside, Mrs. Blackwell, and she'd love to catch up with you. She wanted me to let you know next time I saw you all," Justin said.

"Oh, how lovely. These old bones would do better there than trying to get around in the sand anyhow. You kids go have fun and we'll catch up with you later." She headed inside and Natalie gestured to Mel.

"Guys, this is Melody. Melody, this is Justin, Travis..." She pointed out each in turn, but with as many new faces as there were, Melody quickly forgot most of their names.

She followed them down the path to the dunes and saw there, thankfully, were lounger chairs spread around the area as well. She told Natalie, "I'm not super coordinated with stuff like this, so I'll probably just watch."

"Oh, girl, me too. I'm not about to jump around and get all sweaty. But I will happily watch all of these beautiful men do so." As they took a couple of front row seats, the guys split off into teams and promptly ditched their shirts.

Melody let her gaze trail over Nate's body, eating up all of the flesh on display as if she hadn't just let him fuck her senseless a few hours ago. As the months passed, she kept waiting for the moment when his effect on her lost some intensity, but it just hadn't happened so far. She would feel embarrassed if her own effect on him weren't so bodily evident as well.

Natalie snorted as she caught where Mel's attention had gone. "Cold shower this morning aside, from a women supporting women perspective, good for you. Get it girl." Her own attention snagged on Justin as he talked to his teammates.

The group had split into two, with Nate and Nash on the team opposing Justin. Both had huddled up with serious looks on their faces as if this game held high stakes that the rest of them weren't privy to.

The display of well-muscled bodies had started to draw a crowd, and several women leaned against the railing of the dock above them to watch. The game got underway, with plenty of jumping and swearing, but thankfully laughter too.

"You know what would make this more interesting? Seeing how distracted we can make them while they play. I guarantee if we start stripping, they will not be able to focus. It would be hilarious to see whether Nate or Justin cracks first." She flashed Mel an evil grin.

Melody laughed and shook her head. "I don't know...but you and Justin huh?" She wiggled her eyebrows.

"He's good fun for the weekend. I took him for a test drive last night." Nat winked. "C'mon, it'll only be fair to both teams if you do it too."

Melody hesitated a moment before caving. "Fine. Don't blame me if this backfires though."

With that, they both drew their tops over their heads, dropping them to the ground beside their chairs. They saw Justin stumble as his eyes landed on Nat, but Nate hadn't looked over quite yet. Feeling devious, Mel stood to remove her shorts as well, bending over to fish some sunscreen out of her bag and leaving her curvy ass in the air for Nate's benefit. She glanced over at Natalie and tried to hold in a laugh. "Sunblock?"

Natalie's laughter was cut off by the sharp sound of the ball being spiked and then hitting flesh. Melody turned quickly at the pained sound that followed and saw Justin on the ground, holding his face while Nate had stalked angrily up to the net and was pointing a finger down at him. "I don't know if you were too busy checking out my wife or my sister but get your head in the fucking game."

Melody heard Natalie say under her breath, "Damn it Nathaniel. You better not have broken his face, I was planning to sit on it later." Then she ran over and knelt over Justin, soothing him.

Nate marched over to her next, and she felt butterflies erupt in her stomach. He didn't say anything when he reached her, only wound her ponytail around his fist to angle her face to his, and wrapped a possessive hand around her hip as he claimed her mouth with his.

The way he kissed her was utterly indecent for out in public and was kind of the equivalent of pissing on her to mark his territory, but the little box that contained her inner feminist was shut tight. She clenched her thighs together to help ease the ache he was stoking with each stroke of his tongue and flex of his fingers on her hip. Her skin felt like it was on fire where it met his. This was madness. If they didn't pull away soon, they were going to put on way too much of a show for everyone else here.

"Hey, Caveman. You can't just drag her back to your cave, okay? Weren't you just lecturing about keeping your head in the game?" Nash's voice broke through the haze of lust.

Reality rushed back in and Melody flushed a deep red as she felt all of the eyes that were on them. Nate however looked utterly unbothered, aside from the erection his swim trunks did nothing to hide. As if finally realizing that development, Nate cleared his throat. "Let's take five." He finally eased his grip on her.

"Pretty sure everyone else already decided that. Between Justin and Nat going to get some ice for his face and your porn star promo, they all took the hint we wouldn't be playing for a bit," Nash said.

Melody dared a glance around and found that the players had mostly dispersed to further down the beach and the female audience was still watching them with mixed expressions of longing, jealousy, lust and definitely some hate thrown her way.

"We're just going to go, uh, walk it off," she said to Nash.

Nate's brow furrowed in confusion, so Mel let her hand fall, grazing against his cock which was still hard and pressed against her stomach. His spine straightened and his jaw tensed. "Right, yeah. We'll be back."

Nash let out a sigh and ran a hand over his face, clearly feeling like they were a lost cause. He headed down the beach to join the rest of the team.

Melody took Nate's hand and looked around. She spotted where the beach continued to run under the dock, or she guessed it was more like a pier – but there was a long stretch of secluded area that could be walked underneath, away from prying eyes. She tugged him after her into the gloom.

"Where are we going?" Nate asked.

"Somewhere private to take care of *that*."

He let her pull him along until they were out of sight before he said anything. She felt him stop and turned to look at him. "I'm sorry. I'm not sure what came over me. I'm not usually that guy who can't handle anyone else even looking at his wife. I just saw you there in this," he drew a finger lightly over one of her straps, "and all rational thought fled my brain. I just knew I needed to touch you, and I needed everyone else to know that they couldn't. Nash wasn't wrong in calling me a fucking caveman."

She slowly ran her hands up his chest to circle behind his neck. "I know I should be upset and have this whole speech about how you don't own me prepared...but if I'm being honest, you do. I'm yours. And as much as I don't want to be that jealous bitch either, I can't deny that seeing all those women look at you and want you just as much as I do, only for you to utterly ignore their existence while you choose me...I've never been into any kind of voyeurism, but knowing that they have to sit there and know that you're mine, is so incredibly hot. Because yes, I am yours. But you're mine too." She stretched up onto her toes to steal a kiss.

He groaned against her lips. "What you do to me..."

She huffed a small laugh and released a hand to run down his abdomen. She felt his muscles tighten under her touch and swept her hand into his swim trunks, gripping his cock between them.

He let out a strangled, "*Fuck,*" as she began to pump him.

His hands began to wander too, and she pulled back slightly, but didn't pause her movements with her hand. "I'm not looking to get sand in any unfortunate places." She saw him glance around, noticing the wooden posts that supported the dock. "Or splinters," she said before he could suggest it. "Right now, we're just going to take care of you. You can return the favor later if you want." She winked as she knelt and pulled him out of his shorts.

"Mel," he said as she started teasing touches with her tongue. "You already went down on me this morning. You don't have to do this."

She let out a hum and held his eye. "Did it ever occur to you that I just want to? The things you do to me too..." She cut off any further conversation, taking him into her mouth.

He gripped her ponytail again, letting himself fall into the rhythm they set together. "Mine." He groaned.

Mine.

She would take as much of this man as he would give her, but she was his, body and soul.

When they rejoined everyone later, the game had started back up, but Natalie and Justin were seated off to the side, still applying ice to his face.

Nate went up to them and said, "I'm sorry, man. That wasn't cool of me. I didn't really intend to hit it that hard, but I knew you weren't looking and I had no reason to lose my shit over nothing like that."

Justin stood and held out his hand for Nate to shake. "You're good. You were right; I was distracted. If I had a sister or wife and someone was ogling them, I'd be pissed too. So, I'm sorry for any disrespect." He glanced at Melody and Natalie during the last sentence, including them in his apology as well.

Natalie broke the tension by saying, "I take no offence to being ogled. It's not your fault that I'm hot."

Justin laughed while Nate rolled his eyes and shook his head.

Melody just chuckled before telling Justin, "Thank you. I'm sorry we were being ornery and caused all this drama."

"Well, if you two are done being horny teenagers, did you boys want to rejoin the game?" Nat asked.

They exchanged shrugs and headed back into the crowd. Nash shoved Nate, clearly giving him shit before accepting him back into the team.

"I don't know what you've done with my brother, but you've got him acting like some lovesick kid again and I don't know whether to laugh or gag. I guess I'll let it slide though. It's just good to see him act like a person again," Natalie said.

"He's got me acting like an idiot too. I've never felt like this about anyone before. The things he –"

"Ahh! Ah! Nope. No details. I'm happy for you and all, but he's my brother and I want no details. Ever." Natalie waved her arms.

Melody blushed and laughed nervously. "Right, sorry. I never used to be an oversharer either. It's like I don't know how to act anymore."

"God, you guys are just nauseating. But like in the best way."

"So, Justin is nice."

"He is. I think I'll play nursemaid tonight, that should be fun."

"But is that all it is? Just some fun?"

"Yep. I know my family hates it, but I know what's best for me. Use 'em and lose 'em. There's way too much baggage long term and nothing lasts anyway."

Melody's face scrunched as she considered this. Naomi wasn't far off, clearly there were lingering issues from their dad leaving that played a part here.

"Not to say anything against you and Nate – it's obvious you guys have a good relationship and I'm happy for you. It's just not in the cards for everyone," Natalie said.

"I didn't take it that way. But I think some things do last. Nothing is ever guaranteed, but I think you can make things last as long as possible if you try."

"Well, that's the other thing, isn't it? You can do everything right and still get fucked over. Life can just take it all away at any time. So why bother letting someone get that close if it's just going to destroy you later?"

Ah. Melody realized there was more to this than the rest of them realized. It wasn't just their father that had left Natalie on the defensive. Losing Angela, and watching Nate lose Angela, affected Natalie deeply.

"Enough of that though. I'm not crying over it, so no one else should either. I take care of myself just fine."

Melody knew that pushing in this moment would not be wise. She needed to let Natalie talk more about this when she was ready.

That evening, they all sat around the fire together. As Nate had predicted, Nat was making s'mores, Nash was strumming his guitar softly while their mom swayed and hummed along. Nate had pulled out a pocketknife and was working on the carving he had started the night before. Melody was content to just sit there, watching them all and enjoying their presence.

The song changed and caught Nate's attention. "John Moreland." He smiled at Nash.

Nash nodded as he started to sing. To everyone's surprise, Nate joined in too. Their deep voices twined together, but they had a faraway look in their eyes as they sang of breaking hearts and scars on their soul.

Melody didn't want to move, afraid to break the spell they were casting. She held her breath as she studied Nate's face in the glow of the fire. As he sang a verse about not being able to let go, his focus turned to her, and she could feel heat where his eyes traveled over her face. Goosebumps erupted over her arms and she suppressed a shiver. The final notes played, hanging in the air, and they all remained quiet for a moment.

Naomi broke the silence, clapping. "That was beautiful, boys."

"Oh, shit," Natalie said as she realized she had left her marshmallow in the fire for the entire song. It was nothing but a hunk of charcoal by that point. She shook it off her skewer with annoyance.

Naomi chuckled. "I think I'm going to call it a night, kiddos. Sleep tight."

They called their goodnights after her as she made her way inside, and Nat brushed her hands off. "Well, I'm going to head out to see Justin. See you guys later."

"Really? You're cool with just popping over and being an obvious booty call?" Nash asked.

She scoffed. "Oh, silly boy. He's the booty call in this equation. And I'm a grown-ass woman, I can make my own decisions. Have a nice night." She raised a peace sign over her shoulder as she walked away, not waiting for any further reply.

Nate let out a sigh but didn't call after her. Instead, he looked over at Mel and said, "Actually, there was another spot up the way I wanted to show you while we are here. Want to go with me?"

"Sure," Melody said.

"We'll see you in the morning," he told Nash.

Nash went back to strumming his guitar softly and watching the fire. "Sounds good. Have fun."

She stopped in to use the restroom before meeting Nate at his truck, where he was closing up the tailgate. It was too dark to see what he had loaded though. They climbed into the truck, and he started up the road, further into the wooded hills than they had been before.

After a few twists and turns, he said, "Close your eyes."

She did as he asked, and felt the truck drift to a stop, before backing up and parking. The sound of his door opening came, and he said, "I'll be back in a second. Just wait here and keep those eyes closed."

Melody desperately wanted to peek but didn't want to spoil whatever surprise he was planning, so she waited a couple more minutes until he opened her door and took her hand. "I've got you," he said.

He led her towards the back of the truck, his arm around her waist, and her hand trailed down the side of the truck. Finally, he said, "And open."

From up here, the moon was bright, and she could see miles and miles of the forest below with the lake peeking out between. This was the other side of the coin from this morning – instead of everything painted in gold, it was gilded in silver. She tipped her head back and saw more stars than she could've imagined. "I forget how much the light of the city blocks out the night sky."

"I know. I don't think we get away from it all enough. We miss stuff like this in the hamster wheel that life is sometimes, so I wanted to share this with you too." He steered her to the end of the truck and gestured to the truck bed. "I tried to make it cozy so we can stargaze and enjoy the view."

He had filled the back of the truck with blankets and pillows so they could lay there and look at the sky together. "It's wonderful," she said.

Nate helped her hop up into the truck, and she kicked off her shoes before crawling up into the pile of blankets. He followed behind, laying on his back and pulling her down to lay beside him with his arm around her. She let herself melt into his side and rest her head on his shoulder.

They quietly laid there, pointing out constellations and sharing stories they had heard about them in the past. It was so peaceful out, only the sounds of crickets and the occasional owl to be heard.

She could feel the temperature dropping, little by little too. She shivered and burrowed further into

Nate's side. He pulled another blanket over them both, rubbing his hand over her arm to help warm her.

"Can't have you catching a cold," he said.

She tilted her head to look up at him, finding him already studying her. "Thank you for this."

He gave her a small smile. "You're welcome." He leaned in to kiss her, and she let her eyes fall shut. Unlike this morning, which had felt so frenzied and desperate, as if they would die if they didn't touch each other right that second; this time was soft.

He kept this kiss tender, and as his hands skated over her, his touches felt reverent, like he was trying to memorize every curve of her. The slow passion was building and building, and she wondered if maybe this wouldn't be more intense than all the other times.

They took their time, slowly removing their clothes as they went and only breaking their kiss when absolutely necessary. Once she was bare beneath him, she could feel him everywhere and it stole her breath. He traced a hand over her cheek and down her neck to rest on her nape.

His tongue danced with hers, and heat pooled low in her belly as he wound her tighter and tighter. She was beginning to feel the need to move, to relieve the ache building in her core with friction, and the feeling of him cradled in her thighs was becoming too much to bear.

As if reading her mind, he began to trail his kisses down her throat, flicking his tongue over the sensitive areas that always caused her to squirm. Her back arched, causing her nipples to rub against his chest, and she let out a soft moan.

He continued his gentle kisses down her body, his beard scratching in just the right way. Her breasts were aching and ready by the time he reached them, and he worshipped one with his mouth while palming the other. The sensation sent a jolt of electric need between her thighs, and she rolled her hips in response. She felt his moan on her breast and repeated the action.

"Don't worry, I'm heading that way." He ducked under the blanket, making sure to tuck it back up to her shoulders and stave off the chill.

Now, she couldn't see him and could only rely on the feeling of him as he moved over her. His breath brushed her navel and then she felt the sweep of his tongue again. The anticipation of not knowing where he would touch her next heightened the feeling, and she cried out when he finally flicked his tongue over the spot she needed him most. He let out another groan of appreciation and dipped his tongue inside of her.

Her head fell back as she rode his face, feeling like she was going to burst at any moment from the pleasure. He kept up his leisurely pace, letting her build and build before he replaced his tongue with two fingers and resumed swirling his tongue over her clit. He kept the pressure light, still not sending her over the edge yet.

Her limbs began to tremble as the pressure inside of her kept climbing, and the burning need for release consumed her. Finally, he curled his fingers deep inside of her as he sucked her clit into his mouth and she erupted. Her back arched fully off the truck bed before she settled back down into a pool of relaxed muscles. She felt him kissing a line down her thigh and then back up her body. He paused again at her breasts, stoking the fire inside of her higher once more.

He released her, his sex-mussed hair popping out from under the blanket. She threaded her fingers through it, drawing him down to kiss her again. As he reached down to line himself up with her, she wrapped her legs around his waist and rolled her hips in time with his thrusts.

Like he had all evening, he took his time and kept his thrusts slow and deep, branding every inch of her with his body. She clung to him like a lifeline, unsure how much more pleasure he could wring from her.

The pressure was building again though, and she could feel another climax looming as they finally broke their kiss to catch their breath. He held eye contact as he hovered above her, keeping the same thorough pace with his hips. The intensity in his eyes had her inner walls fluttering around him, and she came again as he watched. She breathed his name in the aftershock and felt him still and pulse deep inside of her, his grip on her tightening before he collapsed with her.

He laid there for a moment and placed a kiss on her collarbone. Shifting onto his back, he pulled her to his side again, and she felt his fingers combing through her hair in soothing strokes. His movements slowed along with his breathing, and she glanced up at his face, realizing he had dozed off.

Melody tentatively reached up and smoothed a hand over his cheek, but he didn't stir. "I love you," she whispered.

She didn't have the nerve to say it while he was awake, but it had been bubbling up inside of her for a while now. It felt good to admit it out loud, even if she was the only one to hear it.

He could sleep for a little longer. She would wake him in a bit and take him home.

Chapter 30

Nate

The next morning, Nate woke up with his face buried in Melody's hair and could feel her heartbeat where her back was pressed to his chest. She had woken him last night after he had fallen asleep in the back of the truck, and he had blearily driven them home before stumbling into bed.

Now he didn't feel any particular motivation to move. There was something peaceful in just lying here, listening to her breathe. The rest of the day was sure to be filled with things to do and places to go, but he could steal away a few more moments first.

Part of him understood that he was getting in over his head here, that his possessive display yesterday and how he could never seem to get his fill of her was a sign that he was not staying as detached as he should. He didn't know what to do about it though, and if he was honest, during moments like this, he wasn't sure if he wanted to.

As soon as the thought surfaced though, it was followed by a pang of guilt. Angela's face flashed in his mind and he stiffened. Where he had felt comfort just moments before, he felt shamed and stifled instead. He slowly released Melody, careful not to wake her as he sat on the edge of the bed, pinching the bridge of his nose and closing his eyes. He needed some distance.

Quietly as he could, he dressed and left their room. Since he always seemed to wake up so early, no one else was up yet. He made his way up to his morning place of solace, sitting down to breathe in the dawn air. Now the memories here were a mixture of missing Angela and sharing pieces of himself with Mel.

He had hoped to clear his mind, but instead the two women flooded his thoughts. They couldn't be more different honestly, but it seemed they both had a hold on him that he couldn't shake. He missed Angela like someone drowning misses air, but Melody was beginning to *feel like air*. Like she was breathing life back into him. He had told everyone for years that he was fine, and for the most part, he had believed it.

Nothing would ever be truly fine with Angela gone, but he was as fine as could be expected. He had grown used to this half-life, and remaining there felt like holding onto the last shred of Angela he had left. Now Melody was part of his life, and he had no idea what he was doing.

All of those old feelings for Angela remained, but new confusing feelings kept popping up surrounding Mel, and he kept trying to shove them down without looking too closely. He knew it was a losing battle, but he didn't know if he was brave enough yet.

The thoughts kept going round and round without any resolution. He sighed in frustration, wishing that he could have just slept in for once instead of tormenting himself.

A small voice in the back of his mind told him that Angela would not want him to torment himself either. There was no universe where she would have wanted him to be alone for the rest of his life or that she would resent him for getting remarried. He tended to ignore that voice though, because thoughts like that made him feel sick. He would resent himself if he ever moved on as if she hadn't existed.

He stood to pace back and forth across the clearing. Trying to find a balance these last few months was more difficult than he had imagined. Refusing to move on from Angela, while growing closer to Melody, felt like two conflicting paths. He kicked a rock over the drop off and heard it distantly splash in the lake below.

Heading back down the path, he paused at the firepit and picked up the carving he had started over the weekend. The small figure of Fredrick was just about complete, with only a few details remaining to finish. He had planned on giving it to Melody today since they were planning to leave tomorrow morning.

Grateful for a distraction, he sat and whittled the last touches into the wood. Once he was satisfied, he went back into the house and found Nash sipping coffee in the kitchen.

"Couldn't sleep?" Nash asked.

"When you're used to waking up early, it's hard to break the habit," Nate said. "I'll be right back."

He let himself back into the room he shared with Mel, finding her still sound asleep. Seeing her peaceful face finally quieted his mind. Pressing a whisper of a kiss on her forehead, he set the tiny Fredrick on her bedside table and went back out to join Nash.

"She's still out," he said.

Nash nodded and poured him a cup of coffee. "Mom and Nat are too."

"Why are you up so early?" Nate asked.

"I don't know really. Just felt restless."

"Everything okay?"

"I mean, yeah, I guess. It's weird, though. I'm like, really happy for you man. But seeing you with someone again and watching Nat go about her whole approach to men, it just sometimes makes me wonder what I'm doing. I don't fit in either category. But you two have someone to go off with this weekend, and I'm just here. Don't get me wrong, I love spending time with Mom, and I don't begrudge either of you for it. I just... I don't know. I don't even know what I'm trying to say here. It just always feels like I'm searching for something, but I don't know what it is or how to find it. Times like this really make me feel it though. Like there's this need to keep looking for somewhere or someone that feels like home. Where I'm meant to be. And that makes me restless. Am I making any sense at all?"

Nate was quiet as he thought it over. "I wish there was some easy fix I could give you. But finding where you're meant to be in life and finding that person are things that can't be rushed, can't be forced. All I know is, when you find it and it's right, it's right. You feel it in your soul."

"I know. Every time I travel, I wait for that feeling. That spark. Every time I try dating too. I know I'm technically doing well in life – I have a successful career and our family is close, but sometimes I feel like I'm behind and life is just passing me by. I mean, you've managed to find that person, not just once but twice now." Nash shrugged and looked out the window.

"Right." Nate swallowed a lump in his throat. "Look, please don't hold me up as some kind of shining example. It's not like it's anything I did. I just got lucky. Shit, I just knew from the time I was seventeen that I wanted to spend the rest of my life with Ang. She was all I had ever known. Losing her is the hardest thing I've ever gone through. Finding Melody was...a surprise. I didn't see that coming. Life doesn't look the way we expect most of the time, sometimes not even the way we want it to look either. But you keep going and eventually you'll find what you're looking for. Or life will show you what you needed all along."

Nash was quiet as he considered Nate's words. The sound of footsteps came from down the hall, and Natalie came into view. "What is this early morning meeting that I wasn't invited to? Solving all the world's problems?"

"Something like that," Nate said.

Nat poured herself a cup of coffee and leaned against the counter. "Every once in a while, I miss things like this. Running into you losers in the kitchen and giving you shit on a regular basis."

Nash snorted. "It's good to spend time with you too, sunshine."

Without needing to say anything, they all made their way over to the couch and sat together. Quiet moments with the two of them grew rarer the older they got; they were all busy with their jobs and lives, but whenever they had the opportunity, it was sweet.

Being able to talk about important things, like he had been with Nash, or talking about nothing at all, there was a comfort in spending time with them. No one understands you quite like a sibling. Maybe it's the shared trauma, maybe it's living together for eighteen years and seeing literally every side of them as a person during that time, but there was a deep-seated bond that linked them. Even when Nate tried to distance himself, like when he would try to step into his dad's shoes in his youth, or after Angela died and he just couldn't talk about it all, that bond never broke.

He listened to his sister's laugh and watched his brother's eyes light up, and he was thankful that it hadn't.

Natalie interrupted his thoughts when she said, "So are we going to talk about the absolute menace you have become now that you're having sex again, Nathaniel?"

"I'd really rather we didn't." He grimaced.

"Dude, she's not wrong. I don't think I've ever stumbled upon you about to, in the middle of, or having just finished fucking in my entire life. It's kinda disturbing." Nash shuddered.

"Okay, okay. Both of you can fuck off." Nate laughed. □

"To be fair, Nat, you're not much better. But you at least don't choose public places, which has somehow become Nate's favorite pastime," Nash said.

Nate put his face in his hands with a groan. "I don't even have an excuse. I feel like I've lost my fucking mind lately."

"No shit." Natalie snorted. "I mean, I want to pluck out my eyeballs and scrub my brain clean of some images, so you really should work on the whole privacy thing, but it's good to see you smile again. Like, really smile." She squeezed his arm.

He leaned his head against the back of the couch with a sigh. "It still feels wrong to smile at all, honestly."

"It's not though," Natalie said.

"Nothing can ever make Angela's death right. But that doesn't mean that you deserve to never be happy again," Nash said.

"It's not about whether or not I deserve it. Though, if I'd noticed she was sick sooner, maybe things would have turned out differently. So maybe I do deserve to stay miserable. But regardless, being happy without her just never made much sense. I've never known how," he said.

"Now hold up, her getting sick was not your fault. You know that, right? You did everything you could. Hindsight is always twenty-twenty, but there was no way for you to know in the moment. Do not carry that guilt, Nate," Natalie said.

"All of us think we are invincible when we're young. We're stupid and we don't take care of ourselves, we don't go to the doctor enough, and sometimes that bites us in the ass. We all learned a hard lesson here, but it's not anything you did wrong," Nash said.

He had never voiced these thoughts to them before, and he wasn't sure what to say now. Their responses didn't necessarily surprise him, and they weren't entirely wrong. But that didn't ease the guilt he had lived with over the last few years. Finally, he said, "I know all of that in my head, but it doesn't make it feel any easier."

"Sometimes you have to just tell your heart to shut the fuck up," Natalie said.

Nate laughed. "Oh yeah, because that works. Nat, you can lie to yourself all you want, but you have feelings too. You can't go your whole life keeping everyone at arm's length and hope that it means you'll never get hurt. Pain is part of life, and if you keep it up, you'll miss out on the good parts along with the bad," Nate said.

"We aren't talking about me." Natalie crossed her arms.

"We do need to at some point, but she's right Nate. Don't deflect," Nash said. "I don't know how to make feelings catch up to logic, but I do know that I can tell that the more time you spend with Melody, the better. I finally feel like I'm catching glimpses of *you* again. It's like you're slowly but surely coming out of a fog. I know you'll never be the same as before, but the last few years have felt like you weren't really here, like you were on autopilot through life, just going through the motions. And I don't blame you, man, but I've missed you."

"Me too," Natalie whispered.

Nate's voice was choked as he said, "I love you both." He pulled them in for a hug, and for once, no one objected.

He had heard someone in the hall a bit ago, but he wasn't sure if it had been his mom or Mel. Poking his head into their room though, he found that she was awake. She was sitting on the bed with the figurine in her hands, examining it with a smile.

She looked up when she heard the door, her smile growing even wider. "You made Fredrick."

He closed the door behind him and leaned a hip against the dresser, returning her smile. "I thought you'd like it."

Melody stood and rushed over to him, catching him off guard as she jumped up and wrapped her arms and legs around him. He caught her with a laugh and she said, "I love it. Thank you." She kissed him and his hands tightened on her thighs reflexively.

"I do have slightly bad news though," he said once they parted.

Her brow furrowed. "What's wrong?"

"I kind of lost in rock, paper, scissors, so we have to go last for showers this morning. Sorry." He cringed.

Melody laughed. "Oh, okay. I thought something serious had happened. But I mean, we do kinda owe everyone for using up all the hot water yesterday."

"I make no apologies. But I suppose this does mean we have some time to kill...I talked about all my plans for this bed, and yet I've managed to make love to you everywhere but here." He raised an eyebrow.

There was a look on her face he couldn't quite decipher, her eyes searching his as she seemed to hold her breath and he realized that was the first time he had referred to their having sex as making love. But last night...that hadn't felt like fucking. That had been *more*. Maybe that's why he had been so out of sorts this morning. But his subconscious had clearly realized it and he called it for what it was without thinking.

But she didn't ask, and he didn't offer to say more. Instead, he kissed her again and walked them over to the bed. He settled over her, deepening the kiss and felt her melt under him.

He released her briefly to throw his shirt off, and she said, "Well, I'm glad I snuck out to brush my teeth while you guys were talking." She ran a finger down his chest, and he leaned into her touch. Her lips trailed down his neck, leaving soft bites as she traveled.

Tilting his head to give her better access, he let his eyes fall closed, and all of his attention focused in on the feeling of her lips on him. Her fingers dug into his back as she blazed a path down his neck and across his shoulder, finally running her tongue over the tattoo on his bicep.

He opened an eye at that, and she shrugged. "I've just always wanted to do that."

"By all means, feel free to lick any part of me that you'd like." He smirked.

Taking it as a challenge, she leaned up and flicked her tongue over his nipple next, and he made an involuntary noise in the back of his throat at the sensation. "My turn," he said.

Leaning down, he captured her hardened nipple through the silky fabric of her nightgown and sucked. He felt her hips jerk beneath him, and he swirled his tongue next before lightly raking his teeth over her.

She turned her head and bit down on his arm to stifle her moans, eliciting a moan from him instead.

"Everyone is awake, so we do need to be quiet this time," he said.

"I'm trying."

"I have an idea." He grinned. He stood and dropped his pants, gesturing for her to shimmy out of her nightgown as well. Once she had, he rolled her onto her side, settling behind her as if he was about to hold her.

He snaked an arm under her head and across her chest, palming her breast. He used his other hand to pull her flush against him, enjoying the feeling of her curves pressing against him. "You can bite my arm or bury your face if you start to get too loud."

As soon as she nodded her agreement, he hooked her leg over the top of his and raised it, spreading her wide for him as he ran a finger through her slickness.

She did as instructed, releasing her moan into his skin, and he increased the pressure of his fingertips. He felt her back arching and her legs trembling the longer he circled her clit. When she finally came, he kept her legs firmly parted and delved two fingers inside, letting her clamp down around them as he continued working her.

Wanting to feel her come on his fingers again, he started up a rhythm, thrusting with his fingers and letting the palm of his hand press into her clit with each motion. He matched his movements on her breast with those below and he felt her bite down on his arm to keep the moans in this time.

She was so close, and he wanted her to let go. "Come on, baby. Let me feel you squeeze me again," he breathed into her ear.

He let out a groan as she bit down harder, feeling her climax rushing through her. "Good girl."

She released his arm and let out a soft whimper.

His lips travelled down the column of her neck, and he gave her a moment to catch her breath, but he wasn't anywhere near done with her yet. Slowly, he pumped his fingers in and out again, and she began to squirm. Her ass was pressing into him with the most perfectly torturous friction, but he kept going. His other hand resumed playing with her breast and she buried her face into his arm just in time to stifle another moan.

His eyes drifted closed as he got lost in the feeling of them moving together – the slide of his hands over her soft skin, the slickness coating his fingers, her hair draped over his arm and emitting the familiar scent of lavender. His tongue flicked out to trace her sweet skin, and she filled all of his senses.

"Nate, please," she whispered.

He opened his eyes. "Please what?"

"I want you now."

He kept moving and ran his nose over the shell of her ear. "Hmm, well you did ask very nicely. But I think I need you to come one more time for me first."

While he had paused his attention to her clit until now, he moved his thumb to roll over it again. Her hips jerked, and he sped up the motion. He watched her face as another orgasm tore through her. She melted into a puddle in his arms and he kissed her cheek.

"Mmm, there you go."

He gently removed his fingers, gripping his cock and rubbing it against her, letting her feel how ready for her he was and slickening himself before he lined himself up to ease inside.

Her breath caught again as he sank inside slowly, letting her adjust to the angle. This time, he bit into her shoulder to stifle *his* moans. She always felt so fucking tight and perfect.

Once he was fully seated, he waited a moment for them both to adjust, and he felt her begin to squirm. He dropped his fingers back to her clit as he began to pump his hips and resumed caressing her breast.

He continued for a while, her trembling growing with each movement of his body. She buried her face into his arm again, barely muffling a cry in time. As much as he wanted to keep going, when she came again, he couldn't hold on. He buried his face into her shoulder to muffle his own bellow.

Utterly spent, he lowered her leg back to the bed but kept his arms around her. "I don't know how you do this to me. It's like I have no self-control and it doesn't matter that we had sex multiple times yesterday. I just can't get enough." He pressed a kiss to her shoulder.

"I know. It was never like this with any other man in my life."

He couldn't help the surge of satisfaction that filled his chest at her admission. This was a dangerous topic they had started though. "They should all be done with the bathroom by now. Want to join me for a shower so we can hopefully both have some hot water?"

She laughed. "Sounds good to me."

Chapter 31

Melody

Since they would be out on the water today, Melody dressed in another swimsuit, choosing a bikini in deep green this time and throwing her hair up into a bun to keep it out of the way. She pulled a little black dress over her head to wear as a cover up and joined the rest of the family.

Nate and Naomi were in the kitchen, packing food into a cooler while Natalie and Nash were playing some card game that featured slapping the pile of cards and more often than not, each other's hand.

Once the food was loaded up, they headed out to Nash's car and Natalie grabbed Nate's arm as they walked. "Oh my god, are those bite marks you heathens?" She examined both of his arms before turning to Melody and spying her bite mark, peeking out from under the strap of her dress as well. She shook her head. "You guys are ridiculous."

"Shut up." Nate laughed. "At least we kept it to our room this time."

"I mean, you're still scarring me psychologically, but I guess this is a step in the right direction?" Natalie slid into the car.

Melody adjusted the strap of her dress to cover the mark, but Nate seemed utterly unbothered. They drove down to the dock and found the Johnsons carrying their own supplies on board.

"Welcome, welcome!" A man called out. She assumed this was Justin's father.

Justin's head popped up from below at that, and a woman followed him up to the deck.

"Thank you for having us," Naomi called back as they approached.

"So glad you can join us," Mrs. Johnson said.

They climbed aboard, storing the cooler of food below and introducing themselves to Melody. When Natalie had mentioned "the boat", she hadn't really known what to expect, but this felt like a small ship. Every surface glittered, and the hardwood floors shined in the bright sunlight. Cushioned seats lined the open deck, where the two mothers had already settled and were visiting over drinks.

Nate and Nash were listening to Mr. Johnson as he told them about the vessel while Justin and Natalie talked quietly a few feet away, exchanging heated looks. As Melody watched, Natalie brushed a hand down his arm while looking up at him from under her lashes. She bit her lip to keep a straight face, but watching Nat work was impressive.

Mr. Johnson drew her attention back to him as he said, "We have three jet skis, so I was thinking you boys could follow the boat out on them. That way you kids can have some fun on those this afternoon."

The guys exchanged wide grins. "That sounds awesome," Nash said.

Nate turned to Melody. "You ever been on one before?"

She shook her head. "No. It looks fun though."

"It's a blast. Just hang on tight," Nash said.

Justin and Natalie had rejoined the group, and he said, "We should be ready to head out as soon as everyone tops up their sunscreen and stows their stuff."

"Yes, children, please make sure you use sunscreen today. All those sunbeams hitting the water will fry you up like a lobster otherwise," Naomi said. She had pulled on a wide brimmed sun hat and was currently rubbing lotion into her own arms.

Justin pulled off his t-shirt. "Here, I can put our clothes below if you guys want to give me yours.

The rest of them followed his lead, and he went to put their clothes somewhere safe as they started passing around the sunscreen. Melody had finished up the front of her body when Nate took the bottle from her hand and gestured for her to face away from him.

His hands glided down her back, covering her skin. He said quietly into her ear, "You and these fucking swimsuits. If I didn't know any better, I'd think you're trying to drive me to insanity."

She hummed as if considering. "Well, maybe I'm just repaying the favor." She took the bottle back from him, to take care of his back next. She glanced around to make sure that no one was looking their way before placing a brief open-mouthed kiss on his tattooed shoulder blade and flicking her tongue once over the inked skin. He grunted low in the back of his throat before he turned back to her and gripped her hip.

"Now listen, you. We're going to be out here all day, surrounded by people and there's nowhere for me to sneak you off to. So, we are going to have to keep a lid on it. Which means I need you to keep that phenomenal tongue of yours to yourself for the time being." He arched a brow at her before turning back around to let her apply his sunscreen.

"And if I don't?" she asked once she finished.

"Then you better hold your breath."

"What?" That was all she got out before he turned and picked her up, running towards the edge of the boat and leaping over, taking her with him.

A squeal escaped her as they fell, but she managed to plug her nose and shut her eyes before they hit the cool water below. They bobbed back up the surface, Nate throwing his head back and laughing when they hit the air. She smacked his shoulder but couldn't stop herself from laughing too.

He kept his grip on her waist, and she gripped his shoulders, their legs brushing as they both kicked to tread water and stay afloat. He gave her a playful grin and a quick kiss before pulling them back over towards the jet skis where the others were getting ready.

Nate climbed onto the unoccupied jet ski and pulled Melody up to sit behind him. Once she was settled and everyone was ready, they followed the boat out into the open water.

The afternoon passed in a series of races, water games, and snack breaks. Once the sun started to set, they tied the skis to the rear of the boat and climbed back aboard. Clothes were pulled back on, food was passed around, and they all got comfortable to wait on the show.

Night had truly set in, and Nate pulled her into his lap, settling her back against his chest so that her head could rest on his shoulder as she watched the sky. The first of the fireworks popped, and she watched as it streaked across the sky. It exploded in a shower of sparks, stark in the utter darkness out here. More and more bursts of color joined the sky and as they reflected off the water around them, she felt as if they were almost trapped in a snow globe.

They were going to head home in the morning, but she knew she would never forget this weekend. She curled further into Nate's arms, thankful for this man and the memories they made here. They would make many more if she could help it.

Chapter 32

Nate

Vacation always cast a spell – a perfect bubble that traps those feelings of being relaxed and carefree. But the bubble always bursts once it's over. It begins on the drive home, and reality slowly sets back in the closer you get to home, like skin that feels too tight.

They were both quiet in the truck, unsure what to say after everything they shared this weekend and all the feelings that were simmering under the surface. He had the odd sensation of not knowing what to do with his hands. Was this how he normally gripped the steering wheel? He resisted the urge to nervously drum his fingers incessantly.

He glanced at Melody and found she was looking out the window, watching the scenery flit by. She at least seemed peaceful, if lost in thought. He turned some music on with the volume low and felt some of the tension leave his shoulders as he focused on the lyrics.

After a while, her breathing changed and he saw that she had fallen asleep. She was curled up with her head resting against the window, her face relaxed, though he was worried she would have a kink in her neck by the time she woke up. After warring with himself, he ended up letting her rest.

Melody was still sound asleep by the time he pulled into Emily's driveway, so he ran a thumb over her cheek and tucked her hair behind her ear. "Mel, we're here. We need to go get Fredrick now."

She inhaled deeply and stretched, looking around groggily. "I didn't mean to fall asleep."

"It's okay. I just didn't want it to scare you awake when he jumps into the truck with us."

She pulled down the visor to tame her hair in the mirror and then opened the door. "Thanks. I'll be right back."

He watched her walk up the sidewalk and ring the doorbell. Emily opened and Fredrick burst forth, so excited to see Melody that he nearly knocked her over. He could hear her laugh from where he was sitting and couldn't help but smile. She gave Emily a quick hug and then headed back to the truck.

Fredrick ambled right in as soon as she opened the door and grumbled in Nate's face as if to express his displeasure at being left behind for the last few days.

"I know, I'm sorry buddy." He pet his ears the way he liked. "You would not have liked the fireworks though."

Melody climbed in behind him, shoving his butt when he made no move to let her have room on the seat. After some finagling, they got him seated in the middle of the bench seat with his head on Melody's lap. He was surprisingly quiet and calm on the way home, thanks to her continuous pets and attention, but Nate could tell the moment he recognized their neighborhood. His ears perked up, and his eyes darted around, while his tail thumped a happy rhythm.

They all spilled out of the truck, hauling their bags inside, and the relief to be home was palpable despite his feelings of being unsettled. There was just something about being back in your own space and sleeping in your own bed after being away.

Once their bags were unpacked, Melody gathered up the laundry and headed to load the washing machine. He poked his head out of their bedroom door to call after her, "Are you hungry? I can whip something up for dinner."

She smiled over her shoulder. "Sure, that sounds great."

He headed into the kitchen and took a look at what they had on hand. Not much, since they hadn't been home and needed to go to the store, but they did have everything for grilled cheese sandwiches with tomato soup, so he got to work.

Melody's steps sounded down the hall, but by the time she padded into the kitchen, he was finishing up and slid a plate over to her. He ladled soup into a bowl and handed it to her next.

She reached up and kissed his cheek. "Thank you." Food in hand, she made her way over to the couch and got comfortable. She flicked through show options while he finished dishing up his own meal and settled in beside her.

Once they decided on what to watch, they ate their food and were content to spend a lazy evening that way. Melody nestled into his side, and he tried his best to relax and shake off the tension that wouldn't seem to dissipate. The quiet that followed them home from the lake did not leave.

The next few days were stilted. He knew it was mostly his fault, but he couldn't seem to snap out of it. He felt in over his head and was doing everything he could to try and regain some self-control when it came to Melody. At the same time, he felt a little bit lighter after talking with his siblings. He hadn't realized how long it had been since they'd all been honest like that without walking on eggshells or avoiding certain topics, and he knew a large part of that was on him.

It wasn't like it was wholly intentional or that he could've necessarily done anything differently – he'd done what he felt he needed to in order to survive after losing Angela – but that didn't make it easy on the rest of them. All he knew was that he would do his best to not shut them out from here on out. He'd probably fail more often than he'd like, but he'd try all the same.

It was a confusing mixture of feelings that plagued him as he went to work or the gym and then came home to Melody. He could tell that he was overcorrecting, withdrawing, being distant. It wasn't fair to her, but everything just felt like too much.

Luckily for him, Melody seemed distracted too. She was as warm as ever, but she was spending extra time in the studio, absorbed in whatever project she was working on. He was grateful for that because he didn't want to hurt her just because he couldn't get his head on straight.

By the time the weekend rolled around again, he finally felt like he had a handle on his emotions again. The ever-shrinking wall around his heart was back up, each concession he made chipping off a block here or there, but it hadn't crumbled completely. All he had to do was hold fast now.

They hadn't had sex since the lake, which probably helped clear his head too, if he was honest. He ached for her though – this was the longest they had gone since they started all of this. She hadn't brought it up and neither had he. Even without the sex, his body was still drawn to her without him even being conscious of it. He still woke up every morning, wrapped around her, limbs tangled and her hair spilling over his chest or pillow. The moments of peace he felt upon waking were ones he tried not to read too much into.

It was Friday and he was finally done with work, so he sang along to the radio as he drove home and did what he could to relax and clear his mind. He hoped that maybe they could get back to some semblance of normal over the next couple of days.

When he got home, he poked his head into her studio but didn't find her there. Fredrick ran to greet him from down the hall, and he stopped to pay the pet tax before he headed towards their bedroom, following the sound of a hammer that was now pounding a steady beat on a wall. He found her there, standing precariously on a step stool so she could reach the spot she was working on.

"Hey," he said.

He should have known better, but she jumped in fright, a hand flying to her chest and the hammer clattering to the floor. Her perch rocked precariously, and he rushed forward to steady her. Once she was secure, she let out a nervous laugh. "You scared the shit out of me."

He closed his eyes and shook his head, a chuckle escaping him. "Sorry. Do you need help with that?"

"No, I got it. Thanks, though. I just need to hang this. What do you think?" She slid the canvas into place and stepped back, biting her lip as she waited for his reaction.

He hadn't bothered to look at the art yet, but now he couldn't look away. It was his lake spot. *Their* lake spot now. The brush strokes brought it to life perfectly, everything golden and peaceful. She didn't usually work in realism, but the details were breathtaking. It was a perfect moment, caught in memory and preserved here for them forever.

"It's perfect," he whispered.

"There's one more." She gestured to the opposite wall, and he turned to look there next.

It was the lookout spot where he'd taken her stargazing. Another snapshot of their life, brought home and rendered painstakingly onto canvas. The moon hung full and heavy in the sky, etching the landscape and lake below in its glow. He felt like he could hear the crickets and feel the breeze over the water.

The two paintings felt like part of a whole – the sunrise hung on their East wall, the moonrise on the West, ready to help them greet the day or draw it to a close. He would forever be in awe of her.

"They're incredible. You're incredible." He cupped her jaw and made her meet his eye when she tried to look away.

A blush crept over her face as he held her gaze. "Thank you. I just want to make sure I always remember those moments."

"Me too." He drew her to him and kissed her softly. She melted into his arms, and they picked right back up where they left off like no time had passed.

As he laid her down on the bed, and they fell into a rhythm that felt as natural, as vital, as breathing – he could feel the wall crumbling.

Nate's birthday was at the end of July and this year his family came over to their house. They ate lunch and played games, during which his siblings became overly competitive as usual. Natalie used every opportunity to spoil Fredrick, giving him table scraps when she thought they weren't looking. The day was full of laughter, and they eventually settled in around the living room to watch him open gifts.

Melody had gotten him a Frieren t-shirt featuring a confused looking Stark, captioned, *I don't understand.*

Nate laughed and turned to Mel seated next to him on the couch, squeezing a hand on her thigh. He smiled as he leaned in to kiss her. "Thanks baby."

"You turned my brother into a nerd?" Natalie asked before pausing and holding up a hand to Melody for a high five. "Nice job."

They moved onto cake next, and Nate went to help Melody dish it out in the kitchen. She turned to him, pressing up to whisper in his ear, "I do have one more present for you to *unwrap* later."

He felt his cock stir in anticipation and tried to subtly adjust his pants. He whispered back, "Well thanks for telling me now. There's nothing like sporting a semi while your family is right fucking there."

Melody stifled her laughter against his shoulder and tried to collect herself. "Hey, just a little payback teasing to build...anticipation." She winked and then walked away, carrying two plates of cake with her.

He grumbled a curse under his breath and followed shortly with the other plates of cake.

What felt like hours later, his family hugged them goodbye and made their way home. He was boxing up the leftover cake when Melody said, "I'm going to slip into something a little less comfortable."

Nate decided that the cake was secure enough, hounding after her down the hall to their room. She shut herself in the bathroom to get ready, and he wasted no time stripping down. He climbed into bed to wait and a few minutes later, he heard the door click open. He tried to take her in but didn't know where to look first.

She had changed into a lacy bustier, which propped her breasts up even further than normal. His eyes trailed down to the little lace thong she wore as she slowly spun in a circle for him, her beautiful ass on display. Thigh high fishnet stockings were secured with a garter running down her thighs and finally she had shiny stiletto heels on below.

He rose to go over to her, his cock jutting out before him, hard and insistent. Before he could close the distance, she twisted around him to back towards the bed, where she reclined, leaning back on her arms and looking up at him with a wicked gleam in her eyes. "How do you want me?"

He wordlessly started forward again, only to be stopped by her stiletto pressed to his chest. This line of her leg drew his attention to her parted thighs where he saw the open gusset in the lace. Logical thought fled his brain as all of his focus fixated on that point. She asked again, "How do you want me?"

She pushed him back, sliding to the floor to kneel in front of him and running her hands up his thighs. "On my knees for you?" He was at a loss for words. She turned and crawled back onto the bed, her ass in the air as she looked back over her shoulder. "On all fours?"

The fragile thread of his restraint snapped, and he was on her. He gave her ass a light slap and heard her gasp as he kissed away the sting. Without giving her time to prepare, he sank down behind her and began to feast on her. From this position, he was able to work her into a frenzy quickly, her legs trembling around him. By the time he added two fingers, she immediately clamped down, coming apart for him. He didn't slow, forcing her orgasm to roll into a second before he allowed her to catch her breath.

He rose to his knees and thrust into her with one deep stroke. Gripping her hair in one hand, he tipped her head back, causing her to arch her back and tilt her hips up even further, intensifying the angle.

"Yes. Harder," she pleaded.

He pumped into her, hard and fast, feeling as if he just couldn't get enough. Needing more, he used a hand to circle her clit as he continued his ruthless pace. The trembling in her legs grew and she let out a moan of "I can't –" as she came on his cock. He still didn't slow. Finally, after a few more thrusts he reached his breaking point, and with a groan, he held himself deep inside while he finished. Melody released a cry as she came one more time, and he slowed his fingers to a stop. He released her to the bed and collapsed down on top of her, careful to not press his full weight down so he didn't smother her.

"Happy birthday, Nate," she said breathlessly.

He managed a contented "Mmm." And placed a line of kisses across her shoulder blades.

They laid there for a while, catching their breath, and Nate propped himself up on his arms, admiring the lace and skin on display. He felt himself hardening again where he was still buried inside of Melody, and she let out a gasp. "Are you...?"

He rolled his hips in response, hitting that spot deep inside that drove her crazy. She let out a moan. "Oh my god."

He continued his leisurely pace, content to draw it out slowly this time. He catalogued every time she tightened under him, every gasped breath, every moan. Pulling out of her, he sat back and said, "Roll over for me, baby. I want to see your face."

She did as asked and he slid home once more. He resumed his slow strokes, rolling his hips to grind his pelvis against her clit each time he was deeply seated. He felt her winding tighter and tighter, like a spool about to come undone. When the tension snapped, the pressure undid him too.

He kissed her tenderly and said, "This has been a good birthday. Thank you."

"I'm glad. And I'm glad you like the lingerie I picked out for you." She laughed.

"This is fucking hot. But honestly, all it does is help emphasize the parts of you that are already sexy to begin with. I will gladly let you play dress up for me anytime you want, but it's you that I want. Whether you're in a dorky t-shirt, some crazy leather get up or in nothing at all, I always want you. Though if I'm being honest, you being completely naked is probably my favorite. If you wanted to run around like that more often, I would definitely not complain."

She snorted a laugh and lightly slapped his shoulder in response. He caught her hand and kissed her fingertips before resting their hands on his chest. "Just being honest."

"So, what do you want to do for the rest of the evening?" she asked.

"You know, honestly I would love to just heat up some leftovers and watch more Full Metal Alchemist, if that's cool with you.'

"Don't threaten me with a good time." She winked.

A little later, they curled up on the couch together, bellies full, and a blanket tucked around them. Quiet moments like this really were the best birthday present.

Her birthday was coming up in a couple of weeks too, so he started forming a plan to make her birthday just as wonderful as she had made his.

Chapter 33

Melody

Melody's birthday arrived before they knew it; the balmy August weather perfect. Nate had been working a lot lately, and she had her suspicions it might be related to her birthday, but she had no idea what to expect. She was excited to celebrate with everyone today though.

By the time the doorbell rang with the first guest, Nate was just about ready. He carried more food out to the table as Melody opened the door and greeted Natalie, who was not only on time, but was the first one there.

Her voice spilled out through the space, "Happy Birthday! And hello my handsome, fluffy man. I missed you so much!" To Nate, she simply called over, "Hey."

Nash trickled in next, and finally Naomi, giving Melody a long hug, swaying back and forth in place. "Happy, happy birthday, Melody. I'm so glad we get to spend it with you."

Melody felt a lump form in her throat as she returned the embrace. She was getting used to Naomi's affection, and sometimes if she closed her eyes, she could pretend it was her mom hugging her. While

Naomi couldn't replace her, she extended her own motherly love to Melody, and she felt it in her bones. "I'm grateful for you," Melody said.

Naomi leaned back without releasing her and pressed a hand to her cheek. "Oh, my dear. I'm grateful for you. Not just for the light you've been bringing back to my son, but because you are a kind, loving, and thoughtful person. I'm so thankful to count you as a daughter."

That did it. Unable to stop the rising tears, Melody buried her face in Naomi's shoulder and let them come. Naomi squeezed her tight, smoothing a hand over her hair until she had composed herself.

Once she felt a little more in control, she released Naomi with a watery smile. "Thank you."

Naomi tapped a finger on her nose. "Anytime, love."

Nate approached, saying, "We're going to do things a little differently today and start with presents."

He gave her a mischievous smile when she looked confused as he took her hand and pulled her back towards the front door. Melody heard everyone else trailing behind them as if they knew exactly what was going on.

"My present first. It's on the porch," Nate said. "Close your eyes."

Melody obeyed, letting him guide her outside. After a few steps, he said, "And open."

Before her was Aunt Bea, smiling widely and sitting on a brand-new porch swing that hung from the roof.

She squealed and ran to hug her aunt. "You're here! How are you here?"

The rest of them laughed and Beatrice said, "Well, your young man had the idea, and Ms. Naomi was kind enough to keep me for the weekend."

"Yes. We're being girlfriends this weekend," Naomi said.

"Mom, I beg of you – don't say that. Unless you want everyone to think that you guys are a couple." Natalie laughed.

Naomi scoffed and waved a hand in her daughter's direction without replying.

Releasing her aunt, she stepped forward to look more closely at the swing. It was beautiful and had delicate carvings across the top. "You made this?" she asked Nate.

He nodded. "I remember when we first looked at the house, you saw the porch and said how much you'd love to have one."

She wrapped her arms around his neck and felt his arms band around her tightly. Those pesky tears were threatening to spill again. "Thank you for doing all of this. I love it."

And I love you.

"I was glad to. Here, try it out." He let her go and steered her to sit down. He joined her, setting the swing to gently rocking as he held her hand.

"It's perfect." She smiled.

"Okay, okay, before you two get overly affectionate – it's time for the rest of the presents," Natalie said and headed back inside.

Nate stole a quick kiss before they filed inside, too. He made her sit in the middle, and everyone gathered around her.

Aunt Bea had gotten her a book she had been wanting to read; Naomi had crocheted her an afghan and Nash had found a beautiful candle during his last trip, with the thoughtful intention of it being set with her parent's photo.

Finally, Natalie handed her an envelope. Melody's brow furrowed as she opened it, and then she couldn't help but smile. "You got us tickets to the anime convention?"

Natalie winked. "I heard it was a thing and naturally thought of you two dorks."

"That's amazing. Thank you, everyone. You all were so, so thoughtful." She glanced around at each of them.

Nate smiled. "You guys ready to eat now?"

A resounding "Yes," followed, and they made their way over to the table to enjoy all of Melody's favorite foods.

As everyone left a few hours later, Melody stood on the porch and waved. Their taillights were fading in the distance, and she felt Nate press in behind her, resting his hands on either side of hers on the rail. His beard tickled her cheek and he said, "You know, your birthday isn't over yet."

"Oh? You've got more planned?" she asked.

"Well, no birthday is complete without hot birthday sex." He ran his mouth down the column of her throat. "I may not have a special outfit, but I promise many orgasms."

"Hmm, well in that case, you've convinced me." She smirked.

He pulled her inside, tossing Fredrick a treat as they passed to distract him as they closed the bedroom door behind them.

Nate paused, leaning on the door and watching her back into the room, his eyes wandering over her body. All at once, he was walking towards her and pulling his shirt over his head. She eyed him in return, never tiring of the view.

When he reached her, she wound her arms around his waist and angled her face for a kiss. He tangled his hand into her hair and snared her lips. Her scalp tingled with the delicious friction, and she opened for him, teasing his tongue with her own.

Their breaths grew heavy as they stayed like that, and his other hand skated down to grip her ass while she dug her nails gently into the muscles of his back. Each sweep of his tongue against hers made her ache to feel it elsewhere. The bulge in his jeans pressed against her stomach, and she let her fingers drift down to his waistband, working their way to the front. When she felt the brush of the hair leading down from his navel, she pulled back enough to start undoing his belt.

"You have far too many clothes on still," he said. She got his belt buckle undone and then he was helping her out of her shirt.

Nate placed a kiss on the curve of her breast, biting down and quickly soothing the sting as she moaned. Her bra went next and then he was sliding the rest off of her too. She reached for his pants again, and this time he obliged.

Once they were both naked, he settled her onto the bed, kneeling between her legs. Her breath hitched as he started a trail of bites and kisses up her thigh, and then he was right where she needed him. A moan escaped her as she focused on the sensation of his tongue swirling over her and his hands holding her hips in place, not letting her squirm an inch away.

He didn't let up, keeping a steady rhythm as the pressure built and built, her muscles coiling in anticipation. Finally, she came with a cry.

Nate hummed his approval. "You're always so fucking sweet." He started the delicious torture again, releasing his hold on one hip so that he could add two fingers inside of her as well. The full feeling and the movements of his tongue had her rocking in time with him, letting her desire climb higher and higher.

She trembled as another climax loomed, and she gave in to the bliss. He didn't slow, drawing out her orgasm as long as possible and spurring another. Her back arched as she tried to regain some control, but he was merciless. His fingers curled deep inside of her, and he sucked her clit sharply. She couldn't breathe as tremors racked her body and she fell limp onto the mattress.

Finally, he gave her a reprieve from the intense pleasure, climbing onto the bed with her. "You good?" He smirked.

"I'm great."

"Get over here then." He winked and settled onto his back.

He didn't need to ask twice. She swung a leg over him, letting herself settle over him and sinking down onto his cock. She rocked her hips, loving the feeling of him inside her. He watched her move for a minute, jaw ticking with restraint. After a moment though, he leaned up to capture one of her nipples in his mouth and worked a hand between them to tease her clit again. It was still overly sensitive, and she clenched her thighs around him as tension bracketed at the base of her spine again.

"Nate!" she cried as another climax consumed her.

"God, I could live off hearing you scream my name like that." He groaned.

His hips continued working in tandem with his fingers, and she was sure that she was spent. A bead of sweat rolled down her spine, and she didn't know how she could possibly come again, but as she felt him pull her down sharply one last time and hit that spot deep inside of her while he stilled and held her there, she did. She came with a guttural moan that she would have been embarrassed of if she'd had more self-awareness in that moment, but currently she didn't feel all that capable of functional thought.

She collapsed down onto his chest as they both fought to catch their breath, and he ran a hand through her hair and over her back. "Happy birthday, baby."

"Today was perfect. Thank you." She gave him a soft kiss.

"You're perfect," he said, giving her another gentle kiss in return.

Her heart swelled, and she laid her head on his chest, wanting to savor this moment. All she could think was, this felt an awful lot like being loved. If this was all he could ever offer her, she would be happy.

A couple of days later, she decided that it was time to return the journal to the attic. Nate wasn't home, and she couldn't bring herself to read more. It was just too much. She already felt guilty about what she had read.

She pulled down the attic stairs, and climbed up, setting the journal on the floor as she searched for the string for the light. Once she found it, she knelt to find the box that the journal belonged in again.

As she located the correct box, she paused to look at the journal one last time. It was then that she heard the footsteps on the stairs and glanced up to see Nate's head breach the opening. She gaped like a fish out of water, not sure what to say as he came to a stop before her.

"What are you doing?" he asked, his brow furrowing as he saw what she was holding.

"Nate, I...I found Angela's journal and I read it."

"You what?"

"I accidentally knocked the box over when I was trying to put some stuff away a while back, and when I saw what it was, I read it. I'm sorry." She handed him the book.

Nate's eyes narrowed as he gripped the journal. "You had no right to read this. No right."

Her shoulders slumped and she looked down at her feet. "I know. I crossed a line and there's no excusing that. All I can say is that I'm sorry. I just wanted to get to know who Angela was, and I wanted to experience you through her eyes. I wanted to see you before the weight of this grief changed you. And I'm so sorry. I'd give anything if I could help take that pain away. If I could trade places with Angela so that you could have her back, I would."

He tossed the journal on the floor, causing the loose photos and papers that had been tucked between the pages to spill across the floor around them. "Damn it Mel, stop. That wouldn't solve a fucking thing. Just like you can't fill the hole she left, she'd never fill the hole that you'd leave in my life now. I lov–" He cut himself off, eyes going wide and then began to pace, running his hands over his face.

"Nate –" Melody reached a hand out towards him.

"*Don't.* I can't. I can't. What the fuck is wrong with me? What, now that she's dead, I'm just going to *move on?* Like she didn't mean anything? Like she was never here? God, what does that say about me? Am I so broken that I just couldn't love her enough?" He fisted his hands in his hair.

"Nathaniel, stop." Melody gripped his face between her hands to stall his pacing. So many emotions were storming across his face, fear, anger, disgust, sorrow, confusion. "You are only human. You loved Angela so well, and she knew it. There are countless pages in this journal talking about how much she loved your life together. You have the biggest heart of anyone I've ever met. You keep Angela's memory alive, you love your family the best you can, and if you found room in your heart for me too, I'm so incredibly honored." Her voice broke as she continued, "I never dared to hope that this would happen, that you would love me like I love you. Loving me does not diminish your love for Angela and it doesn't replace it. Just like she and I are very different people, the love you have for us is unique to each of us. But all I've wanted these last few months was to help you pick up all these broken pieces and make something beautiful out of them. I want to help you keep Angela's memory alive and carry her with us. You wouldn't be who you are today without her. Love is never gone; you carry it with you always. You carry *her* with you always. If I've learned anything, it's that this is what it means to be a widow's wife – it's beautiful and it's painful, but I will help you honor your love and your loss as long as you'll let me."

Nate sank to his knees, curling in on himself to resemble the sculpture he had made. From where his face was buried, Melody was able to make out, "I don't know if I can do this again. I don't think I can handle it. I can't go through all of this again." He raised his head to look at her, and she saw tears had begun to stream down his face. "I don't think I'll survive losing you too."

She knelt down in front of him, resting a hand on his shoulder. "Nate, I can't promise that nothing bad will ever happen. Life is often unfair, and tragedy strikes when you least expect it. We've both been on the receiving end of that. But what I can promise is that I'll do my best to stay with you. And I know in my heart that getting to love you, for however long I may have you, will always be worth it. I refuse to miss out on time with you now just because it may hurt later. I know this will be hard and it will be scary for us both, but in the end it is worth it. *We're* worth it."

He studied her face, breaths coming shakily, and Melody caught sight of one of the pages that landed next to where he knelt. It was folded and in a handwriting that she had come to recognize, was his name.

"Nate," she whispered.

She held it up for him to see, and his eyes widened. He shook his head slightly and looked at her in question.

"I don't know what this is. I didn't see it before. Do you want to read it?"

His voice was hoarse when he answered. "I don't know if I can."

"Do you want me to read it to you?"

Whatever he decided, she would support, but these were likely Angela's last words to him, and she had the feeling that he should hear what she had to say.

He was silent for a moment. Finally, he jerked his head in a nod. She gingerly opened the paper, took a deep breath, and began to read.

"Nate, this is a letter I never wanted to write. I wanted us to grow old and fat with twenty grandbabies running around us as we sat in rocking chairs that you made for us back when your knees still worked. I wanted so much more time with you. You are the love of my life. I'm so incredibly grateful for the time we had together, and I'll forever be sorry that I'm leaving you with so much pain. Please don't hold onto it forever. We did everything we could, and sometimes life just isn't fair. I wish more than anything for you to find joy again someday. It may be different than you pictured, but I know it's possible. You have so much love to give, and I want you to. I want you to love and be loved. I want you to feel your heart race and laugh and work through fights and clean up messes and just live. The good, the bad, all of it is precious. If you're reading this, I'm not in pain anymore. So, please, let someone in someday. Share all of that love I know you have inside. There will never be enough words to tell you how much I love you. I always will. And I know, no matter what, that you'll always love me too. Yours always, Ang."

He fell forward to rest his head in her lap, the tears coming faster and jagged sobs tearing out of him. She held him as the dam burst, and he released the years of pent-up grief, anger, fear and love he had stuffed down, his hot breaths rasping out against her knees. She didn't know how long they sat there, only that she was content to stay until he had spent every tear he needed to.

Running a hand in soothing circles over his back and the other through his hair, she began to hum the melody of Dust to Dust by the Civil Wars. He wound his arms around her waist, and she softly sang bits and pieces of the lyrics, just continuing to hold him until he was able to collect himself.

Finally, he pulled back, sitting up and wiping his face on his sleeve with a deep breath. “I’m sorry. I think I knew that I was falling in love with you from the beginning, but it just felt like I was betraying her, and I was terrified of being in love again. I thought if I could keep you at arm's length, it would be fine. And then when I couldn’t do that, I kept bargaining – if I only give you this piece of me, but no more, I’d be fine. But I was lost all along whether I wanted to admit it or not.” He took her hand. “I love you, Mel. I do. From the first day we met, I felt at home with you. Joy has been such a rare emotion in my life in the last few years, but then you came into the picture, and it was like the sun came back out after hiding behind the clouds for so long. I’m sorry it’s taken me this long to figure it out, or to be brave enough to face it. I’m nowhere near healed, but I’m yours if you’ll have me.”

“We all have healing to do. That’s what being human is. But I would be thrilled to be by your side as you do. I love you so much. You’ve become my home too.”

He kissed her tenderly, and they picked up the scattered pages, tucking the old journal back in its box. As they made their way back down into the house, he turned to her and with a smile doing its best to break free. “Mel? Umm, I didn’t want to say anything earlier and then I got distracted by everything, but you do know that when it's a man that lost his wife, the term is *widower*, right? Widow is technically the female term."

She had a blank look on her face for a good thirty seconds, as if her brain was trying to process the information. Finally, she slapped a hand over her face and said, "Oh my god. I totally forgot that was a thing."

She could tell that he did his best to keep a straight face but watching her slowly lose it snapped his self-control and they both gave into a fit of laughter. After emotions running so high today, it felt good to laugh. Her face hurt and her stomach was starting to ache, but as she wiped tears from her face, all she could think about was how thankful she was for this man that she could both laugh and cry with. He pulled her in for a hug, breathing her in. Her arms wound around his waist and after a moment, he pulled back to kiss her softly again.

She could see the truth shining in his eyes before he said a word. "I love you so much, Mel."

"I love you too."

They knew that everything had changed. And for once in their lives, it was a change for the better.

Epilogue

Nate

Six Months Later

Their first anniversary was coming up soon. It was crazy how different life could become in a year. The freedom that came with loving Melody was breathtaking. Their love story was no longer a lie; they had met, fell in love and gotten married – sure, they would probably never broadcast the ad he had placed, but it was something they could look back and laugh about now. A private joke just for them. To the rest of the world, they were just two broken people who had found each other in the chaos of life.

They were in the process of buying their house from Shirley and all set to open their own gallery soon. A joint space to sell their art, his sculptures and her paintings filling the place with their love and passion. He couldn't be more proud of her, or more grateful for her support. Letting the world see his work fully was nerve wracking and exhilarating. Taking odd pieces here and there to the farmer's market was a far cry from establishing himself officially as an artist separate from his regular store. The launch party was in the works, and then they would be open to the public. The first thing everyone would see when they walked in the doors would be the pieces they had made of each other – her painting that was the color of his eyes and his sculpture of her agile hands. They were accompanied by a plaque that introduced them to the world and set the tone for the space.

Tonight though, they had allowed Natalie to drag them back to the karaoke bar. She seemed to be in the midst of some feud with a man in the crowd, but Nat being Nat, she wouldn't talk about it. She just glared daggers at him while she sang and he heard a muttered, "Fucking Brad," when she took her seat again. Nate decided to stay out of it.

Nash joined them too, content to sit back and watch the drama unfold with their friend Riley. She had been friends with Natalie since high school but had lived abroad as a traveling nurse for a long time. It was nice to have her back in town again.

When Nate's turn was called, Melody joined him onstage for a duet. He didn't even notice the crowd as he watched her take the mic, the noise of the bar fading to a distant roar.

The beginning notes played, and he began, the words to I Got You by the White Buffalo rolling off his tongue. Melody's part came next, and she tossed him a smirk when she sang the line about being sick of him being drunk – amused by the irony, considering the one and only time she'd ever seen him drunk was in this very bar. Though she didn't seem to have any complaints about what had come afterwards that night.

Their voices danced, rising and falling together until the end of the song. He pulled her in for a kiss, not caring if they had an audience, but the crowd shouted their encouragement anyway.

They made it back to their table, where Nash raised a glass in salute and Natalie was quick to roll her eyes and say, "You guys make me gag." But Nate noticed she couldn't help but smile. He had the same problem these days. With Melody by his side, he just couldn't seem to stop smiling.

Want more of the Blackwells?

Check out Natalie's story in...

A Warm Welcome

Listen to Nate & Melody's music here!

Acknowledgements

Dear reader, I can't thank you enough for taking the time to share in my first novel. Nate and Melody's story was one that wouldn't leave me alone until I brought it to life, and I'm so glad you joined me. As someone who has unfortunately gone through several untimely deaths within my personal life in recent years, it was very important to me to shed light on some of the realities of grief that don't always get talked about. It's different, and deeply personal, to each of us, but my hope is that if you have experienced any of this too, maybe you'll feel a little less alone in the world.

Pair that with my love of romance, and here we are, roughly 83,000 words later.

I never could have done this without the love and support of my husband and best friend, both of whom have listened to countless hours of rambling about my fictional world. The feedback, help with editing and brainstorming whenever I got stuck will always be so very appreciated. Thank you, thank you, thank you!

www.ingramcontent.com/pod-product-compliance
Lightning Source LLC
LaVergne TN
LVHW100508110826
845146LV00002B/558

* 9 7 9 8 9 9 4 6 6 7 7 0 5 *